Critical Acclaim for Robert Levy's *No One Dies from Love*

"Levy delivers a viscerally unsettling collection of 12 horror shorts rooted as much in human psychology as in the fantastical and speculative... Levy's stories are made all the more powerful by his unwillingness to shy away from the illicit. By embracing the taboo with the tools of horror and speculative fiction, he at once demystifies these subjects while imbuing them with a magic of his own... The result is a triumph."

—*Publishers Weekly*, Starred Review

"Robert Levy's *No One Dies From Love* may well end up being the book of the year for me. There is a frankness, a boldness, and a compassion in these stories that give real weight to the darkness they hold. It's easy to caricature human pain and vulnerability in service to a horror story, but Levy writes with honesty and depth, and it makes all the difference. I saw some of my own dark corners reflected back to me in this book, and felt the peace that comes from recognition. And that, to me, is what stories are all about."

—Nathan Ballingrud, author of *The Strange* and *North American Lake Monsters*

"Robert Levy's *No One Dies From Love* is a masterful collection of dark fiction—a consecrated and intimate ceremony of human loss and longing. With sumptuous prose and a keen understanding of how grief reshapes us, it's impossible to not be enthralled with Levy's macabre vision."

—Eric LaRocca, author of *Things Have Gotten Worse Since Last We Spoke*

D1590515

NO ONE DIES FROM LOVE

DARK TALES
OF LOSS AND LONGING

Other books by Robert Levy

The Glittering World

NO ONE DIES FROM LOVE
DARK TALES OF LOSS AND LONGING

ROBERT LEVY

WORD HORDE
PETALUMA, CA

An extension of this copyright page appears on page 245

First Edition

ISBN: 978-1-956252-06-4

A Word Horde Book
www.wordhorde.com

TABLE OF CONTENTS

No one dies from love
Guess I'll be the first

—Tove Lo

INTRODUCTION

BY PAUL TREMBLAY

I f the first story we're told as a child isn't a horror story (the fun kind with all manner of human or beastie threatening to eat children) then we're told a love story. Most of us, even the unfortunate ones who grow up trapped in a cruel and real version of a horror story, are taught to view the world through the distorted lens of love. Or, more accurately, the lens of distorted love. It would be an understatement to say Western mainstream culture celebrates and projects simplistic, moralistic, problematic, non-inclusive love stories, ones that often serve as the worst models for adult relationships. Beyond the baked-in cisgendered, patriarchal themes, even as a child, after watching a Disney-fied love story, I remember thinking, okay, great, the heroes are wed, but then what? Won't there be more dragons and poison apples to deal with in their happily ever after? Wouldn't it be disappointing if there weren't? And how long does happily ever after last anyway? (Yes, I was an annoying child.) What about my grandparents, the ones who'd been married for fifty years, or my other grandfather who lost his wife in the mid-1960s and never again dated never mind remarrying, and what about my parents who sometimes fought and ignored each other and sometimes hugged and laughed and hid in their bedroom (ew), and what about my aunt and her partner and why couldn't they (at the time) be married, and what about the quiet uncle who lived with my grandparents and had never been on a date, and what about my divorced aunt? What about me and the rest of us, who aren't princes and princesses? I can't say that the child-me understood the glimpse of awe, horror (what is a love story without horror?), and beauty within the existential binding of desire, love, and loss, but I could sense I had yet to be told anything close to the *full* story.

As adults, we learn that love is both complex and simple. Love is ephemeral and perhaps more precious because it can be lost so easily. Love is also, if not eternal, then spiritually akin to it. One can't describe love (like I'm trying to in my own hackneyed way) in a line. We better communicate love and loss and their ineffability in art and in story. Most stories are love stories.

Robert's brilliant collection, *No One Dies from Love*, gives us a glimpse at love's fuller, gloriously messy and harrowing story. The title itself is a bold statement of literary purpose and a dare to the reader. Is it a lie? Is it a truth? The unity of effect will fill and ache your heart.

"Little Flea, Little Flea" opens the collection with a brief, heartrending glimpse at the vastness of grief at love's loss and how it shapes our lives. Later in "The Cenacle," the weight of a widow's grief becomes an obsessive, haunting, self-destructive vigil. Queerness and *who are we when we love or when we deny it* are themes Robert expertly explores throughout the collection, including the erotic dark fantasy of "My Heart's Own Desire;" a man's desperate visit to an ex-partner of his newly missing lover that veers into cosmic horror in "DST (Fall Back);" and "The Closet Game," a wrenching coming-of-age story as a teen's denial of his desires and his denial of self echoes throughout his possible pasts and futures. "The Oestridae," "The Vault of the Sky, the Face of the Deep," and the haunting "The Rental Sister" pose difficult questions about the lengths we might go to in defending and defining the bonds of familial love. In "Ceremonials," feminine desire and righteous rage flower into grotesquely beautiful vengeance. "Conversion" is an utterly disturbing, unflinching extrapolation of the horror of gay conversion therapy. "Giallo" is a show-stopping fever dream in which desire runs gloriously amok.

These stories showcase Robert's breathtaking range as a writer, equally adept within historical and grounded settings as he is in the fantastic. He writes the quiet, exquisite character piece as well as unleashing grotesque visions that could make a splatterpunk blush. He writes with a fearless integrity of vision, yet as dark or as heavy as the stories get, they're still fun to read. How does he do that? I wish I knew. What I admire most about Robert as a writer is the humanity he imbues within his characters, all of whom are outsiders, just like us. If all stories are love stories, the best ones are always about outsiders.

I haven't even gotten to his *tour de force* novella yet.

Presented as a lost collection of her famous diary entries, "Anaïs Nin at the Grand Guignol" begins with an ending, the end of Nin's relationships with Henry Miller and his wife June. Distraught that she won't see June again, Nin seeks solace in the Grand Guignol theater, where she meets actress Paula Maxa, "The Most Murdered Woman of All Time." She also meets Maxa's destructive demon lover. The voice and writing style are revelations; a perfect amalgam of Nin's and Robert's. The story is as thrilling and titillating as it is ingenious. The novella encapsulates the collection's themes and concerns and is as empowering in the dual faces of love and grief as it is horrifying. The novella is the *full* story, and demands more than a single reading.

While reading this collection, I found an old saying about joy/love and grief was rolling around in my dusty head. I don't know where the saying originates, but it goes something like this: grief shared is divided and joy/love shared is multiplied. Sentimental, yes, but also, true. Or it's true enough that I want it to be always true. In the context of story, dividing grief and multiplying joy/love is an apt description of what writers at their best, at their most challenging and formidable can achieve.

I'd like to thank Robert for sharing his stories with us.

Paul Tremblay
12/29/22

LITTLE FLEA, LITTLE FLEA

The last time I saw my father I was five years old. After a series of abortive stays with various acquaintances and increasingly distant relations, the two of us found ourselves up in Seal Rock, crashing at the beachfront timeshare of his old college roommate; it was only later that I learned we were in fact trespassing, that my father had shimmied his way in through an unlocked window. He was already far gone by then. Major recalcitrance, off his medication, a typical recidivist bipolar case with a severe paranoiac streak to boot. We spent much of that summer scream-singing "Manic Depression" as we collected driftwood along our small stake of the Oregon coastline.

His latest obsession was aliens. It was the late '70s, and alien-related conspiracy was everywhere—abduction, invasion, *Close Encounters*, you name it. Dad considered himself an ambassador to our inevitable interplanetary visitors, someone who could best explain humankind's myriad customs and foibles. Many mornings he'd take to the beach to draw what he called pictograms in the sand, akin to cave drawings and large enough to be seen by Those Watching From Above. "So they know we're a civilized people," as he put it, a staged smile on his face that indicated they might be listening as well.

"I believe you," I told him. And I did.

Of course, back then I had no idea he was sick. I thought he was a blast, at least when he was capable of getting out of bed to meet

5

the day. One of our favorite games was our own version of Marco Polo called Little Flea, Little Flea, where the seeker would exclaim "Little flea, little flea, where can you be?" to which the hider would reply "Big flea, big flea, you'll never find me!" I was the one who hid, and upon finding me he'd shout "You can't fool me!" and spin me in the air until we'd both crash laughing together down to the water. Sunburnt and delirious, we would play for what felt like hours, until it was too dark to go on.

Little flea, little flea, where can you be?

I awoke one morning to find the house empty and trundled out to the deck. Dad was at work on his pictograms, this time of assorted tools, hammers and screwdrivers and wrenches and the like, rows of them in the sand. He shielded his eyes from the sun and waved me down, drawing stick in hand. When I reached him, I could tell he was more off than usual, his eyes wide and round as half-dollars.

"I wanted you to be here. For this. Don't you see? Here." He pulled me over to examine one of the drawings. A bulldozer, perhaps, or maybe some kind of scale? I couldn't say.

"Is that another tool?" I asked. He laughed, the sound broken and brittle, like ice cracking.

"It is, Donnie, it is." He chewed furiously at his lip. "Last night, in a waking dream? *They came to me.* Sent me a vision, to show how they're going to take me." He tapped the picture with his stick. "The name is unpronounceable, but it's essentially a sophisticated transporter device. It's going to reduce me to energy, then beam me up, up through the clouds and inside their ship. I'm supposed to meet them, out there," and he pointed the stick toward the ocean and the horizon beyond.

"Can I come?" I asked.

He laughed that odd laugh again, and bent to kiss the crown of my head. "You're a good kid," he said, his eyes ticking away, toward the water and the waves. "But I need you to stay here and protect the pictograms until I'm gone. Otherwise they won't know where to find me. Can you do that?"

I nodded. He handed me his drawing stick, peeled off his T-shirt and shorts, and ran naked into the water.

"Isn't it amazing?" he shouted from the surf. "They chose *me*."

I watched as he swam out, unsure of where exactly he was going, and when he was going to return. He soon grew invisible, the sun rising brilliant over the water until the entire ocean was one massive sheet of silver, like freshly fallen snow.

I sat in the sand, looking away from the water only to check on the pictograms, the tools in their proper place. We *are* a civilized people, I thought, and rested my head on my knees, the sun yellow and swollen in the sky. I stood to ward off curious gulls, swung at them with the stick, and by late afternoon I grew drowsy. Eventually, I fell asleep.

I awoke past nightfall to a low rumble, to bleach-white lights approaching from the lip of the shore, so bright against the darkness that I threw my arms over my face before I could be swallowed whole. The hard sound of metal on metal, of a hatch opening and shutting, of unsteady movement scuttling across the sand. Water lapped at my feet, the pictograms breached—had I protected them enough? Was it enough for my father to be found?

A new beam fell upon me, stark and blue and carrying an unearthly heat; I didn't know just how cold I was until it found me. Beyond the brightness, the suggestion of an approaching figure wending its way from a large transport of some kind, shadows against the waves. I fumbled for the drawing stick, but it was gone.

You can't fool me, I thought, and squinted into the light.

"Son?" He knelt down. I could make out the dim outline of his ranger hat, the glint of the flashlight, his metal badge. "You all alone out here?"

I looked up and past him, up toward the night sky and moon and planets, to the many stars above.

THE CLOSET GAME

You know the game, don't you? All you need is a closet, and a book of matches—and a willing participant. Not much to it, considering. Jesse first heard about it at twelve from his older sister, after she came home drunk from a party and was trying hard to scare him. Sleepover shenanigans when you lacked a Ouija board, bullshit kid stuff, he knew that much. A game of pretend. Still, she managed to strike a nerve.

You can open a door to another dimension, she whispered across the kitchen table, breath thick with the tang of spiked Red Bull. *You can conjure up a demon from hell.* He smiled with an air of disinterest, but his arms goosefleshed nevertheless.

Later a longhaired spindleshanks at seventeen, forehead splotched with a constellation of acne, Jesse is popular enough to be invited to parties of his own. Up in Craig's parents' bedroom sharing a joint with Tina and Beth, the four of them seated in a rough circle as the kegger rages below, he takes a slug of beer from his Solo cup as Craig explains the rules.

First, you turn out all the lights. Next, you stand inside the closet and close the door. You wait for at least five minutes, and if it's time, you hold out an unlit match and say,

Show me the light, or leave me in darkness.

How will you know when it's time? Tina asks, and Beth reaches over and takes hold of Jesse's hand. Beth is not the one whose hand he wants to hold. *What are you supposed to be waiting for?*

You're listening. For something inside the closet. His eyes tick toward Jesse, who looks away, shifts in place on the spongy carpet. *You might hear whispering, or scratching. Or maybe something else. But when you do, you have to light the match as quickly as possible. If you don't...*

If you don't, what?

Craig taps the joint into the ashtray. *If you hear something and you don't light the match, they say you'll be plunged into everlasting night.*

We could play seven minutes in heaven instead, Beth says, and slides Jesse's hand into her lap.

I'll do it. Jesse grabs the matches and leaps up, wipes his damp hands on the seat of his jeans. *I'll go.*

He enters the closet in darkness. Barely large enough to call a walk-in, but he can stand inside well enough, the airy flutter of clothing and the cling of dry-cleaning plastic lapping from their hangers. He closes the door, rocks on his heels, and he waits. *Okay,* he thinks, *this is going to be, like, nothing.* Pulse loud in his ears, his brain judders back in time, to last week and making out with Beth on a dilapidated lawn chair behind her house. The hungry way she straddled him, the pasty icing taste of her lipstick as she fumbled with his belt buckle.

Don't, he'd said, and grabbed hold of her wrists. *Let's wait until Saturday night, okay? At Craig's party. We'll do it then.*

And soon the intrusive thought appears. The one his mind has conjured too many times: Craig's mouth pressed to his instead, the smell of his best friend's beery breath as his tongue snakes its way between Jesse's teeth. The very thing he has wanted for over two years now, but will never fully admit, not to himself or anyone else. God, he wants Craig so bad he thinks it might kill him. Everything is so fucked up.

A creaking noise behind him, and he starts. The house settling, someone jumping up and down on the improvised dance floor, the dull bass thump from the speakers below. Still, he turns to look.

All that's here is the silent and expected gloom on all sides, and he faces the door once again, stares up at the ceiling. He wonders how long he's been inside, whether it's been long enough for him to give up. The creak from behind again. Only this time it's more like a scraping sound, a large dog scrabbling across floorboards, and Jesse spins. A mouse trapped in the walls, a squirrel or something, and he's had his fill now. He's done. He reaches for the door, his hand flailing forward into empty space. He tries again, this time to the left and right, thrashes around for a wall, for the hanging clothes, anything. There's nothing here to hold onto anymore, nothing at all.

Oh shit. *The match.* Hands shaking, Jesse fumbles with the matchbook, equilibrium dissolving so he is no longer certain what is up or down, whether he is standing on solid earth or floating in an ink-black void. The touch of a hand upon his neck, and he yelps and drops the matches. How far they fall he cannot say. Maybe feet, or light years, or eons.

Cold and impossible fingers begin to stroke at him. The touch firm and familiar, as if the hands are his own, amputated and soldered to the arms of a stranger. Terror floods his brain, and the scrabbling increases, the air permeated with the pungent scent of clove. *It's measuring me,* he thinks absurdly, and he cannot scream, cannot breathe as a white-hot pain sears into his chest like a brand.

An unearthly pressure on his spine, and for a moment there's the sensation of another figure passing through him, a rippling shadow but more like an antishadow, a being made of unseen light. Jesse is jerked forward, while some essential part of him is dragged back into the endless dark.

And just like that, the door is before him again, exactly where it should be. He stumbles shaking from the closet and falls forward into his small circle of friends, the ashtray upended as he gets to his feet. *What the fuck, dude?* Craig says, but Jesse doesn't answer, doesn't look back, only races to the bedroom door and thrusts it wide. He staggers down the hall, knocks a framed family portrait from the wall as he descends the staircase, breathless as he bounds down the steps two at a time. He dodges bodies on the dance floor, his classmates leering and wasted and delirious, and Jesse's here with them now, but also not here. It feels as if he's split between worlds, this and another one increasingly far away.

He closes the front door behind him, the night crisp and scentless as he drops down onto the porch swing and greedily sucks air into his lungs, his thirst for it that of a drowning victim. Heart pounding, he tries to shuck off the fear, to find an adequate explanation. It was just the weed, the beer, his imagination. *Chill. Try to chill. It was nothing, nothing at all.*

Only why did those hands feel so familiar?

He spreads his palms wide and stares down at them, flexes and straightens his fingers. For a fleeting moment, he doesn't recognize these hands as his own.

Jesse? Beth appears in the doorway, her features washed out in the muted glow from the porch light. *Are you okay?*

Yeah. I'm good. He swallows and stands, and what's left of Jesse smiles. *I'm ready now.*

He takes her by the hand and leads her back inside.

It's six weeks later that Beth drags him to the pharmacy for the pregnancy test, and of course the line on the pee stick turns baby-bold positive. If she didn't get knocked up at Craig's party then it was a few days later at her parents' place, but either way she missed her period, and this is really happening. Jesse's father is his anti-role model—the man disappeared for good into the never-never land of the Central America surfing world when Jesse was a toddler—so at least he knows what not to do. He offers to marry Beth, and to raise the child together, already resigned to his fate by the time she reluctantly agrees.

They get hitched over the winter, and it's well into spring when Kayla is born and the three of them move into a small apartment over Beth's parents' garage. Jesse didn't know he could love anything like this—he certainly never cared all that much for babies before—but here she is, his little pride and joy, and by the time Kayla's one month old he's already bringing home the bacon (well, some bacon anyway) at his cousin Sherman's auto body shop, where Jesse does the inspections and tune-ups, changes the oil and windshield wiper fluid, all the things that don't require too much knowhow, not yet. He's not going anywhere, unless he screws up and gets fired. He still has time to learn.

When he's not at work or at home helping Beth with the kid, Jesse drinks down at the Barrel Inn off Exit 25. They don't care that he's not of age, as long as he's respectful and tips the bartender and doesn't appear too trashed when he heads out for the night. He forms a little circle with some of the men there, and next to them he's a real goody-two-shoes, even if he also smokes weed now and again. Decent stuff too, a lot better than the shwag he and Craig used to score from the dealer behind the 7-11. Jesse makes a mental note to call his old friend and invite him out some night, just the two of them, but the thought soon evaporates.

Ever since that party, he can't shake this strange feeling of being watched. At home, at work, even at the bar, a pair of narrowed white eyes staring out from the hidden corners of mirrors and picture frames and, yes, closets too, their cracked-open doors an eerie invitation to some unknown place. Jesse tries not to look, to forget what happened that night in the dark. And still the shadows threaten. As movement in his periphery, shifting and fleeting figures that cannot be seen straight on but nevertheless haunt the edges of his vision.

He learns to live with these unnerving and quivering beings, until he grows so used to their presence it's as if they're a part of the natural environment, his everyday world. So Jesse tells himself his vision is going, that he should get his eyes checked, or maybe his brain, something. He tells himself these things as a kind of story, one he's trying to convince himself is true.

As for Craig, he and Tina get married after high school and have a kid themselves, and after Craig's parents die one after the next (his mother of cancer, his father of a blood infection) he and Tina move into his old childhood home. They have another kid, as do Jesse and Beth, the two couples on a similar trajectory though they've fallen out of touch. Occasionally they run into each other—Craig and Tina have their car serviced at Jesse's shop, though usually it's Tina who brings it in—but other than a passing hello, their paths largely go uncrossed.

Jesse consigns his old friendship to a figurative cardboard box beneath a bed, along with his baseball trophies and comic books and browned-out bong. Kid stuff all, part of some other life, another time now vanished into the past.

Eventually, he forgets about the closet and the game, forgets that he'd ever been attracted to Craig, or to any man at all. It was a phase, of course, a typical one for kids that age, isn't it? So what if when he and Beth sleep together (on Friday nights, the ones when they manage not to pass out first) Jesse imagines someone standing just behind him, another one of his shadowy figures doing to him what he's doing to her, just to keep himself up? It's no big deal. That's just the way it is.

Years later Jesse, now twenty-seven, comes home late from work on a Tuesday, the kids already asleep in bed, to find Beth crying at the kitchen table, a half-drained bottle of red wine in front of her. When he asks what's wrong she has him sit down, and she takes his chapped and worn hand in hers.

Tina Fisher called, she says. *She came home from dropping the kids at school this morning, and found Craig in the garage. There was an old gun of his dad's in the house, a rusted pistol they kept in a lockbox under their bed. Craig waited until she'd left, and then—*

Beth clears her throat. Rough, as if there's something stuck there. *He killed himself.*

Oh, wow. Jesse's stunned, he doesn't know what to say, and a chilly feeling creeps over his skin. It's almost like déjà vu, but that's not it exactly. It's more like he's forgetting to forget something he never knew in the first place, and the odd and uncomfortable sensation throws him into cold shadow.

It's horrible, Beth goes on, her eyes on the table. *I met up with Tina for coffee last year, she told me things had gotten bad between them. He spent lots of late nights at work, then would come home freshly showered, she could smell the soap on his skin. She found porn on his computer, and it was all...*

She looks up at him. *It was all gay.*

Oh, wow, Jesse says, again, like an idiot. He risks a glimpse past Beth, where the dim and narrow space above the refrigerator shimmers, a crouched and otherworldly figure made of darkness and light peering out at him from the gloom. They stare at each other full on.

He swallows hard, and forces himself to look away, and back at his wife. *That is horrible.*

I know. Beth pours herself another glass of wine and shakes her head. *I can't imagine what she's going through.*

The funeral is family only, but the wake is open to anyone, and a few days later Jesse finds himself back at Craig's house for the first time in years. For the first time since that party in high school maybe, when they were all so young and stupid, instead of old and stupid. The kids take over the backyard, and Beth plants herself at the table in the kitchen doorway, where she helps Tina's mom unwrap and serve the many dishes that keep arriving: macaroni salad, meatballs, rolled-up slices of ham and bologna and cubes of cheese on platters from the Stop & Shop. Jesse's not hungry though, not thirsty either, not feeling all that great to be honest. He tugs at the collar of his starched dress shirt and excuses himself from the heat of the grief-heavy room, and he heads upstairs to be alone.

At the end of the hall is Craig's parents' room, which of course is now Craig and Tina's room, or was. Now it's only Tina's room, and when Jesse eases the door shut behind him the smell of her perfume lingers in the air, a spiced scent, almost like clove. His eyes flit to the corner, where a sheath of dry-cleaning plastic hanging from the back of the closet door shudders in the wake of his entrance.

The closet door. He remembers now: the strange party game, the unforgiving darkness, the thing that had touched him inside the closet. As he recalls the sensation of its cold and appraising fingers, Jesse's arms gooseflesh, the hair there standing on end. Despite himself, he's still afraid there's something out there watching him, waiting for him, something he brought forth from the closet, and in truth there's been times the feeling has damn near made him lose his mind. Now that he's back where it started, he can finally admit that much to himself.

There's a danger in not being honest with yourself, isn't there? A real danger, not some kind of metaphorical one. Isn't it this very same danger that had finally gone and killed Craig? *Craig.* His stomach lurches, the depth of his feeling suddenly more than he's allowed himself until now. The loss of his onetime best friend is so… immeasurable. Jesse hasn't let this kind of raw emotion pass through him in far too long. Maybe as long as it's been since he was back in this very room, and still in love with Craig. It was love, yes. He can admit that now too. It really was love.

Without another moment's thought, he strides over to the closet and grasps the doorknob, the dry-cleaning plastic rustling again as he opens it.

In the light from the doorway he examines the closet's contents, one length of the hanging clothes made up of Tina's orderly and bright assortment of skirts and dresses and pants, while the sloppy side is Craig's, a dark palette of slacks and patterned shirts and a sports jacket or two hanging in disarray from the metal rod. Jesse runs his hand down Craig's half, until he reaches hard and cracked leather hanging at the back of the closet.

It's Craig's old letterman jacket, the one he earned for junior varsity wrestling. Jesse would have joined the team their senior year, if he hadn't knocked up Beth and dropped out for his job at Sherman's. He takes hold of the lapel and leans in to smell it, but it makes him think of that gay cowboy movie where that dead actor who played the Joker did the same thing with Jake Gyllenhaal's shirt or whatever, and he takes a step away instead.

Back in the day, Craig looked damned good in this jacket, and he knew it too; he used to wear it to pool parties in the summertime, even in the blazing heat, nothing underneath but a pair of skintight swim trunks and maybe some flip-flops. Jesse grins at the memory before his smile fades, and he wonders for the first time in far too long if there ever could've been something between them. Even something so unlikely as a kind of future together, like the ones they both made with Tina and Beth. Maybe, maybe not, and now he'll never know, will he? For Craig, there's no such thing as the future anyway, not anymore.

Jesse turns to leave the closet, and his shoe crunches down on something. He lifts his foot up, and in the light from the open doorway rests a book of matches on the carpeted closet floor. *How funny*, he thinks, *it's just like from that game.* Only it's not so funny at all, is it?

He knows he should leave it alone, but even as he tells himself to walk out the door, to head back downstairs to his wife and kids and the others that have gathered to mourn their collective loss, he finds himself reaching for the matchbook. Jesse fingers it in one hand, and uses the other to draw the closet door closed, just as he did ten years earlier. Sleepover shenanigans, he tells himself, bullshit kid stuff, and he tears away the cardboard matchstick.

He knows that he's lying to himself. He's become so good at it, and at this point it would be out of character for him to believe the truth, close to an impossibility. He was right about the game in the first place, after all. Like so much of Jesse's life, it's only a matter of pretend.

He can't remember the rules, but he can remember what went wrong: he never lit the match. This time he waits for a minute or two, and goes ahead and rakes the match head across the striker. Once it flares, he squints past the golden glow and finds the closet door before him, not a single thing different or strange.

Show me the light, he thinks, *or leave me in darkness.* He reaches out for the knob and turns it, and pushes the door wide open.

The bedroom, it's darker now and heavy with the sticky-sweet scent of weed, and the energy in the air has shifted. There are three people seated on the carpeted floor in front of him. It's Craig, and Tina, and Beth, all young again, teenagers in the dirty ripe bloom of budding youth.

It's all Jesse can do not to cry out, in both shock and in relief, and he clamps a hand over his mouth. Because now he still has time to make braver choices, to tell Craig how he really feels about him. It isn't too late for things to turn out differently.

How long is he gonna be in there? Tina says, her voice a smoke-thick rasp as she exhales in a thin gray cloud. *It's been, like, half the night.*

He's not coming out of there, not any time soon. Craig takes the joint from Tina and rolls it back and forth between his thumb and index finger, loosening it. *He's in there hiding from Beth.*

Shut up, Beth says, and she laughs, but it's only a performance of laughter. *You're such a jerk, Craig.*

H-hello? Jesse says from the doorway, the match twitching in his grasp. *Guys? Can you hear me?* But there's no response whatsoever.

Oh, come on, I'm just kidding. Craig smiles, and Jesse's heart catches. *But seriously, did you see the way he jumped up before? Looked like someone lit his ass on fire. Makes you wonder what's really going on inside his head.*

A rush of air and a thud, and something shoves hard into Jesse from behind. He lurches back and reaches out to steady himself with his free hand, the other still pinching the lit match. His hand finds the column of a tapered neck, then, lower, a knobby shoulder too, the touch of a warm body beneath thin cotton. *It's one of those things*, he thinks, the antishadows at the corner of his vision, he recognizes it by its dark and shivering form. Only this one, it's made physical, turned to flesh and blood.

As he feels his way around it, the figure shirks him off and barrels past him, out the door and into the center of the room. It's not a shadow at all, though, or at least not anymore. It's Jesse. His younger self, as young as the others, and he watches this other version of him spill to the floor, overturning the ashtray inside the circle before he stands and rights himself.

What the fuck, dude? Craig says, no answer as the boy races from the bedroom without looking back.

From the closet doorway, Jesse looks over at Craig. He squints past the dwindling match, and in the hazy light from the dimmed lamp atop the dresser Craig's face is newly desiccated, his features receding into his skull. For a moment, Craig appears to return Jesse's stare, only he has no eyes anymore, just hollowed-out sockets that peer from the dim with a cold and unforgiving sight of their own.

The match burns his finger, and Jesse howls, dropping it. A wisping scent of sulfur, and he's plunged into a new and complete form of dark, empty and soundless. Everlasting night.

Jesse gasps hungrily, filling his lungs with oxygen that he fears will soon evade him. Still, he palms the matchbook in his clammy hand, he's not going to lose them again, not like last time. Fingers trembling, he fumbles with the matchbook before he manages to light another, the closet door shut before him once more.

Show me the light, or leave me in darkness. The match held in front of him, he reaches out with his free hand and turns the knob.

A woman stands at the dresser, alone. It's Tina, the age she's supposed to be now. She's taken off her dress from the wake, and is turned away from him, busy removing her makeup with a cotton pad. Her arm works in a furious blur, the fingers of her other hand digging into the edge of the dresser so hard her nails score the wood. Jesse steps from the closet, a floorboard creaking underfoot so that she spins around to face him.

Tina's face is gone. It's blank but for her grimacing mouth, she's removed all trace of her eyes and nose, her eyelashes and eyebrows.

What are you doing here? she screams. She charges at him, the pad in her hand matted with hair and gristle and pus. *What are you, some kind of pervert? My God!*

I'm sorry, he says, *Tina, I'm so sorry*. But it's no good, and she batters at him with her fists and that menacing pad, bits of her paring from the cotton and coating his dress shirt in gore.

Go away! she cries, and he stumbles from her. *Go away! Go away!* She slams the closet door shut between them, the sound of her screams rattling the wood in its frame.

The match burns his fingertips, and he drops it. Palms slick with sweat, he dries the matchbook on his pant leg and plucks another from the frayed cardboard.

Show me the light, or leave me in darkness.

He lights a match, reaches forward, and opens up the door.

An adult Craig, seated on the edge of the bed. Beside him is a lockbox, the flaked tan lid already lifted and facing Jesse so he can't see what's inside. But he knows. He knows what's inside and his blood runs cold, he watches frozen with dread as Craig reaches into the open box for his chosen weapon of self-annihilation. Jesse thinks *don't do it don't do it don't do it,* but the words don't come out, no sound whatsoever as Craig continues reaching inside, his arm disappearing up to the elbow, followed by the shoulder. Craig lowers his head, and soon the whole of him gushes forward in an unreal tide of thick ooze, down into the dark of the box.

The light in the room flickers and dims, the rushing onset of a time-lapse dusk, and the match in Jesse's hand burns out. He fumbles for another, lighting it and hitching forward to open up the closet door.

He stands on the edge of a narrow precipice, and when he stares out into the distance there's nothing but a starless and cold night, vast and dark. A dank and fetid smell of rot, he looks down past the lip of the jagged cliff. Far below is a sunken valley, or possibly it's a dried riverbed, filled edge to edge with splayed corpses as far as the eye can see. Some an ancient scattering of bleached-white bones, others so recently perished they are the very picture of sleep, the bodies are stacked so high they seem to melt into one another, innumerable and of every age and race and size and shape. Jesse knows, in his heart, that these countless dead over countless centuries are those who have played the game and lost. Every one of them unable to escape from the endless dark, to survive this fatal contest of pretend.

Is Craig down among them? Will Jesse be one day himself? Or is there even some part of himself already there, lost a decade past now?

High on the cliff, Jesse weeps for them all, and through his fractalizing tears their bodies appear to glow. With lost promise, or with righteous anger, or maybe with a lingering pain, he doesn't know. The secret parts of themselves they kept hidden away for so long shine on undiminished like embers in the valley below. They burn from within, a thousand thousand beacons in the otherwise impenetrable gloom.

The match scorches his finger, and Jesse drops it over the edge, the faint light winking out as he's thrown into darkness.

He lights another match and holds it out, a flare and a half-hearted flutter amid the dim before it too is extinguished. A faint sulfur smell, and the heavy night surrounds him.

He lights another match and waits. It burns out as well, again with that sulfurous scent. Darkness.

Match. Sulfur. Darkness.

Match. Sulfur. Darkness.

His shoulders wracking with sobs, Jesse says *come on come on come on*, his voice raw as he squats on the ground and keeps lighting what seems an endless series of matches, each one burning down to his fingers and throwing him back into the dark of the closet, of his very own life.

Maybe the next match will be the one that changes everything, that gives him the present he so desperately craves, away from this world of terror and fear and cruelty. Or maybe the future he dreamed of, the one that was never meant to be but haunts him just the same, the phantom limb of a life unlived. Where is a past he can still return to, to try and change everything for the better? A world where Craig still lives, where they all do, each one of them their own bright flame in the everlasting night, a galaxy of stars loosed upon the earth like scattered sparks. That's what he wants. That's all he wants. For all of them, each and every one.

In his mind's eye, these many lights keep shining, and still he's left in darkness. There has to be another way.

He lights another match, and he waits.

THE OESTRIDAE

White dust rises from the road like tobacco smoke, followed by the grinding of car wheels on dry Pennsylvania dirt as a silver compact rumbles into view, up the hill on its way to the house. "Who's that?" I say, but Dara only shakes her head and continues to chew at her hair. The spit-wet strands fall from my sister's lips, her gaze lifting until she rises, pulled from the Adirondack chair as if hefted on a rope. It's an August scorcher, the space between us and the road shimmering with heat as we wait for the sky to shift like a sieve and let the rain tumble through, the air a thick wool blanket. It's been humid like this for a month now, ever since our mother disappeared. And just when I think I've finally run out of hope, one last drip of it leaks out to ruin everything.

Near the end of the drive the car stops, about thirty yards from the house. We move as one to the porch steps, the windows of the compact filthy with bone-gray dirt, windshield so impenetrable it's hard to believe the driver can see at all. The car door swings open and a woman emerges, her tangled mane of tight blond curls tamed by a lime green scarf wrangled over her hair and tied underneath her chin like a golden age movie star. She wears oversized shades as well, big black lenses in lacquered Hollywood frames. Her tattered red T-shirt and cutoff blue jeans, though, they're pure country, lean browned limbs bent in two sickled crooks like a grasshopper's legs before she straightens and turns her face toward us.

She lowers her sunglasses, just as Dara gasps beside me. Beneath the headscarf and blond hair, the large glasses and down-home getup, the woman appears to be our mother.

"Billy," Dara says in a whisper.

"Don't." My hand slides in front of her, but she brushes past me and down the steps. The woman, still as a scarecrow, waits beside her car, the sky and distant mountains behind her a matte pane of gray against her vibrant clothing. A soft smile forms upon her achingly familiar face as we approach.

"Hi there," she says. "You're Marlene's babies, aren't you? William and Dara." It's only once she speaks that I'm sure it's not Mom, not really. But this stranger's voice, husky and damp, it looks to be spoken between our mother's lips, and I feel Dara tense on the other side of the dulled silver car. "You must be wondering who I am."

"Are you going to tell us?" I say, and she laughs, really throws her head back and lets it rip.

"I figured *you* wouldn't remember me. What about you?" she says, and looks at my sister. "Might you have a guess?"

"No," Dara says, but I can see her searching the woman's face, dredging the shallows of her memory for an answer. "But you look just like our mother…"

"Yes. Well, I'm not surprised by that one bit. Although it sure has been a while." With a swift blur of motion she unties the scarf and pulls it artfully from her head, a cascade of long tendrils springing out in a bottle-blond wave. "I'm your mother's sister. Your aunt."

"Our aunt?" I say, the words foreign to me. "Mom's an only child."

"Wait." Dara chews at a split end, and she's nodding now, only a little but it's there all the same. "I think I do remember hearing something once about a sister. An older one."

"Younger, thank you very much. But only by a year. The neighbors used to call us Irish twins. Not real ones like you two." She presses a palm to the side of her skull, makes a couple of curls bounce. "My proper name is Lucinda Leigh. But you can call me Aunt Lacy."

"Aunt Lacy," I repeat, as if commanded. It doesn't sound as wrong as I would imagine.

"So, where's your mother at?" She looks toward the house. "I traveled a long way to get here. She'd sure be a sight for tired eyes." Dara and I stare at each other, then away, at the car, the road, the trees and mountains beyond.

"What is it?" Lacy says. "She not here? Don't tell me I came all this way for nothing."

"Our mother…" Dara starts, then stops and looks toward the fence and the road beyond.

"She's missing," I finish. "Twenty-eight days now. She works at a store at the mall, and her manager said she never came back from her lunch break. No one knows what happened to her, or where she might have gone." That sweltering afternoon I pictured her passed out in her car, overtaken by the humidity, but her hatchback was found in the mall parking lot unoccupied.

"Dear lord." Lacy pales and lists, her hand releasing the headscarf as she leans on the hood of the car for support. "Oh my dear sweet lord."

Dara goes to her, puts her arm around Lacy's shoulders and holds her firm. "Come," my sister says, sounding sure of herself for the first time in weeks. "Let's go inside and I'll get you something to drink."

As we mount the porch steps, Aunt Lacy stares over her shoulder at me, her black eyes hard like the lenses of the glasses that had obscured them. Her irises are like polished stones, like our mother's eyes. They're tough to look into so I turn away, toward the lawn and Lacy's scarf as it snakes across the grass, the wind newly baleful.

The hot breeze lifts the scarf into the air before dropping it to the earth once more, where it continues to slither through the dry turf until it catches on the bottom of a fence post and coils there, dead. The screen door snaps closed behind us with a clap, just as it begins to rain.

Dusk settles over the mountains. It will soon be time for dinner, and for three, no less. Storming bad now and I head out back before it gets any darker, soaked through by the time I fetch the hatchet from the woodpile at the side of the house and make for the board-and-wire coop out back. "Shhh, don't worry, okay," I say, "it's going to be okay," the chickens screaming and kicking up pine shavings and running wild from my reaching fingers until I manage to snag one and wrestle it from its cage. I place the bird between my knees, stroke its soft brown feathers until it calms a bit; I cradle it in my arms like a tender thing and walk the green mile to the hemlock stump. Still, I can smell its fear. I stun it with the axe handle and cleave its head off, hold its jerking body up by its feet until it's done fighting, done bleeding out. Mom used to do all this, but now it's down to me.

By the time I've dried myself off and plucked and prepped the chicken, Dara and Aunt Lacy have set the table and parked themselves there over beers and a summer salad of greens from our mother's garden. As I cook they chatter about Lacy's cross-country trip to New York to visit an old cosmetology school friend who opened her own salon, and how Lacy had to make the detour to stop in on her only sister, her only niece and nephew, whom she'd never even met. How startled she is to see them grown, and to learn her sister has vanished.

Once we've had our fill, we let the weight of the meal sink us back in our seats. Aunt Lacy lights a cigarette, and I glance at my sister; Mom never lets anyone smoke in the house, but Dara appears unfazed. I was supposed to leave yesterday for college, but I decided to stay here instead. Me and Dara, we take care of each other. And in the four weeks since Mom went missing, I've imagined the most terrible things.

"Four weeks," Lacy says from the head of the table. She taps the lip of her empty beer bottle against her front teeth. "I can't believe it."

"No trace, no nothing," Dara says. "She just walked on out of the mall and never came back. There's security camera footage of her heading down the road on foot in the direction of the river, but that's all we have."

"I still can't believe Mom has a sister," I say, then flinch, not meaning to say it out loud. I stand quickly to collect the dishes, avoiding Lacy's too-familiar face, afraid of meeting her head-on.

"So, Lacy," Dara says, all her attention on our new aunt, "tell us more about Los Angeles."

"Oh, it's a grand place. Just grand. The people though... They aren't quite up to snuff, if you ask me. They aren't *real*. Some of their parts aren't, neither." She huffs out a smoke-ringed laugh. "Take this one fella I was dating. He was real nice, real generous too. But what an ego! He was a *general practitioner*," she says, annunciating the words with disgust. "You know doctors. They all think they poop out angel feathers. Every last one of them."

I swallow hard and turn from the kitchen area. "I'm actually studying to be a surgeon," I say with as much calm as I can muster. "I'm supposed to go pre-med this semester."

"Well look at you!" Lacy smiles, her teeth stained yellow, like antique ivory buttons. "So it turns out this doctor is still married. Has a wife and family out in Pasadena. Can you imagine? And here I am, sitting there like a fool just waiting for him to make an honest woman out of me. *Actors*. All of them actors out there, even the ones that aren't."

"Really coming down now," I say as I peer out the little window over the sink, and make a point of rattling the stack of dirty dishes against the tiled counter, turn the tap on loud to cause more of a racket, anything to disrupt her nattering. "Aunt Lacy, you should get a move on before it gets much worse. The flooding around here is brutal. I'd hate for your car to get stuck on your way out of town."

"Billy, that's rude." Dara places her beer bottle down on the table. "She's come a very long way, and had a terrible shock."

"It's true," Lacy says, her head wobbling in a gyroscopic shimmy, a bobbleheaded doll. "The shock has been terrible."

"Aunt Lacy," Dara says, shifting closer to her, "I'd like you to stay the night with us. It would be lovely to catch up some more."

"Oh. Oh, honey, that would be swell," Lacy says. "Just the night, and I'm gone."

"You can stay as long as you want. Isn't that right, Billy?" Dara says, her face turned away. Lacy, though, she looks up at me, her stare penetrating, the electric glow of the overheads forming two crescent moons in her shark-black eyes. I feel her on my skin, trying to crawl inside my head. I turn back to the window over the sink and the darkness beyond.

"Sure." What else am I supposed to say? I go back to doing the dishes, scraping away the remains with renewed aggression as they return to their small talking.

"Dara, honey," Lacy says, "when was the last time you washed your hair?" She reaches for my sister but stops. "It's so beautiful, but honestly…"

"What, this?" Dara takes a shoot of her greasy locks in her fingers and stares at it appraisingly, as if through new eyes. "It's been a while," she admits.

"Well, tonight's your lucky night. Because I am going to do it for you. I'm gonna use a deep treatment that will bring its natural rich luster to the surface, where it will really shine. Show me where your bathroom's at, will you?"

"Okay." Dara smiles, really smiles, something I haven't seen in too long. "But it's not going to be pretty."

They rise and glide across the room. Dara disappears up the steps, while Lacy turns back for a moment, clutching the banister with the sinewy talons of a nighthawk.

"Nice to meet you, Billy," she says, her voice sickly sweet. There's no joy in her face, though, her expression as unreadable as her eyes of hard jet. "And thanks for letting me stay. Looks like it might rain for quite some time."

She lengthens and continues her ascent, leaving me and the night to ourselves.

It rains for three days straight. Mostly I spend it in my musty bedroom, playing video games or thumbing through the moldering Introduction to Anatomy textbook I bought at a tag sale a few years ago, the one that first made me curious about how a person looks when he's been opened wide for the world to see; after I showed interest, Mom made sure I got a scalpel set for Christmas, and a model skeleton for my next birthday. I'd bring home things to dissect, frogs from the pond or stillborn rabbits from my friend Barry's hutch. The only thing my mother warned me never to mess with were the botflies that gather in black clouds around the chicken coop, particularly during an Indian summer. It's bad luck to kill those.

Lacy and Dara shut themselves up in Dara's room. I don't know what they get up to exactly, except sometimes at night I can hear them both laughing behind the closed door, the only real laughter we've had in the house since Mom went away. I've stopped saying vanished, or disappeared, or went missing, because it doesn't feel like that anymore, not to me; now it feels like she knew something bad was on its way, and took off before she had to meet it face to face.

On the third night of rain, we gather for a dinner of rice and beans. Heavy bags have swollen under Dara's glassy eyes, dark and brown circles ringed like bird nests. Her mood is buoyant, however, almost manic, and I start to wonder if my sister is sleeping at all. "Tell us more about California, Lacy!" she shouts. "Tell us everything!" Dara claps her hands hard enough to put out the tapers, the ones in the silver candlesticks Mom got at work for next to nothing. And Aunt Lacy is happy to oblige. She's all saucy stories and little winks and butter-scented smiles, but it's hollow, so hollow. I want to say something is very wrong, but I don't. I know no one wants to hear it.

Just before dawn it's finally not raining for one goddamned minute, although it's already hot enough in the day to bubble the paint on my bedroom wall. I head down the hallway to pee, and on my way back I notice my sister's door is cracked open. Just beyond is her bed, three lumpy and worn mattresses piled atop a fiberboard platform. Bent at its foot is Aunt Lacy. She's wearing a blood-red slip dress and hunched over so I can't see her face, only the corkscrews of her near-white hair. She lifts herself into a sitting position and unfurls a black stocking on her long tanned leg, her red lacquered toenails visible through the sheer. I can't imagine why she wants to wear stockings in this weather; even shirtless I feel a fresh slick of perspiration as it forms on my skin.

"Like what you see?" Aunt Lacy says, and it takes me a moment to realize she's talking to me. She teases the second stocking up her thigh, then faces me with her same put-on smile, her same eyes of glossed black onyx, familiar but not. "I'm guessing the answer is no."

"Where's Dara?" I step closer to the doorway but Lacy leaps up and makes it there before me.

"Dara's busy right now. Girl stuff." She steps into the hall and shuts the door behind her. "Is there something I can help you with?"

"It stopped raining, at least for now. I was wondering…"

"Whether I was going to hit the road anytime soon?" Her smile remains, but if there was ever anything behind it that's gone now. "It's not that simple. Your mama has something of mine. A very special thing. And I'm going to need it to get better."

"Are you sick?"

"Something like that." She stretches her hands above her head; her arms tremble, they shake.

"Maybe she left it here. We can help you look for it."

She laughs a little laugh. "You don't understand. That's why she went away. She knew I was coming, and she put it where I couldn't get at it. Maybe she took it. Or maybe not."

"What is it that's so important to you? Or to her?"

"It's a real piece of me. One I can't be whole without." She gives me a strange look. "You can't comprehend," she says. "It's not a matter for men. Let alone little boys."

"Who you calling boy?"

"You, Jack-be-nimble." With a sharp flick of her wrist she slashes a fingernail across my left cheek. I put my hand to my face, stunned. "Play with fire and you just might find a candlestick up your ass."

Before I can speak, she spins on her heel, scuttles back inside and eases the door shut once more, this time with a clicking of the lock.

I stagger back and down the hall to the bathroom, where I grip the edges of the sink to stare at my reflection in the mirror. My face is shocked and pale but there's no mark, and I appear to be unmarred, as if never scratched to begin with. But I feel the wound nevertheless, just beneath my sweat-coated skin. I press the meat of my palms to my stinging eyes as I try to steady my breath.

I wait for them to show for dinner, but they never come. So I remain downstairs at the table until long past midnight, a bottle of beer warming in my hand as I listen to the rain pelt the tin roof. Eventually a door creaks open overhead, followed by the groan of wood risers as a body gradually descends the stairs, its gait awkward with the provisional unsteadiness of the infirm.

"Dara?" I squint through the gloom at the figure, and she stills at the bottom of the stairs, her nightgown pale pink and hung lifeless over her narrow frame. She's too tall to be Aunt Lacy, but she doesn't move like my sister, not at all.

"What? Oh, yes," she replies, my sister's voice after all but spoken in a scratched-vinyl rasp. "I was just going to…" She points toward the kitchen with a spindly arm, skin pale blue in what little diffuse moonlight manages to filter inside the room. "May I?"

"Please." I wonder why she's asking permission, it's her house as much as mine.

She shuffles over to the refrigerator and reaches inside for the water pitcher, the spout of which she brings directly to her lips. Dara drinks for an interminable length of time, until the pitcher is drained and returned empty to its shelf.

"Thirsty, huh?" I chuckle lamely.

"Yes," she says, "thirsty," and laughs in vague imitation. Her black hair shines in the dim, but not her eyes, which are hooded and obscured as she turns toward the stairs.

"Hey." I rise from my seat, which makes her stiffen, as if I were a wild animal she knows she can't outrun. "Don't you ever wonder why Mom never said anything about Aunt Lacy?"

"But she did, she did." My sister slowly nods, and continues to do so. "She told me something once, about how you can't ever stop what's coming. That when it's your time, you have to open yourself up to it and let it do its work. She said those exact words."

"And you think she was talking about Aunt Lacy?"

"Of course, silly," she says and gives another little chuckle, her head still nodding, nodding. "What else would she be talking about?"

"Dara…" I step closer and she steps back, but now I see just how skinny she is, her nightgown soaked through and clinging to her chest like a false skin. "You look like you've been having night sweats. Are you feeling okay?"

"Yes. Oh yes." She smiles, her teeth gray in the moonlight. "Oh yes."

Her wet eyes swim with glaze before she turns away again and heads up the stairs, the sound of bare feet padding against wood steadily diminishing until the only sound is the beating of the rain.

I ease the screen door closed and step onto the porch, breathe in the steaming wet smells of late summer as it continues to pour, the rain a thick curtain off the eaves and overflowing gutters just this side of the vast darkness beyond the house. A snap and a flare of light and I start: Aunt Lacy, seated beside me in one of the two Adirondack chairs. She lights a cigarette, her dark eyes trained on me.

"Lovely weather we're having, isn't it," she says and smiles, but it's not a question, just like it isn't a smile. "Here." She flicks her chin in the direction of the second chair. "Have a seat."

"I'm good standing, thanks." Looking down on her from this height I note how tiny she really is, almost roachlike, and she repulses me just the same. "Probably should get to bed, so..."

"You think you're pretty clever, huh?" She ashes her cigarette with an angry jab of her finger. "Little doctor man. A real Doogie Howser MD, am I right? *Night sweats*. That's a good one." She leans forward in her seat, and her face widens, eager, its own kind of collection plate. "You don't like me very much, do you? No, I can tell. You don't think very much of me at all."

I shrug, but my skin goes cold. I have no choice, I see that now. I've got to get her gone from here.

"You know that piece of yourself you said you were looking for," I begin, "that one that you said our mother took with her?" I stare out into the dark night, in the direction of the main road. "If you want it so bad, why don't you go look for her or something? It's not here, you said it yourself."

"You see, little boy, that's the thing," and she taps the tip of a sharp fingernail against her lower lip. "I'm starting to think that all I need is right here after all." Lacy reaches for her beer, her fingers skittering over her black plastic lighter and across the arm of the chair like a spider. "Mothers and daughters, they share certain gifts. Certain secrets."

"Like how Dara had heard of you before and I hadn't."

"Something like that." She watches a spiral of smoke snake upwards in the muted light. "Besides, your mother might come back some day. And I want to be here when she does."

"She's not coming back," I say, and as soon as the words come out of my mouth I know that they're true. Our mother is never coming back. And as soon as I know this, I also know that Aunt Lacy isn't all she says she is, and that she's not going to leave, not ever, even if she does get what she's come for. She's an evil thing that's found a dry and deep hole to move into, found a dark void in our tragic little lives that was all too primed for the filling, made her way into a place she was never meant to be. Just like the botflies do, out by the coop. After the chickens peck at each other the flies move in, lay their eggs beneath the feathers, in the scratched and broken skin.

Aunt Lacy, she's just like those flies. She's crawled inside our open wound, here to stay unless I do something about it, and fast. She's a dirty little liar is what she is. I bet she's never even been to Los Angeles.

My stomach contracts so hard that my legs buckle and I fall to my knees, the porch wood and roof tin and rainy night sky all spinning out around me. I can't breathe, not enough air to take in, nowhere near enough. I can't breathe. I bring a hand to my chest, open and close my mouth like a fish flopping on the floor of a boat, and in a flash she's right beside me.

"You feel that, little Billygoat?" she whispers in my ear, and all I can do is moan in response. "That's the pain your mama felt when she shat you out into this world, the pair of you good-for-nothings. And ever since, all the both of you have done is take. That's probably why she ran off. Who the hell would want to stick around this dump with you two?"

"You may look like her," I manage to get out, my eyes fixed on the porch's scored surface. "But you're nothing like our mother. Nothing at all."

"But I'm the one who's here."

I swear I can hear her smile.

"Lacy," I say between wheezes. "Aunt Lacy, listen."

She puts the side of her head against the floorboards, her eyes inches away from mine and peering inside me, hollowing me out.

"Yes?"

"I think there's something you should see. It's where our mom keeps her most special things."

"Oh yeah?" Her eyes turn to honeycombs, her lips quiver and part in pleasure.

"It's around the side of the house, by the woodpile. I'll show you…"

"Finally." She rises and straightens, the sound of her dusting off the front of her dress before the clack-clacking of her heels as she crosses the porch. Nausea seizes me in its contracting fist, and I roll onto my side, use one of the chairs to pull myself up into something resembling a standing position.

"Well?" she says from the porch steps, her bright hair already sparkling in the rain. "You coming or not? And you better not be screwing with me."

"Don't worry, okay?" Lacy turns and heads down to the lawn, and I slip her plastic lighter from the arm of the chair, its deceptively insubstantial weight solid in the palm of my hand. "It's going to be okay."

I take the hatchet to Dara's bedroom door, the axe's blood-stained edge making a pulped mess of the wood around the beveled glass knob so I can reach through and open the door from the inside. I tuck the handle of the hatchet into my waistband and search the room, overturn the bed and move the dresser away from the wall before I find my sister on the floor of the closet. She's skin and bones, her naked body sticky all over with what feels like cobwebs. As I pull away the wet strands, however, it begins to feel more like damp thread or hair. "Dara," I say, "we've got to go," and I haul her up into my arms, her eyes shocked wide and haunted, face sheened with sweat. "Listen to me. Can you hear me?"

"Something hurts," she says, wincing. She puts a hand to her chest and coughs. "Right here, inside of me. I can feel it… moving."

"I'm going to get you better. I promise. But you're going to have to come with me."

Dara nods a little, but then she pushes against me, tries to twist from my grasp and back toward the closet. She's weak, though, and I pull her in close, hustle her out of the room. We head down the stairs and through the kitchen, out the front door and down the porch steps, dodging loosed chickens as we make our way to Aunt Lacy's car. I wonder if my sister smells the meat cooking above the scent of cindering pine shavings, the savory odor of burning flesh. It's not raining anymore, but still it threatens.

"Chickens," Dara says in a dazed whisper, as I lay her down in the back seat. "Someone let the chickens out."

"Looks like." I toss the hatchet onto the passenger seat and run back inside the house for a few last things before I climb behind the wheel.

Dara stares up at me. "What about Aunt Lacy?" she asks, her lips cracked and bleeding.

"She's going to stay here for a while," I say, my voice pitched to soothe in my best bedside manner. "As long as she wants, like you said. She's going to hold down the fort."

I start the ignition just as a terrible moaning pierces the damp wet air, a deep and mournful wail that causes me to shake so violently I slam on the gas pedal before taking the car out of park. No, not mournful. Injured. Spiteful. I had hoped dissevering her head from her body, her tongue from her mouth, her limbs from her torso would have brought us some quiet. But even dismantled into pieces and locked up in the chicken coop, the entire structure doused in lighter fluid and set aflame, even that hasn't managed to fully shut her up.

I wanted it to have been easy; instead I bit down hard on my tongue as I worked, wished myself less timid and more bold, more cruel, like her. That I could reduce her to specimen alone. But that's not in my nature, and I know that now as well. What I don't know is why I turned out different from Aunt Lacy, where the branches of our family tree parted and made us into two separate kinds of things. But I am different from her. And I have to believe my sister is as well. We can't all be monsters, can we?

"That sound…" Dara shivers and sits up. "What's that sound?"

"It's only the wind, playing tricks. Close your eyes and sleep, okay? We'll be there soon."

We roll out into the night. The hood of the car is glossed with rain and shimmers in the starlight as we leave our home in the rearview, the bright flicker of flames from the coop burning yellow and blue as we continue down the drive. We reach the bottom of the hill, and I make the turn away from town.

"Where are we going?" Dara asks.

"In the direction of the river," I tell her. That's all we have to go on.

I glance at the hatchet on the passenger seat, where it sits atop my anatomy book, beside my scalpel set and surgical tools, all the things I'd hoped would bring me closer to being the person I wanted to be, the one who could make everything better. But that's probably over now. I've messed where I shouldn't have, and now I'm on call. All that's left to do is finish the work I started.

The scalpels, those are for Dara; if Aunt Lacy left something inside of my sister, I'm going to have to cut it out of her. I'll do the same for myself if I have to, and I touch at the invisible wound upon my cheek. Who knows how deeply she's burrowed inside of us? And the hatchet, that's for our mother if she abandoned us, not to mention any other bad relations we may meet along the way. There might be more of them.

THE CENACLE

The widow waits for the service to be over. The incomprehensible liturgy of atonal Hebrew gutturals, millennia of meaning resonant for so many but not her. She'd never learned the language of her ancestors, never considered that her supposed faith might lend her any comfort until now. Her husband's coffin thirteen feet away and sunk six more, the pine box lowered south from the light of a sun invisible behind dreary February clouds. She can't face the hole so she stares down at her feet in the mud-dirtied snow, stockinged legs like sticks beneath her long coat. Everyone in black, from her stepdaughter to the rabbi to the cemetery attendants and scattered among the Brooklyn gravestones, the land blotted out by the unyielding blizzard that had buried the city in its own white grave. Even still the snow swirls.

She waits for them all to leave. From her awkward brothers to her overattentive coworkers, she nods as they go, each one in turn, moving on to the luncheon, then later shiva, and finally to a peaceful sleep she herself could never bear. She is an onen, in a state of mourning beyond reach. "I'll be along, I'll be along," she says, "I just need some time to myself." A deception. She wants no time alone, not ever. What she wants is her husband back.

Her husband's daughter, born of his previous marriage, is the hardest goodbye. "Why did he have to die?" the girl sobs, her wet face pressed against the widow's breast; the girl's mother keeps a safe distance, frozen beneath a denuded elm far from the plot. "Everyone dies, my love," the widow replies, and strokes the ten-year-old's strawberry hair, her wedding ring snagging in the girl's tangled mess of curls. "Only some go sooner than later."

She waits until the sun sinks behind the horizon of distant buildings before she admits to herself that she's too cold to remain here forever, that eventually the attendants will return to usher her from the premises, tell her she can return in the morning, some widows do, day after day after day. Darkening sky and she moves from the gravesite at last, shuffles through the snow until she's back at the road that snakes through the cemetery in one long and intricate seam.

She steps onto the path, and movement catches her attention: a dark shadow in the distance, hunched and shuffling along a mausoleum-dotted hillock overlooking the snow-caked grounds. The figure progresses slowly across the landscape, shreds of gauzy black cloth flapping like clerical vestments in the wind as it reaches with sickled arms to touch upon each tombstone as if blind and feeling the way forward. The stranger stops and cocks an ear to the side, nose threading the air, a bloodhound seeking a scent.

The widow is chilled by a bitter wind. She lifts the neck of her coat against it, the furred collar tugged up to her eyes as the figure turns toward her and lifts a hand in acknowledgment, the scraps of what seems to be a shawl shifting in the breeze. An elderly woman by the looks of it, hunched in a manner that suggests a kyphotic spine bent by defect or age.

The stranger turns and lowers her head once more before soldiering on, trudging through the scattered stones and disappearing around the side of a large rotunded mausoleum. The widow waits. But when the stranger fails to appear she makes her way up the hill, drawn to the crypt as if toward an answer to an unspoken but persistent question. Her shoes brown with mud as she slides against the wet earth, the still-falling snow. She rights herself, and she climbs, until she reaches the twin doors that announce the entrance to the crypt.

The braided door handles have been wiped clean of frost, and she takes hold of their cold iron and pulls. Softly at first, but then she puts her weight into it, leaning back as she yanks until the doors groan open, just wide enough to pass. Within the slash of muted light an interior wall is visible—much deeper inside than she'd expected, given the vault's outward dimensions—and it's only upon entering the antechamber and daring to ease the doors shut in her wake that she makes out the dim illuminations of candleflame flickering farther inside the crypt. That, and the pleasing smell of cedar smoke, as well as the vague susurrations of voices, just as they fall silent.

She takes care not to trip upon the raised step leading into the main rotunda of the tomb, and she treads forward, broaching the arched entryway as she comes to a halt beneath the rose marble lintel.

Seated in an approximation of a semicircle are two women, one quite old and another young, along with an elderly man. Lit only by votive candles burning upon the crypt's every ledge, the three are dressed in funereal black and huddled about a raised granite slab. Upon the stone surface are a further arrangement of votives, pale wax dripping and pooling into gray swirls along the floor of the rounded tomb.

"Hello, dear," the old woman says from her place between the others, eyes bright in the candle flame as she draws her shawl with a wrinkled hand, brown fingers sparkling with gold and azure rings. "Would you like to join us? We're just having a spot of dinner before it gets too late." The hunched woman casts a hand across the stone block: inside the circle of candles a pile of smoked fowl is laid out, picked at with tiny bones jutting from charred skin upon a bed of unidentifiable berries and roots. The widow knows she should be repulsed but her stomach lurches for a moment like a dog jerked on a chain, and she's shocked by her sudden hunger.

"Who are you?" she asks. "What are you doing in here?"

"What are *you* doing in here?" the old man says, his voice a gravel-dragged rasp. "We're in this together, aren't we?" He gestures for her to sit. She stares down at her feet and the puddle of melted snow they've left upon the flagstone, and she regrets not stamping the ice off them before entering.

"Come," the old woman says, "don't be shy," and so the widow lowers herself onto the near side of the slab. "Excellent, excellent. Happy to see you're joining us here today. We're always looking for a decent fourth."

"Bridge numbers," the old man says. "I tried teaching them rummy, but there's really no convincing these two."

The old woman laughs, then covers her mouth. "Sorry. Bad joke, I'm afraid. We're not really much for bridge."

"What are you, then?" the widow asks, and turns to face the young woman, who remains quiet and still.

"Ah," the old woman says. "Well. I suppose we're many things, of course, no person being just *one* thing. But mostly, we're the ones left behind."

"Left behind by who?"

Even as the widow asks the question, however, she knows. For what is she now, but left behind herself? The young woman's light blue eyes swell with such alarming compassion that it makes her want to weep in recognition.

"How long have you been here?" the widow asks.

"Some time, now," the old woman replies. "After a while, you lose count of the days. You just… stay." Her expectant face shines, incandescent in the flickering candlelight reflected upon the granite slab. "You'll stay, won't you?"

"I… don't think so." The widow makes no move to leave, however. Shadows dance about the curved walls as dusk's last light evaporates beyond the surprising warmth of the stone shelter. "I have to go."

"There's nothing for you out there," the old woman says. "Not anymore."

"I have a stepdaughter," the widow says. "I have friends."

"We'll be your friends now. We'll be your family too."

"I should go."

"We're the only ones who can care for you."

"I should go."

"We're the only ones that can know you."

"Let her go already!" the old man barks, spittle flung from the corner of his mouth as he waves her away. "Let her see for herself what it's like out there, now."

They fall silent. The widow begins to back away from them and toward the doors, but makes it no farther than the step leading to the anteroom when she stills, all the while her eyes on theirs. She has a stepdaughter; she has friends; she drinks two cups of coffee in the morning as she does the crossword with a ballpoint pen. But she had a husband, then. So none of that could now be so.

"Perhaps I will stay," the widow says. "For a little while."

The old woman smiles. "Good," she says, and nods in eager approval. "Good."

So she stays. For a few minutes, and then for an hour, for the evening and then overnight, sleeping beside them beneath an oilskin tarpaulin on the cold and damp flagstones that pave the floor of the crypt. They wake her at dawn and lead her to the evergreen hedges abutting the high flat stone of the cemetery walls to collect chokeberries, which grow there in red clotted bunches, a gift of winter. They show her how they use barbed wire as snares to catch sparrows and pigeons, starlings and other birds too stupid or slow to fly south for the winter. She keeps expecting someone to come looking for her—her family, her friends, the police—but no one ever does.

She spends the day with them, and then another night, another morning and a new day, occupied with the daily business of acquiring food, of learning from the others the customs and rules of their strange and insular world. They melt frost in marble cisterns and drink from ornamental urns, the accoutrements of the dead refashioned for the needs of the living. But isn't it all for the living? The widow casts her eyes across the snow-blanketed graves. The coffins and tombstones, the ritual pyres and monumental obelisks… What do the dead care, anymore?

Most wonderful of all, there's no need for the widow to speak of her husband, for any of them to speak of their husbands, or the old man of his wife. It's enough for them to be together in their grief. Their simple companionship abates the pain of her loss more than she would have ever thought possible.

Early on the morning of the third day, they finish stealing candles from the small chapel near the gates when they come upon a pair of parka-clad workers digging a fresh grave on the south side of the cemetery. The widow, exposed to them in the bright light of day, scuttles behind the obscuring limbs of a weeping willow, but the others continue undaunted along the path toward the mausoleum that is their home. The gravediggers fail to acknowledge them, and after some time she realizes that the workers take no notice of them whatsoever.

"Why don't they see us?" she asks the others once she's caught up with them.

The old woman shrugs. "They don't want to see us, I suppose. It's too… difficult for them."

"They don't have any skin in the game," the old man says, and hocks a dark yellow loogie into the thick paste of snow. "They might as well work at a bank."

"Once the funeral is over, they move on. Everyone does. But not us." The old woman smiles her bright warm smile, but this time there's something sorrowful in it, which feels just right.

By the seventh day, the end of shiva, the widow rarely thinks of the life that awaits her at her former home, doesn't even remember more than a vague outline of what she ever did with her time. Where did I work? she wonders. Was it at an office building? Or was it some kind of school? By the ninth day it's like walking through a waking dream: she no longer recalls her stepdaughter's age, or the color of her hair, and soon the girl's name is lost to her altogether, along with the general features of her face. All she remembers now is her husband, and she clings to his memory like a talisman, a lantern in the dark of night. It's all she has left to hold.

She knows it's because of her new friends. They understand her, in a way others are unable, and she knows this to be true because she understands them the same way. The widow knows that by staying with them—by haunting the hallowed grounds of the cemetery and living off what grows here, and alights here, and is fed by the flesh and marrow of the departed—that she needn't move on, not ever. Because some people never do.

By the tenth day in the cemetery, however, the pain of her husband's absence returns unabated. It surges like a cresting wave and crashes over her, bringing her back to that awful phone call, that moment that ushered her unwillingly into the midnight realm of unmitigated despair. I can't breathe, she thinks, I'll never breathe again, and she runs the familiar distance from the crypt down the hill to the family plot, where her husband's grave, as with the rest, is buried in white. Her chapped pink hands dig at the wet ground, her tears pocking the snow. It's only once she's made her way to the hard dirt below that she stops to wonder whether she's trying to dig her husband out of his resting place or make a grave for herself to crawl into, where she can lie down and pull the earth around her like a shroud. Even the accusation of her stepdaughter's face begins to return, the dark almond eyes the girl shared with her father, the single dimple in her right cheek. She has abandoned her husband's daughter, as she herself has been abandoned. She wants to die.

And what truth this is! As true as the aim of the steering column that had impaled her husband in his twisted metal cage, the one they needed the Jaws of Life to free him from, though there would be no life for him, not anymore. Twelve days gone since the phone call from the police, the race to the hospital to bear witness to his mangled body, her knuckles white against the steering wheel of her own car as she tried to wish it undone the way she had wished Tinkerbell back to life as a little girl, one among many at a crowded matinee clapping her hands at the screen so hard she was sure her numbed fingers would bleed.

Has it been only twelve days? Impossible. Surely it has been months. Twelve days? No. She couldn't do this. No. She could not. Never.

"You can," the old woman says at her side, all three of them here now, her friends. "You will."

"How?" The widow wipes away tears and peers down at the pathetic little pit she's carved. "How can I keep from wanting it to be over, every second of every hour?"

The old woman looks to the man, who slowly nods, just once, his head drooping so that his pallid chin touches the immaculate Windsor knot in his tweed necktie. He looks to the young woman, who nods once herself, the air crisping with electric tension.

"We have a trick that helps." The old woman steps closer, her stale breath carried on the wind. "Would you like us to show you?"

That night after their rounds they trail back inside the crypt, back to the central round chamber, the widow entering last of all. The young woman lights the arrangement of ledge candles, one after the next, as the temple-like room takes on the eerie half-flame of a winter hearth. The old man clears their last meal's detritus from the granite slab to help the old woman as she lowers herself down upon the tomb.

The old man and the young woman gather on either side of her prone form, the pair tugging back the old woman's tatty black shawl. They unbutton her blouse and lower it, unfasten her nude-colored brassiere and shimmy it out from beneath her, peeling off the rest of her mourning attire until she is naked upon the slab. The old woman crosses her arms over her breasts and closes her eyes, as if she herself is laid out in death's final repose.

All along the woman's body are painted intricate black circles. Of varying size and shape, the patterns run up and down her sides in erratic intervals, appearing to spot her the way a leopard's coat is spotted, dark swirls patching her sagging and distended skin.

Mesmerized, the widow steps forward. Inches away now, and she can see at last that they aren't inked-on designs, but are in fact suppurated wounds, the size of bite marks. Just as soon as she realizes this fact a festering smell hits her, and she staggers back gasping from the slab.

"What is this?" the widow asks, and covers her nose and mouth with a trembling hand.

"This," the old man says, "is the trick."

The widow stares at the young woman, who remains silent as ever, only nodding gravely as she lowers herself to her knees beside the older woman's supine figure. Without taking her eyes off the widow, the young woman lifts the older woman's arm, brings it to her mouth, and sinks her teeth into its spongy flesh, the aged brown parchment of skin bruising and blooding a deeper shade of red.

"My God," the widow whispers. "Why?"

"This is our sacrament," the old woman says from the slab, eyes still shut though her parted lips quiver as if jolted by an electric current. "This is the holy of holy, the flesh that binds us together."

"Take of her," the old man says, so close his rotted breath masks the scent of the old woman's wounds. "Take of her flesh and blood, so that you may strengthen grief's resolve. It's the only way, now."

"I… can't. I can't." She wipes away tears and retreats for the doors, wedges her chaffed fingers into the narrow space between them and wrenches them open, ready to flee into the darkness. No one tries to stop her.

But looking out at pale tombstones that litter the dim night like scattered teeth, she hesitates. It's because she knows she cannot face the outside world, not anymore. She cannot face anyone who had ever known her before. She needs to be with her own kind, now.

The widow eases the doors shut, a whinnying grind of iron on stone as she turns back to face them. A thrill prickles her skin, an admixture of terror and fascination as she walks the length of the antechamber and back inside the domed sepulcher, where they wait for her in their strange tableau.

She lowers herself beside the slab. "Show me how it's done."

The young woman wipes her mouth and points with a blood-flecked finger at the old woman's free arm. The widow lifts it, bringing the hand toward her. The smell of the old woman's lesions is gone now, replaced by that of snuffed-out candles, as well as a holier scent, sandalwood, perhaps. The widow finds an unblemished section of skin along the inside of the old woman's papery wrist, brings it to her lips, and sinks her teeth into the flesh.

The taste is revolting, and also extraordinary; it reminds her of her first taste of tomato, of being a young girl and plucking one from her grandmother's garden vines, sliding its tough membrane across her lips before biting down. How surprising the spurting of its contents, the strong perfumy taste of lifeblood and liquefied meat, and she retches now as she did then.

But even as she raises her head from where she is sick beside the slab and stares up at them—the looming old man, the wide-eyed young woman, the mutilated older one whose death mask of a face remains still, save the tears spilling from her closed eyes—even as she wants to scream and run from them and die from anguish and sorrow and the guilt of abandoning her stepdaughter, she knows that she will not.

She will not scream. She will not run away. She will stay, and she will eat. And she will live. Without her stepdaughter, who is better off without the burden of the widow's annihilative grief. She will live without her husband. But for him. For him.

"Think of him as you eat of me," the old woman whispers, her eyes still closed tight. "Think of him, and the pain begins to slip away, like braised meat off the bone."

The widow grimaces, a trickle of blood leaking from the corner of her mouth as she swallows back a bit of fleshy gristle, the taste of it like tomato skin. She lowers her skull to the old woman's arm, and bites down again, more. This she could do. Yes. She could. Forever, even. Yes.

On the seventeenth day, they take of the old man. Of his chalky white skin and sinewy flesh, his tough hide and enlarged veins, a thin cord of muscle snagging in the widow's teeth before she manages to swallow it down. He doesn't remain still the way the old woman had, but rather hums and rocks from side to side as the three women feed upon him, their shadows expanding and contracting against the curved walls of the crypt like their own set of dark wounds. "Think of him as you eat of me," the old man whispers and groans, the scent of sandalwood permeating the musty air. "Think of him. Think of him."

And so she does. Of her husband's coppery thick beard and wire-rim spectacles, his swollen gut that he used to take in his two large hands and cradle as if it were a baby. The old man's blooded flesh travels fast through her system, and she feels a calm she hasn't known in memory.

On the twenty-fourth day, they eat of the young woman. She whimpers as the old woman suckles at her thigh, her little hands pressed over her mouth as if trying to keep something down herself. The widow feels a tremor of unease. But didn't she see for herself how the young woman had given herself over? Submission is a precept of faith, the old woman had said, what the widow's own people would call a mitzvah, or even tikkun olam. Think of him, she reminds herself, and crouches beside the old man to taste of the young woman's bony shoulder, the meat soft beneath its warm baste of blood. Think of him. And she does.

The thirtieth day arrives. The end of shloshim, the traditional period of mourning, the one her mother had practiced, and her mother's mother before her. Back from the chokeberry shrubs she walks weaving through the maze of gravestones, the snow reduced to patches, the sun bright overhead with a faint blossoming scent in the air. Spring is on its way to Gravesend Cemetery at last.

Just as she reaches the turnoff to the crypt, she catches the unmistakable sound of liturgy on the wind, and she slows, a small service taking place on the other side of the road. A Greek one, she believes, the priest droning on in his own devotional recitations, the way her rabbi had in his. A few dozen mourners are arranged around the priest, around the square hole dug into the earth and framed by too-bright astroturf meant to conceal the fresh grave dirt scattered upon the soft ground. None of them see her standing there. Not the priest or the cemetery workers, the mourners or even the dead. She is but a ghost among them, something so raw and terrible the brain stutters upon sight of her, the eye failing to alight before it quickly flits away.

But then one of them looks up, and she starts: a salt-and-pepper-haired man not terribly much older than herself, but with the prematurely aged face and shocked hollow expression of a widower. His glazed eyes narrow and blink, and they stare at each other, the world falling silent of prayer. I see you, she thinks, and nods slowly before she moves on. I see you. She wonders if he'll be lucky enough to find his way to the crypt, or if the outside world will force him into its plastic and deadening embrace, all platitudes and hopeful falsities. Sometimes it's better not to be seen.

She smells the incense the moment she opens the doors to the crypt, that same perfumy scent that seemed to arise from nowhere each time they took of one another. It was as if the very act had caused some unaccountable pheromone to be secreted from beneath the skin, either the consumer or the consumed. Today, she thinks. It must be the day for me to submit to them, so that their own pain might be eased in turn. Today.

But when she passes through the narrow antechamber and enters the main room of the crypt, she's surprised to see the granite slab is already taken. A large figure lies upon it, swathed crown to toe in a tachrichim, which reminds the widow of nothing so much as a last-minute Halloween costume, someone playing at being a ghost.

The others are gathered around the slab, their eyes upon her, watchful. You see me, she thinks, and steps forward to join them.

"Go on," the old man says, and chins toward the head of the shrouded figure. Who else has joined us, then? It never occurred to her before that there would ever be five of them. The widow leans over, and begins to unwrap the dressing.

Even before she has the linen undone, she knows. But still she must see to be sure. She pulls down the folds of the shroud to find his coppery red hair, and only a bit more, only a bit, his skin a dead and dark shade of charcoal around the sunken pits of black and unidentifiable matter where her husband's eyes once were, but no longer are. She finds she cannot breathe.

"You must take of him." The old woman's voice is like a rock hurled against the widow's breast. "To be bound to him forever. The way you've been bound to us."

"This is the night feast," the old man says, "the feast of last partings. The final sacrament of the oldest funerary rites, passed down but occulted from one culture to the next. We have set the table in the sacred space, so that you too might become a part of greater things. This is our gift to you, in the manner we have been gifted by others."

"No." The widow pulls the cloth back over her husband's too-bright hair. "No. I won't do it. Not to him." She looks to the young woman, who only bows her head, whether in prayer or shame it's unclear.

"There must be a feast," the old woman says. "And there must be one tonight." The kindness gone from her wizened face, she rears up from the floor and takes hold of the shroud in two clawlike hands and begins to tug it away. The widow pulls her husband toward herself, and the old woman pulls him back, the corpse rocking between them as if undecided.

She finally reaches over the slab and shoves the old woman, who stumbles against the wall of the crypt, toppling a shelf of candles, the shroud still grasped in one fist. The uncovered body goes with her. It tumbles from the back of the slab, only the briefest glimpse of its hideous decomposition as it falls mercifully into the shadows with a dull thunk.

The widow hurries toward the doors. The old man and young woman are soon upon her, however, dragging her back by her hair and wrestling her toward the slab as they pull away her long coat, her own shroud of winter these past thirty days. The old man thrusts her down onto the cold granite, her head slamming against it so hard she blacks out.

But not for long enough. She awakens moments later to a night-time sea of imagined stars, dancing about her mind. There is a disturbing sensation of icy breath across her naked belly, followed by an acute stabbing upon her inner thigh, where they're already beginning to take.

"Move over, move over," the old man mutters in the near dark. The three are backlit now, the candlelight and shadow a long distant dream; everything looks darker from the slab.

"Give it here," the old woman says. "You're not doing it right!" The woman takes the widow's hand, sinks her sharp teeth into the soft white flesh of her arm and the widow cries out, the worst pain she's ever learned. No, not the worst: even this blinding curtain of agony pales next to that phone call, a month gone. It's still not enough. So that's what she thinks of, the phone call that ended her old life. That and the back of her husband's freckled and sunburnt neck, his wavy red hair as he runs laughing from her and down to the sea on some past and distant shore. Sand whips all around them as she hurries and fails to keep pace, his sunhatted daughter trailing behind them both, a bright yellow bucket dragged in her wake.

The old woman grunts as she chaws her way up the bloodied and spasming arm, and the widow's own mouth goes agape. She forces herself back to the greater pain, her loss a worried scab that's been prized open anew. They take of her, and they think of lost loves, and it should be enough for them all. She will survive this. Think of him.

"Help me! Help!" she screams, and the old man hurries to mount her, bends leering over her and lowers his skull in an open-mouthed kiss. He finds her tongue and fastens his brittle teeth to it, blood spattering his glasses and rushing down both their throats as he silences her. Her tongue severed now, the old man turns his head to spit it slippery and wet against the curved wall of the crypt. The old woman scrambles after it, a starved dog after a scrap of meat, the widow gurgling in protestation as she continues to drink of her own blood. Now she knows why the young woman never speaks.

Help me!

She screams in silence, as they continue to devour her.

Think of him.

A distant shore, a laugh. It should be enough.

His face!

She sees him, again.

His face!

At last, she smiles.

CEREMONIALS

You might be inclined to think that the tree made us do what we did, though in truth it was only an invitation. It wanted us to feed it, yes, to be its pollinating emissaries, but that doesn't mean it caused our righteousness, or our rage. All the tree did was make us see ourselves for what we really were.

We were only fifteen, after all, and already so familiar with the range of indignities that could befall us at any time. Already we longed for power, and for justice, to blossom into our birthright and become something else altogether. Eight weeks away from home was our opportunity to reinvent ourselves—*You can be whoever you want at summer camp*, our mothers told us, we tell our own children that today—and so perhaps our wish to change primed us for the transformation. We were open, and so we were opened further, until we were turned inside out.

Of the five of us—we were six once, before Steph's mono came roaring back and her parents had to drive up from Boston to take her home—it was Melissa who first spotted it. Heat close to unbearable by noon, we were on our way back from the waterfront, lake water already dried from our one-pieces and two-pieces and the skin of our browned limbs. We separated from the main path leading back to the cabins and forged our own desire line through the woods, the overarching boughs of the pines and firs keeping us safe from the midday sun.

After fifteen minutes, however, it was obvious we had lost our way. Sari and Amy argued about which direction to go, Lauren eyeing the beds of her fingernails while Beth did a wobbly-footed plié, relevé, plié, until we collectively grew aware of Melissa, frozen at the lip of our small circle. She faced away from us, still as a statue with her hands pressed to her stomach, as if she were holding something inside.

"Mel?" Amy said. "Hello. What is with you?"

She just stared blankly into the trees, and we looked to each other for answers.

"Melissa?" Lauren took a cautious step toward her. "You okay?"

"You see that?" Melissa whispered, bending branches from her path as she began to trundle her way through the underbrush. Fifty yards into the woods and we followed her until we finally caught up, our paths braiding together as we arrived at the source of her intense focus.

It resembled a rock formation of some kind, a lone stalagmite. Maybe two feet around and a dozen feet tall, it rose from a rutted brown mound, ridged and lichen-dappled and studded with a honeycomb of toothy white seeds. Its trunk or stem or spine reached in a monolithic column to bisect the shading canopy of leaves in a gray and twisted and almost silvered spike. At its midsection was a stratum of wilted appendages, protuberances hanging limp with puckered mouths dangling toward the forest floor where the small bones of unidentifiable woodland creatures littered the ground.

"What is it?" Melissa asked.

"I don't know," Lauren said. "Some kind of messed-up tree?"

"Petrified, maybe. Fossilized." Sari ran her hand along its rough hide, her fingernails tap-tapping against it. "These weird long carbuncle things, they're hollowed out. By insects, maybe? That would be my guess."

"It doesn't look like it belongs here," Lauren said, and shielded her eyes to scan the surroundings. "It's the only one like it around."

"I think it's cool." Beth bent down to inspect its scaly sheen, the individual facets so glossy they caught stray glimmers of sunlight on their gunmetal bark, the surfaces almost reflective. "Freaky-looking, isn't it? I don't know. I like it."

"It looks like a giant dick." Amy leaned over and sniffed at it. "But it smells like a big old vadge."

"Does it?" Mel took a whiff. "Liar. It doesn't smell like anything!"

"Made you try, though," Amy said, and Mel gave her a little shove.

Lauren stared up at the crown, the point of its curved tip barely discernible against the wide sweep of leaves and branches and understory, all backlit by the bright white sky. "It reminds me of a maypole. You guys do May Day at school?"

"There was a maypole at a day camp I went to," Sari said. "We used to sing this song as we danced around it. You know, while we weaved all the ribbon strings together? 'Arise, arise, you fair pretty maid, and bring your May bush in…'"

"That is literally the gayest thing I've ever heard." Amy grabbed the trunk in two hands and started grinding on it. "If it was thinner it would make a dope stripper pole, though."

"Too bad no one would pay to see your skanky ass," Mel said, and Amy flipped her the bird.

"It wants," Beth whispered from where she crouched, and "Huh?" someone said, I don't remember who. She didn't respond. No one said anything, until the quiet was interrupted by the distinct crunching of leaves underfoot.

"Shhh!" Lauren hissed. We slumped down and duckwalked along the forest floor until we were concealed in a nettled bush edging the clearing. A shout, followed by hoots of laughter, and the muffled voices of boys resounded across the woods.

"Yo man, it's gonna be sick," one of them said. It was Bunk Ten, our brother bunk, who'd been hassling us all summer. We bristled as one, memories of snapped bra straps and taunts and undisguised leers goosefleshing our already prickled skins.

"We gotta wait for the counselor retreat," another said, surely Tommy Gardner. "That's soon, right?"

"Tonight. My dad rented out the Lobster Shack." This from Jared Slater, whose father was the director of the camp, which made him as close to untouchable as they came. He had a raging hard-on for Lauren, and was always trying to dance with her at socials, draw her to the back of the meeting house during movie nights, get her alone. We all turned to her, Lauren's eyes frantic with hyper-alertness, the way a rabbit looks just before it bolts.

"Nasty shit," a fourth said, this being Erik Kirsch. "Nasty shit," and their unmodulated voices soon faded, along with their lumbering footfalls.

We remained silent and still long after their departure. How cavalier they were! How heedless and free and unburdened. The ease of young men. We had moved through these same woods with a similar ease, of course, only just before. All that had brought it to an end was them.

"Assholes." Mel slapped the pine needles from her haunches as she rose. "Sounds like they're planning their next circle jerk."

"Gross," Amy said. "Don't make me think about their tiny baby cocks. I'll lose my tater tots."

"Yeah, sure. Like you're so picky."

"I know, right? I'll take what I can get!"

Mel and Amy carried on, to Sari's begrudging amusement. Lauren stood and considered the strange tree again, before she turned back to Beth, who stayed sitting by the edge of the clearing.

"Hey," she said. "They're gone."

"You sure?" Beth laughed, but there was nothing behind it.

"Yeah. I'm sure." Lauren smiled and reached out her hand, and Beth took it, used it to help herself up. We touched our restless hands to the smooth trunk as we made our way around it and back the way we came.

Heat overripe by midnight, well past curfew but our counselors were away on the retreat so we were wide awake, huddled together in the bathroom and talking while we did our hair or our nails or our lips. All except for Beth, who sat with us for the sake of appearances but was immersed in a moldering *Archie Digest* she'd unearthed from the crawlspace beneath the cabin. We sang pop songs at the top of our lungs, Lauren rolling her tube of cherry-red lipstick up and down in time, the smell of sweat and sunblock perfuming the air as everything pulsed in the same hungry rhythm, the same vast organism heaving with expectant breath. We knew something was going to happen, we just didn't know what.

"You guys, keep it down!" Sari whisper-seethed, her own lipstick smeared in a pin-thin line at the corner of her mouth. "I am not doing KP again for you loud bitches. My hair smelled like bug juice for a week."

"Hey, Beth." Lauren reached down and wagged the lipstick in front of her. "Wanna try? It suits your skin tone."

Beth lowered her digest, her wide round eyes blinking her way out of Riverdale and back into Camp Arcadia's second-most-senior girls' cabin. "What? Oh. No, thanks. It's almost bedtime. What's the point?"

"What's the point of anything?" Melissa took the tube from Lauren, squatted down in front of Beth, and proceeded to paint her lips. "We could all be dead tomorrow."

Melissa made her blot, and lifted Beth beneath her armpits until we all faced our reflections in the mirror.

"Well? Lauren said. "What do you think?"

"I think…" Beth looked at herself this way and that, her lips curving up into a devious smile, until the lights cut off and the cabin was plunged into darkness.

"The fuck?" Lauren managed to get out, before the sound of heavy footsteps on the porch silenced her, silenced all of us. Beth clenched Melissa's hand so hard it bled, so hard Mel would take the three crescent-shaped scars with her to the trial. Amy, ever brave, peeped her head out the roughhewn door into the main room, only to be yanked forward with a yelp.

That's when Sari screamed, echoed by more cries, from everywhere at once. The fearful screams of girls, yes, but also the unfettered howls of boys, wild and feral.

"Panty raid!" Erik Kirsch, flashlight swinging at his waist, ran up and down the bed rows flipping mattresses, his face blackened by greasepaint. Jared Slater, his face darkened as well, pinned Amy against the wall and licked her cheek with a fat tongue as Brent Coates rifled through Melissa's foot locker, T-shirts and shorts and bras tossed to the floor. They swarmed the cabin to fill all the empty private spaces, everywhere and all at once.

"Get out of here!" Lauren screamed. "Get out!" She beat against Erik's chest, his face, and finally his back. He laughed, bending to retrieve his fallen flashlight, and she placed her bare foot on the seat of his shorts and toppled him over, his head slamming against the floor.

"Fucking bitch," he snarled. "Ow. Fuck."

"Get out!" she kept screaming. "Get out!"

The boys guffawed as they careened toward the door, as we hurled epithets and bars of soap and tampons and magazines until they were finally gone. Sari retrieved the flashlight from the floor and made her way to the main light switch, the cabin illuminated once more.

Shaken and furious, we surveyed the damage, Sari already putting her sandals on to go wake up the camp director, the nurse, anyone who was still left on camp grounds. But we all stopped when we heard the low moaning coming from the bathroom. We approached as one, and gathered in the doorway where we froze.

Beth lay sobbing on the floor of the shower stall. Beneath her oversized T-shirt, she was attempting to hitch up her underwear, but they were twisted and tangled below her knees.

"Jesus." Mel went to her, but "Don't!" Beth cried, "please," and she waved her off. She pulled her underwear up, then wiped her eyes with the heels of her hands and bent to retrieve her now-crumpled comic. "He tried… to take them. I'm fine, okay? Give me a minute." Mel backed out of the bathroom, and Beth swung the door shut, latching the tarnished handle.

"We've got to do something," Amy said once we regrouped on the other side of the cabin, Sari dragging a cot against the door in case the boys returned. It had been ten minutes, and Beth still hadn't come out of the bathroom. The unspoken problem was that Jared was the director's son, so how much punishment could they really face? There had to be another way.

"We can't let those little shits get away with this," Mel said, Sari nodding along beside her. "We've got to fuck them up, or they'll just come back for more."

"You guys," Lauren said, her face illuminated by the naked white light from the bathroom door she'd just toed open. "Look."

We crowded inside and stared at the window, its screen pushed through onto an unobstructed square of black night beyond. Beth was gone.

We fanned out through the woods, took turns calling her name into the darkness, the gloom unbothered by the feeble beams from our flashlights. Stumbled over rocks and brambles, wove our way through the trees until it felt as if we were fleeing from something, rather than seeking it out. All the while, we were alerted to the skitterings of small creatures and the stridulations of insects, each individual being reaching out to others of its kind. A wetness hung in the air, a pregnant stillness heavy with heat and the faint odor of night blossoms that scented the forest with traces of sweet sap and musk.

But not just any night blossom, no. Even as the aroma enveloped us, as the faint green glow led us between the trees, we knew exactly where it was we were going, where we were meant to be all along. The alluring scent and erratic incandescence were accompanied by a soughing noise, a distant whistling like wind through pipes of slender wood, and soon we reached the gleaming provenance of such otherworldly sensation.

Beth was there, drawn as we had been drawn. Seated at the center of the clearing, where nothing seemed to grow (it was plain to see now, how had we missed the surrounding barrenness before?) but the succulence she now held fast, nothing around her and the tree save a wide and cautious circle of scattered brown needles, the bed of pine dead where it fell.

"Beth?" Amy ventured, but like the rest of us Amy was focused solely on the plant, and the way Beth was stroking it from her prone and demure and worshipful position.

The tree had changed since the afternoon. Now, the heady growth was in full splendor, slicked with a silver-yellow viscosity that glowed in iridescent waves. It was crowned with a flowering blue spadix, the mossy green spathe spilled open around it in a dramatic sweep of leaves luxuriant with yellow fur, the drape of tongue-like fronds shuddering in an approximation of pleasure—whether due to Beth's stimulation or through some other means it was impossible to tell—and curled in a way that made the tree appear to return her rapt attention.

The smell was stronger here, so much stronger, and the whistling took on greater clarity, a little lilting tune that wordlessly chanted of holy and faraway places, of bounty and lushness and escape. A song of ecstasy. Sari stepped into the clearing, and a moment later Melissa did as well. All of us followed to join Beth, to be a part of this sanctified moment, this most divine form of communion. We were intoxicated.

Beth stripped the shirt from her skin, Lauren unclasping her own bra and letting it fall from her shoulders as Amy reached the tree and placed her hands on the supple stem. We stepped out of our sandals, our shorts, our underwear, any part of us that had once been hidden now exposed to the moonlight, the providing air. Naked, we caressed the velvet-soft leaves, the damp stamen, the trembling meat of it. We lost ourselves inside its music, its scent, the wet folds of its nature; how long we delighted there was anyone's guess.

The time, it hardly mattered, however. For what was time, anymore? Once, we measured in befores and afters, in moments that might occur and change us forever—our first periods, surely, but also the loss of our dull, aching virginities, not gifts to give away so much as hand-me-downs to shed, a years-long game of hot potato we would never have to play again. Only two of us had yet crossed that threshold, the rest left on the same familiar side.

Now, these milestones were rendered meaningless. The carnival ride of adolescence that, wild, swung us around in wide circles had gone off its track altogether, each recognizable signpost distorted until we couldn't tell one from the rest. In this moment, time had stopped, and no longer held any sway whatsoever. We had gained something enduring, which was each other, finally and at last. We were part of a greater whole. Flowers of midnight, flowers of the moon, we were born of the night blossom, the evening bloom.

The plant issued forth its aqueous tang, redolent with lust, adrenaline jacked through our veins and straight into our cerebral cortexes. We had become one with the tree.

"Do you hear it?" Beth said, and of course we did. How could we not? Its language was unmistakable, written upon our very skin.

"Yes," Lauren said, and nodded. "It's hungry."

"So hungry." Sari's eyes filled with tears. "We need to feed it, now."

"Now," Amy said.

"Now," repeated Melissa.

"Now," we whispered. "Now now now now," until the word folded away from itself, coiled inward, and finally burst apart.

Still naked, we beached our canoes at the boys' waterfront, bare feet plashing the shallows as we padded up the cold shore. Our arms were heavy with scavenged weapons of wood and steel, the sand bleached a blue-silver sheet in the glow from the low zinc moon. Creepy-crawled over the humpbacked dunes and into the trees, red-raw shoulders narrowed between the hides of birches and spruces and pines, the night forest alive with the low humming bass of piping insects and punctuated by the occasional chirrup and whir of a predatory bird as it broached the canopy overhead.

A shifting breeze, and it was no longer just the algal smell of the lake that reached our nostrils but that of sweet sap and lavender, of mildew and sex, all the manifold contents of the inflorescent tree and the ripe bouquet spurting from its perfumed heart. We breathed it in, slow and steady, in and out and in until our lungs were coated and filled near rupture with the fecund and unrelenting scent. The blood rushed to the surface of our skins, our faces and fingers and limbs tingling as if coming to newfound life, and we advanced through the darkness as our own team of hunters.

We smelled them long before we reached their cabin. First, their various glamours and ointments, the chemical kick of roll-on deodorant and mouthwash and athlete's foot spray, all the many scented charms they used to subdue the ministrations of their baser natures. We ourselves belonged only to nature now, and so we lifted the veil upon these minor deceptions, drawn forward instead by the unmaskable odors of unwashed hair and ball sweat and the inebriating funks of boys-becoming-men, both repulsive and alluring in equal measure. We loved it. And we had to have it.

Up the cabin steps single file with Lauren in the lead, though it was hard to see in the

darkened darker darkness we hunger we thirst we yearn we need

dark. But it was not only the dark, no. We were blurring together, each of us barely distinguishable from the rest as we creaked open the door and

scuttle shift stretch shimmy spider

we were inside.

We floated wraithlike across the room, arranged ourselves as one long body

five heads five hearts ten reaching hands fifty reaching fingers

with one mission, one mind. Snaked fast toward the last cots on the row, on the left side, the sinister side. And there he was. Jared Slater, face ghostly pale in the gray moonlight filtered through the window and its tattered screen at the foot of his bed. Untouchable

we must touch we must taste we harvest we lay waste we free
no more.

We slid his sheets down, acknowledged and perhaps even admired the shape of him
chest broad sunken cage of boy with boy lungs with boy heart
and all that was trapped inside.

We embraced his mouth and nose with a firm pillow, pressed down so that it held tight over his face, hands grasping his thrashing limbs as they struggled before he fell still
never to move never to chase never to touch to ruin
forever.

We cut off a handful of his meat with his own Swiss Army knife acquired from atop his dresser. We took his tongue, severed in a needy kiss between our savage
these gifts will please the tree
teeth.

Another one stirred, and Beth was upon him, fast as loosed mercury. It was Erik Kirsch this time, and she bit two fingers from his right hand as he let out a gag of swallowed pain laced with shock. The others awoke in stunned disarray
too late for them far too late
to the monstrous and swirling beauty all around them.

Besides, we could see in the dark by now, every one of us; now, we were lit from within. A third had his head bashed in with a heavy branch from the distant woods, a loving cup formed from the back of his cratered skull, a fourth and fifth run through with a rusted rake from the groundskeeper's toolshed. All finished, each with some part of themselves kept not as trophy or mere sacrifice, but as a true and sacred
these gifts will please the tree
offering.

All save one. Brent Coates. He huddled in the corner, wracked and shivering so hard we could hear his teeth clacking like a woodpecker pecking, his breath wheezing in, out, in. Sated, we left him, without claiming any part of him. He knew we would come back for him should he cry out, should he reveal what aspects of our divine rites he believed he may have gleaned, what

wonder might ferocity delight

small fragments of our vast mysteries his limited capacities might have unknowingly glimpsed. Pity him, most of all.

Our ceremonials, they were not for this becoming-a-man. Just as we were never for him, or for any of his kind, and never would be. No. We belonged only to each other, and to the tree.

And just like that, we were gone. Returned to nature, to the night that was our new home. In all, we took a pair of eyes and the riven tongue, an entire arm torn from its shouldering socket, a gristle-encrusted rib, a half-dozen fingers, a purple and bruised heart still glutted and red, the meatiest of meats, so many parts we could have assembled our very own boy, in the fashion of our own choosing. But this was

all for the tree

all for the tree, for its many eager and hungry mouths to feed and feed. It needed our menses too, our hair and nails, all the excess girl bits we were willing to expend; it needed what we were willing to offer, as well as

chaos leads our orders

the gifts that we took.

We paddled back across the lake to where it waited with everlasting patience. No Venus flytrap, it nevertheless required worship like the goddess of love herself. No corpse flower either, yet needing its own flitting attendants all same; it offered the same deathly attraction. We sang its own song back to it, there in that most sacred of places, the wails and cries and lamentations as if from the holiest of holy temples. We called out beneath its sheltering leaves, beneath the crosshatched pine boughs, a network of intertwining branches that formed its own vast and lashing ceiling overhead.

And did our flesh transmute? Did we become something akin to the tree itself, our skin thickening with striated bark, eyes dewing over with honeyed nectar? Were our disguises peeled back, so that our true natures were exposed to air and moon for the very first time? Yes. Yes, and yes.

Pumping with hot blood and moist with traces of icy lake water, we danced about the tree, cackling and sobbing and cursing in new languages both guttural and elegant. Our bodies stripped of costuming, we who were unadorned and drenched in gore, formidable and anointed and alive. We were alive. We were alive. We were alive.

We awakened at first light, naked and splayed out in a starred pattern upon the bed of dried needles. At the center of our five prone forms was our most beloved tree, now closed into the stony pillar of rough bark and fiber, returned to its state of dormancy, satiety. A thrill of surprise, and almost baffled we rose to our feet one after the next, unsteady as newborn foals.

"What happened?" Melissa said, and "Did we…" Beth said, and "Oh my God…" Sari said. We feigned shame and fright and horror, all the emotions we were taught and trained since early girlhood to feel, but it was a pantomime. We knew exactly what we'd done and why, and once we recognized the performance in one another we allowed the façade to crumble and fall away. We knew, and it was still a thrill.

We gathered our clothes and began to dress under the tree's mighty slab of an obelisk. Soon, men would come for us, separate us one from the next as petals torn from the rarest of hothouse flowers. We would be hunted, and captured, and tried, and punished, our lives no longer our own.

Though it was we who made that fateful choice, didn't we? We who tore flesh from bone, eyes from skull, heart from chest, life itself from the living. We were newly birthed from the tree, it was true, but still we chose this for ourselves. The daughters of mothers and fathers, the sisters of siblings, the girlfriends and teammates and interns and students, the retail workers and ice cream scoopers and, yes, the campers of Bunk Eleven: We made our choice.

As with any choice, we would have to live with it, but at least the decision was ours. And for the moment, we remained free. We couldn't help but smile.

This is what makes us girls, we thought, and traded glances redolent with the authority and primacy of hidden knowledge, gained. We clasped hands, and we twisted our way through the woods, the dawn chorus chittering amid the trees as we moved with ease as one. *This is what we are, in the end and at last.*

Now, we have become women. At least I have; our sentences precluded us from ever contacting one another again. Now, I am a wife and mother, my name a new name that no one from that time in my life could ever find. So I wait. I sit in front of the television, on the living room sofa next to my husband—a decent enough man, who glimpses only the face I choose to show him— and though I watch the evening news in a somnambulant haze, I nevertheless shake my head at all I see. The wars between men, the barbarism enacted against nature, the cruelty inflicted on women, on children, the powerless, the helpless, the hopeless. What to do? What to do? I want to run and hide, to take a pill, a bath, close myself off from the world beyond my front door.

And then I remember that summer. I remember the girls, and the tree, and being part of something larger than myself, and the memory of it causes me to tremble. I clasp my shaking hands between my legs, and I wait. Twenty years gone now—almost twenty-five years, this coming August—and words like *deciduousness* and *cultivation* and *lifecycle* and *regeneration* float like dandelion seeds across the forest floor of my mind. What wants will always want, will always need to blossom to life once more.

We sit, and we wait for the call.

CONVERSION

SESSION ONE

The new patient sits on the couch and stares past the therapist at the long wall of bookshelves, the dimly lit office and all its many reference volumes still heavy with the smell of cigar smoke and pipe smoke and cigarette smoke, from when the therapist indulged in such vices. Only fifteen, the boy's eyes are so alive with raw pain they're almost aflame, and the therapist already knows it will be difficult to bring him through the length of the conversion process without breaking him irreparably. Behavior modification, if it is to be a lasting success, is an arduous endeavor, one that should never be rushed, and needs to be managed with the utmost delicacy. But it must be done, it will be done, he has done it for others thus afflicted so many times before, and the therapist swells with a pride born of duty. His training and experience, as always, will show him the way.

The patient's mother is perched beside the boy. She tugs at her sleeve and hem, her lacquered nails dancing atop her lap, scratching at her starchy green dress. "Doctor, you have to help us," she says, though her gaze remains upon her son. "I've been assured your methods are fail-safe."

"You need to trust me," he replies, and cleans his spectacles with a handkerchief. "No matter where the treatment may take us, if you truly want your son to be whole. Do you trust me?"

She nods her assent, and her eyes widen with limitless possibility, with hope. Now she has become the child.

"Excellent, excellent. In that case, we may begin. If you will." He gestures toward the door. "We have a few matters to discuss, between gentlemen."

Once the mother steps out, the therapist places his notepad on the desk and smiles, leans back in his chair and crosses his arms behind his head. "So," he says. "Let's talk about what happens at school."

"What happens at…" The boy feigns confusion, but there's no real effort in it.

"That's why you're here, isn't it? Because they tease you there, for being different. For being too…"

"Effeminate?"

The therapist nods. "Even your teachers are repelled by you, or so I'm told. And you are different from the other boys, are you not?"

"Not so different," he mumbles, his head lowered in shame.

"We mustn't have secrets, you and I." The therapist leans forward in his seat, his eyes fixed on the patient so firmly that the boy doesn't dare look away. "Not if we're going to work together on your well-being. You have a choice, you see. One path is that of loneliness and deviance and despair, while the other is toward that of integration and opportunity. And you are standing at a crossroads. Do you want to be a sissy for the rest of your life? Or do you want to become a man?"

"I want…" The boy licks his bottom lip, a nervous tic. "I want to become a man."

"Then I promise to do everything in my power to assist you. Do you want my help?"

"Yes," the boy says. "I do."

"Then tell me about your troubles. Specifically, what you think about when you fantasize."

"When I…"

"When you masturbate. You do masturbate, don't you?"

"I can't talk about that. It's too embarrassing."

"No secrets, young man. Remember? Not if you want to get better."

The patient coughs, twice, thrice. A somatization, perhaps? "I think about... other boys. Doing things to me."

"These other boys... What exactly do you think about them doing to you?"

"I think about them... dominating me."

"I see." The therapist retrieves his notepad and pen from his desk, and begins to write. "Please, do continue. And leave nothing out. I want you to tell me everything."

SESSION FOUR

"What do you see when you look at him?"

"I don't know." The boy shakes his head as he stares up at the television monitor, his oily hair tucked behind his pink and jugged ears.

"Go on," the therapist says. Perched upon his tatty armchair, its arms worn with three decades of scuffs from his own restless fingers and discolored by his own sweaty palms, he watches the boy on the couch as he shrugs and shifts, watches the boy on the television monitor as well, the video feed snaking from the camera mounted on a nearby tripod. "Tell me what you see."

"I see... I see all my pimples." The boy laughs, but there's no joy in it, he's as tender as a fresh bruise. The therapist stifles a sigh, but he withholds from speaking further in the hope of teasing out more of the boy's perspective regarding his sorely diminished self-image.

The patient is thin as bones, little more than a skeleton beneath a light shirt and short pants, the only decent meat on him likely dangled between his clasped legs fuzzed with the spectral light down of late pubescence. It is only their fourth session together, and the boy's mother is already growing impatient for results. But you can't make a man out of a milksop overnight, or even in a month's time, no matter how much you're paying for it, no matter how good the therapist's reputation. More extreme measures will have to be taken.

"I see...." The boy stops to bite at a hangnail, his mouth glossed with fresh spittle where he's been licking at his lips. It is a coquette's gesture, an inadvertent seduction; the therapist masks his revulsion and stews in silence. "I see someone who's not happy with himself."

"Yes, yes," the therapist murmurs from behind him, and shifts in his own seat. "What else do you see?"

"Someone who is a great disappointment. To his family, his community. Someone who's afraid of his own shadow. But also..."

"Go on."

The boy swallows, hard, the knob of his Adam's apple hefted and released like a door latch. "I also see someone who wants to be better than he is."

The therapist reaches out to clasp his shoulder, and together they watch his hand on the monitor as he gives the boy an avuncular squeeze.

He will fuck the manhood into the boy himself if he has to, and the therapist's groin stirs at the thought, his cock aroused from its dormancy. He will fuck him if he has to. Lead the spotted weakling across the room and fold him in half over the desk, a clatter of belt buckles as he thrusts himself inside, six inches of steel shoved up the hinged boy's backside. The patient will cry out but the therapist will shove a hand inside the boy's mouth, ride him from both ends until the boy gags and vomits to near-suffocation, thighs running viscous and sweaty and red in a most violent and spectacular deflowering.

"Good," the therapist says, and removes his hand from the boy's shoulder. "That's good."

SESSION SEVEN

"What do you see when you look at them?"

"I see... two men having sex."

The patient sits on the couch, facing the television monitor. On the screen are two men, hairless and muscular. One of them is quite fair, while the other is swarthier, both on a platform bed at the center of a wood-paneled room that brings to mind a suburban basement or perhaps a hunting lodge. The blond man is larger and on top, where he ruts away at the darker one with the impassive and mechanical regularity of a windup toy. It is a scene from *Cabana Boys 3,* one of many pornographic films the therapist keeps on file, locked away in a lower desk drawer so that when his shiftless daughter wanders down here to his street-level office (the rest of their home in the townhouse's four stories overhead), she won't stumble across this most verboten material, she of idle fingers and prying eyes. It is only meant for him, and his patients. It is the third film he and the boy have watched together.

"And does it arouse you?" the therapist asks, and fingers the remote control in his hand.

"I don't know... I don't think so."

"Be honest. No secrets."

"Sure," he says after a while. "I guess."

"What is it you see that excites you?"

The boy only shrugs, but the therapist waits. He'll wait for the rest of the session if he has to.

"Well," the patient finally answers, "I think it's the way the one on the bottom is sort of stuck. He can't get out from under, right? It's supposed to be something fun he's doing, but notice his face. He looks miserable, as if he's just waiting for it to be over. He's surrendered himself to the other man. And he's given up trying, even though he appears to be in pain."

"Interesting," the therapist says, and jots a few notes upon his pad. "And where do you see yourself in this scenario? What position do you derive your pleasure from?"

"I guess I see myself as the one who surrenders himself," the boy says, and he winces as if thus conditioned.

"Yes. Of course." The therapist pauses the film and rises from his armchair. He takes the drawer key from his breast pocket as he walks over to his desk. He bends down and unlocks a lower drawer, not the one containing the pornography but a second that holds a very different kind of stimuli.

He removes the black box and takes it back over to the couch, where he kneels at the boy's feet to plug the EST machine into the socket.

"What is that thing?" the boy asks, pointing to the black box and its many small dials and controls as the therapist fits the grounding clamp onto two of the boy's fingers.

"It's an electrical stimulation device. As you continue to watch, you'll receive a very small jolt of electricity when you become aroused. Just a slight uncomfortable sensation that will have a cumulative effect, rather than an acute one."

"Are you sure?" He appears dubious, and understandably so. But the therapist will start him off slowly, break him in. He's done it so many times before. "How will it know when I'm... aroused?"

"That's simple." He hands the boy the trigger wand. "You're going to click this button yourself, every time you feel excited. It's entirely self-administered. Nothing to worry about, I promise."

"Oh, okay." The patient's face flushes with relief. "So, I just press, right here?"

The therapist nods. "Go on. Give it a whirl."

He presses the button, and jerks in place upon the couch. "Ah!" he says, and lets out a little chuckle. "Funny feeling. It's like... licking a 9-volt battery. But all over my body."

"See? It's hardly anything at all. Now. Shall we continue?"

SESSION ELEVEN

The boy is wan. Dark and angry rings about his eyes, hair

tumbleweed dry, skin drawn where it isn't pocked with acne, he has narrow brown veins singed into his temples and along his chest, his fingers ash gray from the work of the EST machine. Lying on the floor with his limbs splayed in corpse pose, he resembles nothing so much as a deactivated robot awaiting some fresh jolt of energy, for its circuitry to be emboldened to action. Between the electroshock and the ipecac, the last few sessions have taken their toll. This, of course, is all part of the process. There are a number of significant hurtles they need to cross to reach satisfactory conversion.

"You've done such important work already," the therapist says, and he dims the lights. "You must know that to be true. Now. Roll onto your stomach, please."

The film begins. A man and a man, this time on the deck of speedboat, one on his knees with his head nestled in the other's crotch as he undoes the man's zipper.

The therapist lies on top of the boy, presses him down against the carpet's rough weave with his cock against the cleft in the patient's buttocks. Does the boy enjoy this particular form of intimacy? He says nothing to indicate otherwise.

"Do you feel aroused?" the therapist whispers in his ear.

"No," the boy says, barely audible, the side of his face mashed against the thick carpet, though he can still view the monitor.

"Do you feel anything whatsoever?"

"Only uncomfortable. And... nauseous."

"Do you need the toilet?"

"No. Not this time. But I'd rather not look, all the same."

After a few minutes the men onscreen both spend themselves upon the concave belly of the receptive fellow, and the therapist stands, adjusting himself before he replaces the videotape cassette.

Another film, this time of a naked woman, her puckered nipples hard as glass as she plays with herself, a French manicured hand traveling from her waxed and hairless sex up her torso and past her swollen breasts to her sneering mouth, lipstick smearing upon her lips like blood as she rubs herself above and below. Soon, an un-clothed man enters the picture, shot from the chest down, faceless and with a brutally erect cock. He immediately slaps her across the face. It is one of the therapist's favorite scenes.

"Go on," he says to his patient. "Feel at yourself down there. Don't be shy. Take hold of your manhood. It is your mantle. Your birthright."

The boy sits up and undoes his trouser buttons. He begins to masturbate. Breath erratic, he tugs at himself for some time, though his reddening face soon distorts into a steadily worsening contortion of anxiety, colored by no small amount of discomfiture and possibly—no, definitely—rage. He slows and, finally defeat-ed, abandons the endeavor altogether, folding his arms across his chest in refusal.

"I can't," he says, the very picture of frustration. "I can't do this."

"That's because you don't know yet what is to desire a woman. But you will learn." The therapist leans down, his lips grazing the back of the boy's head and his dark halo of curls, close enough to kiss. "Look. How he takes her? His callous hand at her throat, while he calls her debasing names. Is she not a dirty cunt, a stupid whore? She knows she is these things. See? There. Her startled expression of fear? It masks her pleasure to be penetrated, to be possessed. She knows that is her true worth. To bring a woman low, to break her: that is a *real* man's calling, his essential desire. That is what we aspire for."

The therapist leans over the boy, reaching down to cradle the boy's limp appendage. The boy gasps and writhes beneath his hand.

"Shhh, it's alright. I'm not going to take anything. Settle down. I'm a doctor, remember? So. Keep watching the woman. Keep watching her fear."

The boy stills, frozen, his eyes fixed on the monitor and the hu-miliated woman upon it. Eventually, he begins to harden beneath the therapist's steady stroking.

"See?" the therapist says.

SESSION THIRTEEN

The patient sits on the couch, the lights dimmed. Beside him is the therapist's daughter, a foot away but separated by so many things, a world apart. The doctor has enlisted her and her wiles, her physical presence really, and compelled her to obey. It is all in service of the patient. For the boy must be guided in such matters, to learn how best to be at ease around a potential mate, and who better to participate in the process than the therapist's very own in-house assistant?

The girl is seventeen, almost a woman really, and looking more like her mother by the day. How beautiful his wife was in her own youth, the therapist thinks, and blanches at the thought of her current state, her body gone to the dogs in the years following childbirth. Perhaps he will find himself a new and younger wife, once their daughter leaves for university. He makes a note to weigh the logistics further in his free time.

"I feel so silly," the girl whispers to the patient with a smile, but her father overhears.

"What did I tell you?" he admonishes her, his mood already soured after considering his wife's uninviting shape. "You are not to use words of any kind. And you say you want to attend the upcoming dance at school, yes? Or was that just another passing fancy of yours?"

"I do, Father," she says, and lowers her head. "Forgive me."

"Then no speaking whatsoever." He softens his face as he turns his attention back to the patient. "Now," he says, "look at her closely. And tell me what you see."

"I see…" The boy giggles, and she smiles once more, but her eyes dart to her father's face, unsure of whether even this gesture is permissible. "I see a beautiful girl."

"Yes," the therapist says. "And what does she smell like?"

The boy, uncertain, leans in and sniffs at her neck, then pulls away, eyes wet and wide. "Like a delicious shampoo. Like lavender, perhaps."

"And what does she feel like?"

No one smiles, no one laughs, and the patient slowly reaches out to her, his pale and burnt fingers drawn forward as if on silken strings. The girl watches as he lets his hand rest upon her knee.

"Warm. She feels warm."

"Her waist," the therapist says, directing him, and the boy's hand slides up to her midsection. "Now... allow your hands to roam her."

"Father—"

"Silence!" he commands, and the girl shudders as if struck. The patient hesitates, then has his fingers spider up her body, sliding for a few moments across her stomach before they find their way beneath her shirt. She gasps and turns her face away, her expression anguished as he moves from her belly to her breasts, which he holds in both hands atop her brassiere as he leans in once more to sniff at her. He nuzzles against her neck, kisses her there with little pecks, forces himself against her as if attempting to burrow his way beneath her skin.

Finally, she can take no more. The girl leaps up from the couch, pushing the boy away as tears bloom at her eyes. She covers her face and storms from the office, slamming the door in her wake so hard that the doctor's degrees rattle in their oaken frames upon the wall. It seems that she won't be going to the school dance after all.

"I'm so sorry," the patient says, but the therapist shakes his head. "I shouldn't have—"

"Not at all. You did well. Very well. Did you feel how exhilarating it is? To be the dominant one, as nature intended it, to feel the power over woman that is your fulfillment as a man?"

"I did. I really did." The boy grins, for the first time revealing a single sharp canine tooth, and the therapist can see a genuine spark of hope in his patient's eyes. The treatment is working.

"I'm so pleased." He pats the boy on the knee. "You mustn't

allow a girl's reticence to stand in your way. When it is a matter of his entitlement, a real man doesn't rely on permission, on a girl's fleeting whims to take shape. You must never apologize for pursuing what is rightfully yours. You must only seize it."

SESSION NINETEEN

"We need to discuss what happened last night."

"Did I do something wrong?" the patient asks, and licks furiously at his lower lip, his hair damp from the steady snow falling outside the townhouse. By all appearances, the boy has become far more sturdy these past few sessions, as if he's suddenly growing into his body, shoulders squared back instead of stooped. Still, his eyes flit nervously across the room, past the therapist and toward the office door.

"My daughter is very distressed. She's told her mother that she found you at her window, that she awoke in the night to discover you watching her as she slept. This after she repeatedly observed you following her home." Things are still on course, and indeed the boy is well on his way to total conversion. But the therapist caught his own mistake too late, and now the patient has imprinted himself upon his daughter like a newly birthed gosling. Adjustments will need to be made at once.

"Oh." A bashful smile, a flash of that sharp canine. "That."

"When we utilized her in session, she was intended to be a stand-in, a demonstration of womanhood, in the representative sense. She was never meant to become the actual object of your desire. During the last session, you said you would keep your distance from her. You gave your promise."

"I... suppose I just got so excited that I finally found myself attracted to a girl. That I really wanted to be with her... physically."

"Yes, and your youthful enthusiasm is a powerful device at our disposal. But now we must redirect your attentions to other girls, other young women."

The boy nods, though he seems unconvinced. "And how are we supposed to do that exactly?"

"With the help of another kind of professional." The therapist writes the information down on a slip of scratch paper. "Call that number. She'll be expecting you."

He takes the slip of paper. "Who is she?"

"Her name is unimportant. It's what she has to offer of her body that is of significance." The boy eyes the paper in his hands with reverence, a key to a magical new realm. "No need to conform to the conventions of polite society, not with this one. You may treat her as you'd like, as one would treat an animal. Use her as you wish."

"Oh yes?"

"Her capacity for degradation is near limitless. I myself know from personal experience."

"Thank you, Doctor." The boy stares down at the floor, taps the edge of the paper against his dagger of a tooth before raising his eyes once more. "Thank you for everything."

SESSION TWENTY-TWO

"What do you see when you look at him?"

He watches the patient watch himself on the monitor, no trace of the therapist captured in the video feed save the shadow of his right hand, which he quickly guides from the frame.

"I see someone who is becoming his best self," the patient says. He nods at his own image, acknowledging to himself the truth of his words. "I see someone in charge."

"And what is it that you mean when you say that?"

He turns his gaze toward the therapist, his open face bright, resplendent. Even his complexion has cleared of its blemishes, his very hormones at a newfound equilibrium. "I mean that I know who I am now. All the many negative tendencies I first brought into this office? The aberrance, and despondency, the longing for submission? Why, that's all gone now. Because I see how all those feelings were misplaced. Once I aimed my yearnings in the proper direction, I realized that anything I set my mind and heart upon, any *woman*, could be mine for the taking. I have actualized, once and for all. I have become a man."

"And you harbor none of your former impulses or desires whatsoever?"

He smiles, eyetooth glistening. "I have new desires now."

"Excellent." The therapist closes his notepad. "It appears that, as they say, our work here is done."

He escorts the boy to the entryway, or rather escorts the one who is a boy no longer, another success story to be added to the many who have walked through this very door. Successful conversion has been achieved.

"I've learned so much from you," the patient says, and thrusts out his hand to shake. "I really have."

"I see great things in your future, young man. I really do."

"Oh. One thing." He reaches into the inside breast pocket of his jacket and emerges with a simple manila envelope. "I brought you this, as a gift for all that you've done for me. You can open it later. Consider it a token of my esteem."

"Why, I'm touched," the therapist says, and takes the envelope, which is thick with what feels like cardboard stock. "That's quite considerate of you."

"It's the least I can do, Doctor. I would be nothing without your guiding hand."

Not long after the young man departs, the therapist retrieves a letter opener from his desk and uses it to slash open the sealed mouth of the envelope the patient has given him. He carefully extracts the contents, which are comprised of two dozen or so matte photographs, square and rounded at the edges, shot and developed in saturated color. He turns on his desk lamp, and pushes his spectacles further up his nose to examine his reward.

The first photograph is distorted, but when the therapist brings it to his face he can see it is of an eye, in extreme close-up and round with wonder. When he looks closer, however, he sees that the eye is wide not with awe but terror. He flips to the next photograph, and it is the top half of the prostitute's familiar face, one eye still wide, yes, though the other is swollen shut, battered a putrid and grayish blue beneath her tear-streaked mascara. The next picture shows more of her form, stripped naked on her bed and bound with her own ripped black stockings, mouth stuffed with a pair of black panties. At the corner of her lips is a thin strand of blood trailing down her cheek, down to the rumpled and soiled sheets beneath.

The next photograph: her bare back, hunched, skin drained of color. White.

The next: her bare back, the flesh near her shoulder gashed wide by a hideous bite mark, punctuated by a deep and unmistakable rent at its edge from a single sharp tooth. Red and white.

The next: the wound upon her peeled back gaping apart to expose her tender meat, blossoming open in a parted mouth of ligament and gore as if to deliver its own fatal kiss. Red, and white, and pink.

In the blurred background: a vanity table, and in its stained mirror a glimpse of the photographer: the boy turned young man, the therapist's now-former patient, his youthful face leering not at the prone woman before him but at his own reflection, at the camera lens and hence the therapist. The boy is naked himself and fully erect, his unsheathed cock scarlet red. Swollen and shined with engorgement, yes, but also slicked with blood, that and something more solid as well. Mucus, perhaps, or gristle. He is the very image of pride.

By the time the therapist reaches the final horrifying photograph he is on his feet, his free hand at his mouth, where he bites down in shock and revulsion.

He thrusts the obscene images away from his person, where they scatter across his desk blotter in an unholy fan of depravity. A moment later he finds himself racing out his office door to the bottom of the stairs, where the curved mahogany banister spirals its way up toward the topmost heights of the grand townhouse.

"Are all the windows locked?" he cries out. "Are all the windows and doors locked and closed?"

"Of course they are," his wife calls down from above; it is still winter after all.

"What is it?" His daughter leans over the highest railing, her shoulders bare, hair wet from the bath. "What's wrong?"

"Nothing," the therapist shouts up with a little wave, thinking better of it. "It's nothing," and he heads back down the hall to his office.

He locks the door behind him, and approaches the desk warily, as if the photographs might spring from their resting place to alarm him in some new and unforeseen manner. But no, they're still there, splayed out where he had tossed them as if ridding himself of an unclean thing.

The therapist resumes his place in his chair. He takes up the pictures, and lays them out on the blotter before him, one at a time and with care, in a studied and most macabre game of solitaire. Something must be done at once.

He reaches for the telephone and grasps the cold plastic receiver, though he's unsure of who he might call exactly. The patient's mother? Or the police? No, that won't do. He'd be ruined for one, his methods discredited; he'd become a laughing stock among his colleagues. That won't do at all.

Who's to say he even looked at the photographs, even knew of his patient's transgressions in the first place? And what transgressions they are! Blasphemous, and spectacular.

He plucks a photo from the assortment, carries it into the light of the desk lamp. The bite mark alone, how the boy had made his own opening inside of her… Who would think of ruining a woman in such a way, even a common whore such as this? The patient truly had tamed her, that much was certain, not just as he'd been instructed but further, harder, better. He was a master of perversity, and though this was his first, there were surely more to come.

The therapist runs a finger over the surface of the photograph, and allows it to fall into his lap, where his member, unbidden, begins to stir and harden, its own separate kind of monster.

SESSION ONE

The first-time patient, a middle-aged woman, lies upon the couch, the room filled with the scent of fresh peonies from the bouquet that the therapist's new wife uprooted from the garden this morning. He worries about his wife, so young and naïve, so unsuited to this increasingly dangerous world. She's not so very much older than his daughter, who hasn't once returned from abroad since she left for university last year, who never calls or writes or checks up on him, the selfish ingrate. She hadn't even attended the wedding.

"It's my daughter I'm most worried about," the new patient is saying, and the therapist returns from his bitter reverie. "That's really why I came here to see you. I'm concerned she might be forming an unwholesome attachment with a girl who lives on the next street over."

"Interesting." The therapist jots a few notes on his pad. "What makes you say that?"

"She and the other girl, they spend all their time together. It's as if one can't be without the other. I tried to put a stop to it—I ordered my daughter straight home from school, and forbade them from ever speaking again—but just this past Saturday I caught her sneaking back inside the house. In the dead of night! She wouldn't tell me where she'd been, of course, but I knew. There was no question in my mind she was out doing heaven knows what with that girl. I'm telling you, it's unnatural."

"We can't have your daughter disobeying you, that much is certain. And we can't have her out on the streets at night."

"This used to be such a safe district, but now... Well. You know.

They say there's a murderer on the loose."

He grimaces. "I'm not so sure about that."

"It's true. My sister, she does secretarial work for the constabulary? She says there's been five women murdered in the district this past year alone. Ladies of the evening. So far."

"Is that so?"

The woman nods. "The killings are savage, apparently. Just savage. And all with the same terrible bite mark…" She shudders, and for a moment the therapist's eyes dart toward his desk drawer and the eleven manila envelopes locked inside, identical but for their contents. "I'm sorry, where was I?"

"Your daughter. And the other girl…"

"Oh yes. You can help us, Doctor, can't you?" Her eyes flood with hope. "I hear the most wonderful things about your work from the other mothers, I really do. I've even been told your methods are fail-safe."

The therapist smiles.

THE RENTAL SISTER

I'm kind of known for telling this story, and don't worry, it's a quick one. Okay? This was the summer before I discovered acting and moved to the States, when I was still Shinju instead of Shannon. I was living in the Aoyama district, waitressing on and off and pretty much lost in life, working at an Italian restaurant at the time. There's little to no tipping in Japan—only from tourists, really—and I was complaining one day to my co-worker Yoshiko about how I was having trouble paying my bills. That was the moment she suggested I make some money on the side as a rental sister.

I had to ask what this was and the answer was surprising and has to do with the hikikomori. That basically means withdrawal, and it's a big problem in Japan, what you would call a social epidemic. The hikikomori, almost all young men, close themselves off in their rooms for years and years, only coming out in the middle of the night to grab food before going back inside. It's like the way anorexia is here, you know, very popular? Once the family runs out of options, there are a few very expensive treatment companies that you can contract. They send over a girl known as a rental sister, who goes to your house to try to coax the boy out into the world. Yoshiko worked for Fresh Start, which was one of these companies. She said it was easy work and that she would be happy to refer me.

"Oh, and if they give you Koji Tanabashi in Meguro as your

first," she said as she wrote down the address of the company, "don't tear your hair out over it." I didn't ask what she meant.

Once I applied and was accepted at Fresh Start, I immediately started my training as a rental sister. They told me it's not like being a therapist or even an outreach worker, more like just a friend to talk to. Training was basically an afternoon of practice with my supervisor Mr. Suzuki and then a manual to read that evening. As Yoshiko predicted, my first assignment was in fact a twenty-year-old man named Koji Tanabashi, my age, who lived in the Meguro district. That's in the suburbs so I took the bus out there, and read his one-page bio along the way. I also read the manual, which basically was not helpful, just things not to do like do not be too flirtatious, do not be impatient, do not be aggressive, things like that.

I went to the address and found myself at the doors of a large home, two floors and very modern. Or it probably was modern when it was built, maybe fifty years ago? Lots of concrete and very little glass, like an office building or a bomb shelter, but instead it was a house. I rang the doorbell. Mrs. Tanabashi—who turned out to be a very impolite woman—bowed quickly and then made her way through the expansive genkan and into the main hallway. "You are the thirty-seventh rental girl we have hired," she said in almost a whisper as I followed her up the staircase. "Maybe you will be the one." I decided that this was her way of telling me she had already spent a great deal of money.

We passed beneath a large skylight, and I remember looking up for a moment at the darkening sky. We went down the hall to the last door, which was on the right. I turned to Mrs. Tanabashi but she had already pulled away and was heading back down the stairs. I wanted to leave as well. So, okay, I thought, you can do this, it's just like meeting a very quiet new friend, and I've had those before, so why not, you know? I kneeled down on the hard wood in front of the locked door and sat in silence. After a few minutes, I made sure Mrs. Tanabashi wasn't watching me; then I reached into my rucksack for the manual and read from its suggestions for introductory phrases.

"Hello, Koji!" I was trying to sound fun. "My name is Shinju, can you hear me?"

Nothing.

"I was hoping I could talk to you, and I heard you were a good listener, is that true?"

More nothing.

I began to tell him about my day, about my friends, the restaurant, how I decided to join Fresh Start, except I said I joined because I liked talking with people instead of the real reason, which was because I needed the money. I tried anything I could think of that would be helpful and not aggressive, that might appeal to a hikikomori, even slipping a friendly note under the door if he preferred to communicate that way. I told him about the movie I had seen the previous week, the one I hoped to see the next, the book I was reading and how interesting it was; I even read from it for a while. Every moment as a rental sister is a race against time, for the longer a hikikomori is shut in the less likely he is to emerge.

By my watch, I could see that only a half hour had passed, and I was already running out of things to say. I pulled his bio out of my rucksack and looked it over again. There was nothing so very special about him I could grab onto, really just that he liked videogames and only videogames. I hate videogames, because I find them addicting, you know? I would rather use that time to read a book. Anyway, I knew I had a great deal more work to do, so I kept going. A race against time, but also endless time. I can still picture that hallway as if I were standing in it now: the shell-lacquered credenza, the woven bamboo screen, and beside it the traditional watercolor of a fisherman returning to shore. Everything in its place, just so.

Once the three hours were done and there was still no response from the other side of the door, I said goodnight and left the house. As I started down the path to the main street, I turned to stare back at the house, and the heavy curtains in one of the upper windows moved for a moment, before it fell still. It was Koji's room. I gave a little wave and kept walking, sure that I was being watched as I went. I would have felt like a complete failure if it wasn't for seeing those curtains move. They kept me at it.

I spent the next month making three weekly visits. I grew more prepared, more determined, so that when Mrs. Tanabashi would say "Anything?" as I left each night I might eventually have something to tell her, instead of simply apologizing. I really did not like this woman. Her presence was always so heavy, being in a constant state of disapproval as she was, you know? I started playing videogames at home on the computer, and then I would come back to Koji's door and recount what had happened in the game. In my mind I was already improving, and so I talked on and on, endless one-sided discussions of what I was playing, my scores, who I encountered along the way, things like that. I was beginning to worry about my paycheck.

One night, six weeks after I first started as Koji's rental sister, something finally happened. I'd already abandoned my videogame idea, and, having nothing left to share of myself, I started making up stories to tell. I was so bored by then, sitting alone for hours on the small tatami mat I would bring with me; I was surprised there was nothing comfortable already in place in front of the door, me being the thirty-seventh sister to put herself there for hours on end. I began talking about how I was going to move to the United States and become a famous actress and that I would take him with me and we would live in Hollywood together, just nonsense at the time. Now that I say it, I was acting even in that moment.

I talked on and on, and then I feel something push against my hand, which is against the bottom of the door. I look down, and a Post-It note has been slipped out to me, and it says
YOU ARE PRETTY

I laughed. I couldn't help it, I was just so grateful he had written anything at all, and that it wasn't to tell me to go away. "Why, thank you, Koji," I said. "You're a very nice young man. And I bet you are a handsome one as well."

After another minute, he slips a second note under the door, and it says

NOT ANYMORE

"Come now, I find that hard to believe," I went on. "You're so handsome in photographs, and no one loses that much beauty just by being alone." I hadn't actually seen a picture of him. There wasn't one in his bio, or anywhere in the house that I could find. And yes, I was ignoring the advice in the manual, but I got through to him my own way, didn't I? "I'll tell you what. If you open the door a crack I'll tell you if you are handsome or not, okay?"

Another minute passes, then another note, and it says

I CANNOT OPEN THE DOOR

"Koji," I said, going for playfulness. "What's wrong, don't you like me anymore?"

Then, very quickly this time, another note appears, and it says

I AM COLD HERE

"Well, okay, I'll go ask your mother for a blanket and I'll leave it outside the door for you to take after I'm gone."

I went downstairs and found Mrs. Tanabashi in the kitchen, preparing her dinner; her husband was an international businessman and he was away from home a great deal. "You won't believe it!" I said, so excited to tell her of my progress. "Koji started slipping me notes." I handed them to her and as she read them her eyes went wide with shock. Then she looked up at me, and her anger was impossible to mistake.

"Wait for me in the genkan," she said, her back to me as she left the kitchen. I went to wait for her there, and it was almost an hour later—I had nothing to do but stare at the row of shoes beside the entrance—that the doorbell rang. Mrs. Tanabashi came to answer it, and it was Mr. Suzuki, my Fresh Start supervisor. He was furious.

"Shinju," he said, "you are a very irresponsible girl and I want you to apologize to Mrs. Tanabashi."

"What have I done wrong?" I asked him, and he turned to Mrs. Tanabashi, who handed him the notes.

"What are these?" he said, holding them out to me.

"They're notes from Koji," I replied, taking them. "He slipped them under the door when we were talking."

Mr. Suzuki turned back to Mrs. Tanabashi. "I'm so sorry," he said to her. "She won't be coming back here."

"What's going on?" I said, losing my patience. "Tell me what I did."

"Enough of your lies, Shinju. I know you wrote these notes yourself."

"I would never do that!" I said. "Why would I ever do such a thing?"

"Because someone must have told you there's no one in that room." He looked down at the floor, then back at Mrs. Tanabashi, then back at me. "You realize I'm going to have to terminate your employment."

"These notes were slipped under the door!" I said, louder now. "There's someone on the other side!"

"There's no one in there and you know it. Mrs. Tanabashi kindly allows Fresh Start to use this as a facility so that new rental sisters can get practice before their real work with the hikikomori. *This* is your training, Shinju."

"But there's someone in there!" I insisted, shouting this time, and then Mrs. Tanabashi let out a kind of scream of frustration that silenced me.

"Follow me, then, 'pretty' girl," she said, and Mr. Suzuki and I went after her up the stairs. When we got to the door she rudely stepped on my tatami, reaching into her pocket for a ring of keys. She struggled with the lock for a moment before the knob turned, and when she swung open the door a stack of papers on the other side spread across the floor like the opening of a fan.

The room was empty. There was no furniture, no closet, nothing but the heavy curtains drawn across the far wall. I stepped inside, just to make sure, Mr. Suzuki entering after me. It was much smaller than I had pictured. Nothing.

Mrs. Tanabashi left the keys in the lock and headed down the hall, slamming her bedroom door behind her.

"I don't understand," I said, staring down at the papers on the floor. The writings of thirty-seven rental sisters in training, all unread, a rainbow of different colors and styles of stationery, glowing in the light from the open door. "I was so sure. Maybe if she would just look at the handwriting again—"

But Mr. Suzuki interrupted me. "Listen, Shinju, I understand that this was something you wanted to happen so badly that you created your own fantasy. But you've managed to deeply offend Mrs. Tanabashi, and that is not excusable."

"What have I done that was so wrong?" I asked him.

"The reason she offers our company this space is because her own son was a hikikomori. He ended up hanging himself. This used to be his room." I understood her in that moment, the weight of her soul, and longed to console her. I never saw her again.

And then, and this is exactly how it happened, I felt this strange coldness pass over me, almost like static electricity, you know? Something brushed against my hair, back and forth and back again, as if from above. I looked up at the ceiling.

"Time to go," Mr. Suzuki said.

I left alone, headed down the stairs and into the genkan, where I put on my shoes and went out into the cold evening air; autumn had arrived without my noticing. I stopped to stare up at Koji's window, the heavy curtains black and unmoving, before I made my way home.

I try not to think about that stage in my life very often, days of vast emptiness waiting to be filled by something, anything that might show me my way, my purpose in being. But I think about that night all the time. In fact, I still have those notes he slipped under the door. I carry them with me in my wallet wherever I go. Would you like to see them?

君はきれい

もうハンサムじゃない

ドアガ開けられない

僕は寒い

MY HEART'S OWN DESIRE

"**O**ut, you dirty thief! Get away from me!"

From the very top of the steps, the Hierophant, red-faced, gives my suitcase a firm push with his pale foot. Halfway down the stairs it takes flight, splits open because the lock on it has never quite worked, and releases my clothes like pigeons loosed from a rooftop coop. Worn cigarette pants hang lifelessly along the banister, while my only dress shirt flutters to my feet upon the dirt-caked landing. I wonder when I'll have the chance to get it cleaned again. It's not every day you get taken in by a trick with a washing machine, let alone a funny old wizard who loves to get all the street boys high on the Lord's own formula.

"Now leave my sight," the Hierophant says, and through a hazy cloud of sandalwood from the censer he waves me away, gilded vestments crinkling as he turns and slams the door to his private sanctum. So many nights spent waiting outside that room while he crafted his wares, eerie lights pulsating beyond the lintel as ancient invocations sounded from within until he would emerge in an alchemical cloud, dazzling creations in hand. I would genuflect in reverence, then drop to my knees so he could slip one of his magic wafers between my parted lips. Only then did I feel high enough to heaven, so close to God my lips would go numb in rapture.

Once I gather up my things and stuff them back inside my

suitcase I head out into the sweltering afternoon. Heat waves rise from the concrete like treated glass, and the city seems newly loud, almost deafening; I went out so rarely during my stay in the Hierophant's manse. I was lucky to have lasted so long: if I had to play petting games with the old fool one more time I was going to scream, I really was. That must be why I pinched so many of his wafers, the ones with the hourglass symbols he calls saturnalias. They cast a dreamlike spell, let you see who you used to be, before you got so low.

I hurry along the familiar way to the stone park, not remembering when even this tinderbox town was last so damn humid, the thick air already building a nest inside my lower lungs. The park opens up before me, bustling with people because of the heat— misery and company and all that—and I hover until someone vacates my favorite bench. I sit, yank the suitcase next to me and take a good look around. It's been a while since I last saw this place, where all the sweet young apprentices come to meet their sugar mages and lonely sorcerers, their crippled mutant professors and horny sea captains, those who know a thing or two about how to feed a hungry mouth and get something else in return.

In fact, I haven't been here since the Hierophant found me asleep on this very bench, gave me a kick in my side that took me out of my dreams. I looked up to find a tall white man, bony and birdlike in his tufted finery. He said he was a man of means now hidden to the world, and that he wanted nothing more than to take me back to his place. It is safe, he said, and warm. He also let it be known he could conjure the most illuminating things, potion-soaked wafers that gave you crystal visions. The Hierophant's shit is so good, my brother Carter told me later, people say God is his supplier.

"Well, hello Lewis Lewis." My friend Rosa towers above me. She's wearing a black straw hat, the outsized brim decorated with whole clumps of waxed grapes. She pushes the brim back with a naked wrist and gives me her cheek to kiss. "Sorry, love, lipstick," she says, and pulls my suitcase off the bench to sit, folds her endless legs over my lap. "So when did the Hierophant let you out?" and I say, "I let myself out."

"Well good, because Carter was thinking of sending in a SWAT team." She reaches into her gargantuan black handbag, pulls out a candy, and waves it at me. "Peanut chew?" I say no and she says, "Peanut chew peanut chew?" because she is always talking nonsense like that; once she gets the sound of something in her head, it sticks. "I'm off to Pompeii," she says of the hustler bar where Carter works and sleeps fitful mornings on a dirty mattress in the basement. "But, oh, come with me. I'm going to meet your brother, brother." She puts her foot up on the bench and ties a neglected lace on a long blue boot. "He'll love seeing you without that messy old queen shadowing you. For once."

We leave the park, and because I'm squinting Rosa pulls out dark glasses and puts them on my face. "Now you look like that dead guy," she says, and I say yeah, but I don't know who she means.

Across the thin strip of city and we make it to Pompeii, its windows painted black with the overheads off, last night's stenches of spilled beer and male excretions resurrected by the heat of the day. No one in the front room, no one behind the bar but these are the sounds I hear: the industrial fan whipping above the thick steel doors. The clack of a pool cue from the back room, where a sunk ball rolls through the canals. A transistor radio, blaring an ad for a car dealership. And finally my brother's wordless screams, that seem to come from everywhere at once.

In the other room, separated from the front by an arched brick entrance, I find Carter. He's shirtless, faced away from me and crouched over someone as he throttles them, hard. His sweat-slicked shoulders move up and down, his whole body heaves as he beats on a white kid whose face is raw red. Standing behind Carter is another one of the bartenders, Scotto, and he leans on his good leg, chalking his pool cue and surveying the balls on the table. Rosa stretches her arm in front of me and says, "What the hell is going on here?" Which I would very much like to know myself.

Carter turns and looks right at me, a spattering of blood across his cheeks. "Hey," he pants, "Lewis," and smiles that old familiar smile. The same one he had when we were little kids, big-headed boys under wild bushes of hair, let loose on the city streets. "How you been?"

He smiles that wide smile of his and I tremble. I try to freeze my heart from feeling, but it only melts away.

"You should've seen the way he went into the kid."

Rosa has her arm around Carter's waist and is recounting the story for some newcomers. She gestures madly, knocking over a bottle in her excitement. "Junk bitch got caught with his hand in the register. Didn't know what hit him. Hurricane Carter over here!" Rosa hits my brother in the shoulder, and he raises his fist in mock retaliation, knuckles bruised and bloody. It's early evening and a dozen regulars have shown, Pompeii humming with news of the fight. "You should've taken his ear off," Rosa says, "made it into a necklace."

"Screw that." Carter reaches into his back pocket. "I got his wallet!"

He holds the cracked leather high in the air to much laughter. Scotto, behind the bar, snatches the wallet from him and picks through its contents until he settles on an identification card. "Check it," Scotto says. "Sad thing is only seventeen."

Carter turns to me, because that's my age. "You better watch out, Lewis," he says with a grin.

A regular at the end of the bar is holding an ID card in one hand and the emptied wallet in the other. He puts the card to his forehead, spins around in a little dance and says, "Look at me, I'm Dennis Dorst," then falls to the floor like he's been punched. More laughter, and why is that name so familiar? I feel a strange chill, as if the name might be my own, only from some other life.

Carter has turned quiet. He leans across the bar to grab the card away from Scotto, staring down at the scratched plastic before he puts it on the bar in front of me. It's a student ID from our old high school. "You know this guy?" Carter asks, and as I take in the kid's picture I think of chemistry class and a dusty pale boy bent over a flame, trying and failing to cook junk with the rest of the burnouts. I'd see him in front of school sometimes, kicking gravel across the blacktop, always quiet and slow. But I haven't been by school in a while.

I shrug. "Don't look like anyone to me."

Carter turns away, toward the liquor bottles and the mirror behind them. I can still see his face though, the black warrior eyes that had met my own last year after we came home from school to find our mother had left, the house emptied of half its contents, her dying houseplants left behind to rot in the terra cotta pots that lined every windowsill. I watch him now, parts of him, his muscular back and sculpted arms that held countless girls in the dark basements and attics of our youth, groping them alongside moldered cardboard boxes and ancient ratty couches. I can't help but think of those nights we lay in our beds, me on the top bunk with Carter below. Laughing, he would tell me which ones were eager and which were prudish, what he could get them to do. Then he would roll over, pull his pillow over his head, and drift into dreams.

But I never slept. Instead I would watch his face through the darkness until my eyes felt like they were going to be stuck open forever. I would imagine his hands roaming my skin, conjure the smell of his sweet-sour breath, that smile, just for me. Even with my eyes closed, it is still only him that I see.

I turn toward the front door of Pompeii, a bloody handprint left there by the beaten boy as he stumbled out, neat red stripes laid out on the jamb like the painted divider on a freeway. The bloodstains bend away, dissolve as the door swings open, along with the blinding light of day. And who steps inside the bar but the Hierophant himself.

"Oh God." I leap off my stool, and Rosa reaches to slow me but I speed toward the toilets, where I lock myself inside. Soon there is a loud knocking on the bathroom door, and I let it go on for a while before I finally unlock it. The Hierophant, tight-lipped, smiles at me, Carter just behind him. I nod once at my brother and in comes the old man, the door shut and locked behind him. He puts his hands on my waist, and I pull away, go sit on the lip of the sink.

"I want you back," the Hierophant says. "I've seen things. Created a new potion that's changed everything. It's given me a vision for the ages… I know what you are to me now." But all I can do is shake my head. He looks awful, skin clotted like curdled milk, hairless and pink like a plucked chicken. He pleads with me, cries, "Please, please," as he undoes my belt buckle. I can no longer look at him so I look away, into the mirror behind his back. The bathroom lights are fluorescent green and make my own skin waxen and pocked; I think I could pull this sickly mask off my bones with one quick scrape, if I really tried.

The Hierophant kneels and begins to weep, his head buried in my lap. His hands slide my pants down, and he takes the meat of my cock between his fingers like he's about to pluck a flower in bloom, working his tongue upon the opening of my foreskin in practiced waves. I know I have to get hard so I make myself think of that night a year ago, the last Carter and I saw of our father. Our last night at home.

A heavy rain on the sills had made it sound like a holy war waged in heaven, like the storming of a wasted castle, up high in the sky. And lord how we drank that night, dropped the bottle of bourbon on the carpet again and again until the rug ran from green to brown, until it matched the spindly limbs of the dead houseplants still squatting on every ledge in the apartment. I said *Carter*, and he turned to me, lit up from behind by the streetlamp outside the living room windows, the walls barren white since our mother took all the artwork when she left. And he knew. All the lights were off, and we sat in stillness until he leaned into me across the table and took my hand in his.

I said that I was scared. Carter moved his hand to my face and said, Fine, be scared. He gave me the gentlest of kisses, and it moved me beyond words. How often I had pictured this, this sweetness, this beauty. The room began to spin, and I felt him hold me, felt him all over me, everywhere. His fingers, on the gate latches of my hipbones as he tugged down my boxer shorts, my cock springing skyward in newfound release; his own hardness, thick and warm as I brought its dewy tip to my lips, as I took him inside my eager mouth; the smell of his funk and the sound of his sighing as I brought him to the floor beside me.

And what I wouldn't do for him. Walk on parched and jagged ground, walk through fire. That fire grew and raged over me, burnt his hands where they clutched my shoulders. He pulled me up and into his lap, and we were hard against each other, before I slid myself between his legs and thrusted my cock inside him. He almost cried out but then he bit my shoulder, drawing blood, and Go on and scream, then, I said. Go on and scream, since our father was working the night shift at the electrical plant and the whole world was ours, the sky and the earth beneath it. I buried my face in his armpit, licked the dense patch of wiry curls there as he moaned, his hands moving around my neck and holding me there just tight enough that I was sure I was ready to explode.

We were attached, fleshy and inseparable, nails and hair grafted to each other in a living tapestry. An undifferentiated dyad, we burned together, and we made something new as we fucked on the soft carpet, me inside of him, him inside of me. Together we burned, as one.

And as we burned, we radiated waves of energy. I could feel little nicks and scrapes on my skin shimmer and fade; the little white scar Carter had on his temple from a recent fall on his skateboard, it shuddered like a dewdrop before vanishing from his face. The houseplants upon the windowsills—the ones our mother had left behind, to die as we would ourselves one day—they coiled and greened until their leaves unfurled like holy scrolls, scents heavy and fecund, their beds of black soil steadily moistening as they accepted this freshly secreted life. All this I could see in the night. All this I could taste, as I came in a convulsion of heat and liquid, jerking my brother until he came too, everything drowned and weightless and wild.

The sweet darkness turned to light, which I had mistaken for dawn until I looked over my Carter's shoulder and saw the living room lights were on. And there was our father. He stood over us in his company uniform, the drained bottle of whiskey in his hand. He didn't say a word, not one. He just stared, our bodies at his feet. If he had brained us both with that bottle it would have been relief from the unbearable silence. But it never came. Instead, we simply lay there frozen as he looked down at us, the dark outline of our tangled limbs singed into the carpet around us.

Carter, naked, stood and walked stoically to our bedroom. By the time I pulled myself up and ran to him he had already gotten the suitcases down from the closet shelf. We dressed, and we packed, and we left. The heat from his skin still upon me, the wet smells of the resurrected plants heavy inside my head, we wandered the rainy streets until we were so tired that we collapsed in the weeds bordering the stone park. I assumed Carter had felt as shameful as I did, so I kept quiet as he pulled his hood over his eyes and fell asleep, his lips wet with rain. But I never slept.

And that was all. One night of heavy storming and heat, and it was over. Gone down to the place where skin and silence both go to die. Forgotten. But not forgotten. Because I remember. And so does he.

I grunt once, twice, and I spasm and spend in the Hierophant's mouth, hold the back of his skull so he's forced to take every drop of it down his gagging throat, just how the old bird likes it. When he finishes jerking himself off he staggers to standing, pale hand on the lip of the sink to steady himself. "Thank you, my son," he says as he does up his trousers, eyes fixed on the wet floor between us. He turns on his heel and leaves the bathroom, the door swinging shut behind him.

I get down from the sink and pull up my pants, and there's a small glassine baggie of wafers on the floor, an offering of sorts. I hold the baggie up to the grotesque light, and inside the wafers glimmer in beautiful greens and yellows and blues, each surface etched with a clover or a star or a moon like some fucked-up version of Lucky Charms. I lean out the door and flash the baggie, and Carter and Rosa come running. "You best give me my share," I say as Carter divvies up our score. "I'm the one that had to do the dirty work." There's blood caked in the edges of Carter's nails, and I picture that beaten boy again. The thought of his broken face makes me shudder.

Carter hands me my due, maybe five wafers in all. We dose, and all our heads go up, toward God. I ask what kind they are, and Carter shakes his head. "They have little hearts on them," he says. "So maybe they're a new kind of jumpers?" Which I don't really like but are better than nothing at all. I like spreading out into a velvet rug on the floor and burning down into pulp, a slow, simmering crawl into sleep. Jumpers make your love grow larger so you have enough for everyone, but they also make everything race at the same time. Not what I like at all.

"Oh wait," Carter slurs, and squeezes his eyes closed. "Wait just a minute. There's something else inside of this. Another spell building."

"Saturnalia?" I say hopefully, which rolls you out into a sticky sweet paste, so you feel like you did before you were born.

"Not sure," he says, his lips widening into a Cheshire grin. "But it tastes pure." And it's only now that I'm sure the Hierophant really does want me back.

We treat ourselves to a second heart-inscribed wafer as me and Rosa drink beer and watch Carter restock the bar. Darkness

ascends and Pompeii begins to fill with lustful bodies, the air con-
ditioner wheezing beneath the heat. I feel warm and distracted,
unsure of where the new wafers will take me; all I know is every
patron that enters has got a face that interests me. "Hot night," I
say, and for some reason that makes Carter laugh.

"Here, dear Lewis dear Lewis," Rosa says, and pulls two ciga-
rettes from her handbag. She puts them both in her mouth and
lights them before handing me one. "You know, I really mother
the two of you," she says, a helix of smoke escaping her lips. "You'd
be nothing without me."

"We're nothing with you either," Carter says, and she reaches
over the bar to swing at him with her bag. They start bickering,
play sparring the way they always do. I pretend to smile and close
my eyes, let the sound of them drift away as I allow the wafer's
spell to take hold.

And that's when I see him in my mind: the battered boy, lying
on the pavement in the alley next to the bar. I look down as if from
above, lean over him to make sure he's alive, his chest rising and
falling with shallow breath. His face is bent, split sideways across
the nose, but still beautiful in its own broken way. And it is him,
Dennis, the burnout I remember from school. But his tatty image
soon fades from sight and my head begins to spin, the vision reel-
ing with the stuttering speed of a departing express train. I begin
to panic, afraid that I might float up into the atmosphere, never
to return.

I open my eyes and I'm back inside, back inside my body. Carter
and Rosa are staring at me, my brother now on our side of the bar
top. "What's up with you?" he asks. I shake my head and he rests
a gentle hand on my shoulder. "You sick?"

"No," I lie. Because really I feel like vomiting, my spell-drowsy
skull hung so low my chin almost touches my chest. "Well, let's
drink some more then," Rosa says. She slides my beer in front of
me, clinks her bottle against mine.

I look away for what I think is only a moment, but when I turn back Rosa's gone, the Hierophant standing in her place. Bone-thin inside a frayed black velvet smoking jacket despite the heat, he grasps my wrist in a chapped white hand. "My child," he says, "I've seen you in my prayers. Have you seen me in yours?" I open my mouth to reply but no sound comes out. "Soon you'll know, if you don't already." He smiles, and the sight of his yellowed teeth makes me list.

I stumble from my bar stool. The whole place starts to shimmer with an iridescent light, colors throbbing from green to yellow to blue and back again. No sound now as a new fever wracks me, and I press the side of my head against the bar top. Carter passes by with a crate of empty glasses and it's like he's all lit up, skin sparkling with neon energy, with bright and gleaming diamonds. He glows.

It takes all my strength to turn my head toward the Hierophant, whose veins swim like eels beneath his skin. "The new wafers," I manage to say, stomach rattling like spare change in a tin can. "The ones with the hearts on them. What are they supposed to do?"

"Magnificent, aren't they? I call them lockets." He reaches deep inside the pockets of his smoking jacket and produces two heaping baggies. "There's plenty more for the taking. If it's me you see, that is."

"Of course I see you." What does he mean by that?

The Hierophant leers, bares his stained teeth again. "Then all is as it should be."

I creak my head back toward Carter, who is busy wiping up a spill on the bar top. "Hey," I say. "Do you feel as strange as I do?" But he refuses to look at me, fixed only upon the dishrag swirling beneath his glittering hands and their bruised knuckles, rich and purple like dark rock. All of him glows. I want to blow upon these fingers, cool them beneath my sweet breath, make my brother smile or sigh. We can heal him, together, this I know just as surely as we undid our scars that night, the way we raised our mother's houseplants from the dead. But the Hierophant pulls me closer with a bent claw cupped beneath my chin. "Tell me how you see me," he says, his voice lascivious, wizened face inches from mine. "Tell me how you see your heart's own desire."

"My heart's own…?"

In an instant, Pompeii grinds to a halt, as if frozen in time. The four-on-the-floor stomp from the speakers becomes one long and steady thrum, a bass-heavy moan both primal and holy. The Hierophant is talking but I can no longer hear him, his words a mumble that soon forms a song, sung in a language I've never heard before. The tune folds in on itself until it becomes everything, electric sparks flaring inside my eyes. "Here it comes!" the Hierophant shouts with exultation. "Here it is!" I try to blink but I can't, try to move or scream, and just when I think this dizzying enchantment has reached its climax, I see.

It is a taste more than anything else, a peppermint and egg yolk mash that slides over my tongue in a wave of liquid light. Or rather it is a smell, that of lilac and vinegar, gasoline and dew-damp moss. But more than all this it is a person. Oh yes, it is someone that embraces me beneath the shade of a crepe myrtle, white petals gracing us like rice thrown at a wedding. The Hierophant is gone. Instead, it is my love who reaches out for me, and I kiss his hand, kiss the tips of his bruised fingers, rough upon my lips like pitted rock. I'm hard now, harder than I've ever been, and he smiles and looks away, turning from me.

And I want to say no, no, but it is too late. He floats away and I am left behind, screaming his name through the lonely fall of night.

"I'm here, I'm here," Carter says. I squint through the dark and find myself limp in his arms, his palm pressed to my brow. I throw his hand off, shrug off the cobwebbed fog in my head. I push myself away and flee, lurch through the crowd to the emergency exit, beat my hands against the door until I think my fists will breach the steel. As I throw the door open a few patrons stare after me with mild curiosity, but most of them are caught up in their own worlds with their own longings, everyone looking to score.

I start down the alleyway but remember the beaten boy lying there and I can't help him now, can't even help myself. So I backtrack, take hold of the dangling fire escape ladder above me and start to climb its rust-flaked rungs. I reach the first landing, fall against the ragged brick wall and to my knees, too strung out to go on. Instead I sit and wipe tears from my face, using a well-worn sleeve that makes my eyes sting even more.

There is a clattering on the ladder below, someone swiftly rising in my wake. I reach out in front of me and a hand finds mine in the dark. "Shhh," Carter says, wrapping his strong arms around me. I cry for a while, too ashamed to ask what I might have said or done back inside the bar, under the influence of the wafer-induced spell. All I want to say is that I'm an unclean thing, that I'm something dirty and wrong. But when I look into his eyes my breath catches, his black warrior eyes that are not so different from mine. Eyes I've always thought of as flinty and sharklike but are really just wounded, and searching, and scared. I could stare into them for the rest of my days.

I take his face in my hands, close the short distance between us, and press my mouth to his. I kiss him hard, force him to kiss me back. And to mean it.

Carter's arms slacken, and I pull away. "I'm sorry," I say, "I'm sorry. Damn. It's the wafers. I don't know what they did to me but I didn't mean to—"

"You saw me," Carter says. "When you were rolling just now. You saw me, didn't you?"

I nod reluctantly, and he exhales, hard. "The Hierophant," I say. "He started to tell me something about them. But..."

Carter looks away, down at the alley below. In profile he looks softer, and younger; maybe even younger than me. "The ones we took before, with the hearts on them," he says, his voice uneasy. "They cast a spell that shows you the face of your true love."

I open my mouth, but I cannot speak, cannot believe this is happening. It takes me a few moments to steel myself. But finally I ask.

"What about you? Carter? Who did you see?"

He doesn't answer, only waits for a few moments. And then he yanks me roughly toward him. I brace for him to hit me but he lifts me on top of him instead. His hands move over me, traveling my goosefleshed skin until I'm so engorged I can feel a dribble of pre-cum ooze from the tip of my cock. I play with his hair, let my tongue flicker across his neck. We fall against the railing and climb along the stairs like an enormous crab. He holds my face in his bruised hands, drinks from my mouth, my lips. I reach down in the darkness and fumble with his sweat-soaked shirt, yank his pants down and then my own, cover my palm with spit before I grab his swollen cock and slide him inside me with a raw hunger I've never known. And we rock, his long fingers digging into my ass and squeezing me like overripe fruit, the muscles of his exposed back slick with sweat as he pistons in and out of me, a train racing so hard it can't possibly have any tangible destination, not anywhere on God's green earth. Not here.

"This is all I want in the world," Carter whispers in my ear, and he brings me back to his sour and red mouth, his beautiful God-given form, and I bite down on his shoulder as I struggle for leverage. I finally find something solid, hold tight to the metal rails of the fire escape, like a prisoner to the bars of his cage. He thrusts me further open, again, again, and we race together as one, the fire escape rattling away like rolling thunder as we fuck in circles, in spirals, in tightening cords of passion, of lust. We are the only ones left here, the only ones that matter. And together, we begin to burn.

I think of the Hierophant, waiting inside the bar for me. And who can say I will not go back to him? He still has what I want, after all, the sweet taste of oblivion that he parcels out like bones to a starving dog. I think of the beaten boy in the alleyway, his tongue lolled from the side of his mouth, convulsing in a private hell of pain that my brother and I can abate, with our shared heat, together. And who says I will not go to that boy instead? I think of my father hunched over his whiskey and cursing his perverse sons, his abandoning wife. His barren walls still shine in the night, in and among our mother's forsaken plants, dead again or still alive, in verdant shades of green. And who's to say I'll never return?

All I can say is this I will not leave, and Carter's kisses go down in the dark, kisses like lilac and gasoline. Our fire, it brightens and swells, and it melts the cage that encloses us, the flames of resurrection spilling from our bodies in irradiating waves. I will not let this leave.

GIALLO

1

You are in a session with a new patient, at your private offices on the north side of town. She is attractive and paranoiac, the peony scent of her perfume threading the air as she lies on the couch fingering the crucifix at her neckline with a nervous hand.

"Someone has been following me," she says. "I can never see their face, but when I head home from work at night, I often find them trailing me. They do not move like an ordinary person, but rather shiver along, as if they are some kind of a phantasm. I fear for the safety of my child. I fear for my own life. I am so sleepless with fear, I am beginning to lose my commissions, one after the next."

"And what is it you do for a living?" You tap your fountain pen against your lower lip, the hum of passing traffic from the street below seething like a swarm of goaded yellowjackets.

"I'm a mask-maker," she replies, and smiles. "After all, everyone needs to wear a mask now and again."

2

You are in a session with a longtime patient, a painter of impressionist landscapes, at your shared offices by the waterfront. He is attractive and depressive, an aroma of turpentine wafting from him as he sits in the worn club chair chain-smoking and digging

111

into the palm of his hand with a sharp and yellowed fingernail.

"Lately, I've been worried I'm going to do something bad," he says. "I have fantasies of dismemberment, of amputation. I have intrusive thoughts of cutting into taut skin, of rending flesh from bone. The idea of what it must feel like, it haunts my waking hours."

"And who is it that you fantasize about violating?" You tap your fountain pen against your upper lip, the distant bleat of a cargo ship's frantic horn disrupting the silence from the nearby docks.

"Why, myself of course," he replies, and smiles for the first time this session. "Whatever made you think otherwise?"

3

You are in another session. Only here you are the client, in your own therapist's city center offices, the fragrance of yellowing books emanating from the overstuffed bookcases. She has you lying on the floor, the ceiling fan above rotating round, round. You think of your patients, of the crime and filth in the city you've lived in all your life, and you wonder just what it is that keeps you tethered to this damnable place. Regardless, you feel compelled to stay, as if to assuage the wrath of a jealous and vengeful lover.

"Are you still doing your breathing?" she asks, and you nod. "Go on, then. Show me the exercises, as I taught them to you."

You close your eyes and inhale deeply, and attempt to calm your racing mind.

"I am not myself damaged," you say. "I am not paranoid, or obsessive, or otherwise troubled. Though I am enlisted to aid others with their personal despairs, I am nevertheless free of such concerns."

"Good," your therapist says, the sound of her pen skittering across the pages of her notepad. "Very good."

4

You take a yellow cab home, the clap of thunder as rain deluges the city streets on the far side of the glass. Your eyes sting from exhaustion, and "Would you mind not smoking?" you ask the driver. If he heard you he doesn't respond, however, only ashes his cigarette into an empty coffee cup. You face the window again, steam rising from the sidewalk grates like the hot breath of a subterranean beast, an immense and slumbering creature apt to stir and feed at a moment's notice.

As you approach the crosstown tunnel, you glimpse a rain-drenched couple, caressing amorously against the façade of a travel agency. Just as you begin to descend, however, a glint of light catches your eye, and you gasp: the pair appear to be struggling, a carving knife clenched in the man's black-gloved hand.

"Wait!" you tell the driver, unsure of what you've seen. "Stop!" He doesn't listen, however, and soon the taxi is swallowed into the tunnel, the violent crash of rain replaced by the sound of blood rushing in your ears.

5

Your sleep is fitful. Storm-soaked nightmares of gloved hands that stab and strangle and rend, of flesh that bruises and bleeds and bursts open like an overripe tomato. After tossing and turning all night, you awaken to a hazy sliver of dawn and go for a run along the river, yellow light on the rough water shuddering like candle flame. Even from high atop the promenade, the smell of sewage from last night's rain is repellant, and you wonder how much longer the city's precarious infrastructure can sustain the burdens of the heedless populace.

You jog over to your local café. "Did you hear?" the proprietor says as he sets down your espresso on its saucer. "There's been another murder. The body was disemboweled and left in the gutter, with the pancreas nowhere to be found."

"God in heaven," you say. "Tell me: was she found last night in midtown, outside the eastern entrance to the tunnel?"

"Last night outside the tunnel, yes. Only the body was discovered

on the west side, not the east. And this time, the victim wasn't a
woman, but rather a man."

6

You visit the crime scene, a crowd gathered behind a latticework of
yellow police tape. You stand on your toes to peer over their heads,
the pavement and chipped red brick outside the tunnel entrance
stained crimson from the killer's maniacal handiwork. Movement
catches your eye: a filthy and slavering white cat, batting about a
dead mouse in the adjoining alley. As you approach, the cat hisses
at you, eyes flaring and face smeared with gore.

Bloodied prey between its teeth, it darts away, and your gaze
follows to a figure standing at the far end of the passageway. Their
face is obscured by a mask resembling a leering red devil, hands
sheathed in glossy black leather, and you stare into their yellow
eyes before you start down the telescoping alley.

"Wait!" you shout. They turn and flee, however, rounding the
corner and out of sight. By the time that, breathless, you reach the
open mouth of the alley, you find yourself alone.

7

"Sorry I'm late," you say, and kiss your date before settling into
your seat. "I had an emergency session with a suicidal client."

"That's all right." He unfolds his crisp napkin and spreads it
across his lap. "I was late last time, remember? I had to finish
hanging those new canvases."

The restaurant is quiet and peaceful. A fire crackles in the stone
fireplace across the room, red and yellow flames gamboling like
reckless and unbridled spirits. You reach across the table and take
your date's hand, only he winces and pulls away.

"I injured myself." He shows you his right wrist, the pale flesh
freshly bruised. "Someone knocked me over in the street, and I
fell. They never stopped, and I never saw their face. I'm telling
you, this city is really going to hell."

8

You go dancing. The nightclub is bustling, your chest vibrating with the thrum of disco from the speakers, the air laced with the faint and sweet smell of nitrous oxide. You drink and sweat and sway, your date's unscathed hand at your waist as you press yourself to him, the smoke-filled room blazing red, yellow, red from the rotating gels on the lighting grid high above.

He goes to fetch you a drink, and in the pulsating lights you glimpse someone in a sleek devil mask peering at you across the dance floor. You push through the crowd, the figure slipping into an adjacent unisex restroom as you follow. The blare of music dims to a distant and frenetic heartbeat as the door eases shut, and you make your way down the row of empty stalls.

When you reach the last one, you take a deep breath and open it. Inside is a nun in full habit, hunched over lines of cocaine atop the back of the toilet.

"I'm sorry," you say, and she glares at you. You raise a hand in apology before backing away from the stall.

9

You cross the piazza on your way home. Aside from the buzzing of the streetlamps, it's quiet for this time of night, and you pause in front of the imposing gothic cathedral. Footfall on cobblestone reverberates against the church's façade, and you turn, but there's no one else there. As you continue walking, the sound of footsteps increases, and you quicken your pace.

A chatter of yellow lovebirds bursts overhead, and you are forced to your knees as they hurtle shrieking across the piazza. You stumble back to your feet as the birds crash into the cathedral's massive rose window, piercing the stained glass like artillery fire.

You race inside the church, crunching over broken glass and the snap-necked bodies of birds in the dim moonlight from the shattered window. Upon the main altar is an open-armed statue of the Virgin, its head missing as she blindly reaches out to you in palpable despair.

10

You find a gathering of police officers stationed outside your building, siren lights bathing the façade in blue and red. When you ask what has happened, they inform you that there's been a murder. A shadow falls on the vestibule wall behind them, and you brush past and step inside, the many tear-shaped candelabra bulbs that frame the lobby flickering and hissing and popping in their sockets.

Suspended like a pendulum at the center of the curving grand staircase is your landlady's inverted body. Bruised and bloodied yellow, she hangs from an electrical cord fixed to the crystal chandelier six flights above. Her eyes are shocked wide as she stares back at you as if from below, imploring, accusing, a twisting corkscrew of crimson staining the white marble in a grim spiral below.

After you're questioned, you retire to the quiet of your apartment. It is only once you go to check your calendar for the following day's appointments that you find the message, scrawled in blood on the mirror above your desk.

YOU'RE NEXT

11

"They asked if I had any idea who committed the crime." You lie on the worn black couch with your back to your therapist, and you listen to the scratching of her pen on her notepad, bright sunlight slashing through the blinds. "If it's the same person who left the message, there's a chance I might have recently come across them."

"And?" The sound of her pen ceases. "Who stands out in your mind?"

"Well," you say, and tick the names off on your hands, "there is a new patient, as well as an old one. My local café proprietor. Oh, and an occasional date of mine. A few others as well. A taxicab driver, and a nun I surprised in a nightclub bathroom, or someone dressed as one. And the officer who interviewed me. Strangers. This city, it's full of suspicious characters. It births them, and nurtures them. For what purpose, I cannot say."

Her chair groans as she shifts in her seat. "Can you think of anyone else?"

"No one," you say. "Only you."

12

You reach your local café near closing time and plant yourself on a bar stool, the proprietor wiping down the counter with a filthy rag before he pours you a Negroni.

"Did you hear?" he says eagerly, and waves you off when you try to pay. "There's been another murder."

"Yes, I know." You remove the lemon wedge and sip at your shimmering red drink. "She was my landlady. I saw her strung up when I returned home the other night."

He reaches under the counter and retrieves a copy of the evening edition, slapping the newspaper down. "This one is new."

Beneath the headline DOWNTOWN BLOODBATH is a photograph of a young man splayed face-down on the steps of the courthouse. Runnels of blood pool from his body, a pair of gardening shears abandoned at his side with the subhead TONGUE MISSING AFTER SICKO STRIKES AGAIN in boldface below. You glance up at the proprietor, who has already turned away to dust off the bottles behind the bar.

You weren't next after all. What, then, did the bloody message mean?

13

You are in bed watching the morning news, the mayor promising an end to the wave of brutal killings that has rocked the city. "Well, I'm off," your date says, buttoning his shirt cuffs at the foot of the bed. "The gallery isn't going to open itself."

You wait until he's gone before leaping out of bed. Already dressed, you throw on your shoes and jacket and hurry out the door in pursuit.

You track him through the foggy and litter-strewn streets, dodging tourists and joggers, pedestrians and panhandlers, and as you do so you wonder if he was telling the truth about the injury on his wrist.

You're surprised and relieved when you reach the gallery. The shades are drawn, but you peer through a narrow parting and glimpse the new exhibition. A series of abstract oil paintings, bright lurid slashes bursting from a wide palette of flesh tones. Pale flesh, olive flesh, dark flesh but the rending is all the same, a basinful of savage red spattered across each canvas in a violent and uncontrolled rage.

14

You spend the afternoon at the main branch of the library, where you research the murders, the frequency of which is escalating at an astonishing speed. No matter what promises the mayor makes, it is clear the police are baffled and have no substantial leads. One of the older librarians takes pity on you and shows you how to thread the microfilm projector, and when you begin to look back into the history of this place, you are disturbed to confirm the dark fact that this has always been a place of ill will and omen, a place with malice at its heart.

TWIN NEWBORNS ABDUCTED FROM HOSPITAL; PARENTS DISTRAUGHT

"GOOD TIME GIRL" KILLER SLIPS DRAGNET IN DEADLY ESCAPE

DOOMSDAY CULT MASS SUCIDE CLAIMS TWENTY LIVES

Perhaps even cities can be born wrong, you think, and shudder.

"The House of the Red Serpent." The librarian is standing directly behind you, a coffee mug adorned with a yellow smiley face gripped in her hand as she reads over your shoulder, and you jolt; you hadn't heard her approach. "That's what the cult was called. New Age types, they performed public rituals in one of the local parks before they went underground. For the time, they really stood out. Nowadays, everyone and their grandmother thinks they can read the scratches on the wall."

15

"Fifteen. The Devil," the fortune teller says, and taps the card before her, the candlelit storefront thick with the smell of sandalwood incense. "A sign of vice and addiction, of carnal desire and the priority of material possessions. The snake within the tree of the knowledge of good and evil. This is what crosses you. Not only what you are facing, but what challenges your position and your very sanity. You are trapped, and must give up what no longer serves you."

"How can I stop it?" You stare down at the procession of cards and their interconnected symbols and signs, the tarot spread laid out upon the black velvet cloth. "How can I prevent any more of these killings, and keep from losing my mind in the process?"

"There is no stopping it." She shakes her head as she examines the cards, her gold hoop earrings shimmering in the dim light. "You are on the fool's journey now. Twenty-two steps on the path of understanding, a winding road through a wondrous and often dangerous wood, or in your case an unforgiving city. The journey will end in liberation, or annihilation, or both. Regardless, you are certain to be transformed forever."

16

You stand on the crowded metro platform during the evening commute, the underground ripe with the smell of stale urine as you wait for the advancing train to enter the station and shuttle you home. A man approaches along the track: your longtime patient, the painter, whose hand fumbles in his coat pocket as he fixes you with an unsettling leer.

You hold your breath as he produces a piece of colorful card stock, bold red words printed on a yellow background. "How nice to run into you," he says, and holds out the glossy card. "I wanted to invite you to my upcoming gallery show."

As you step forward for the card, a hunched figure rushes past, knocking hard into your shoulder only to reach out with black-gloved hands and shove the painter into the path of the oncoming train.

Your patient pinwheels back, his eyes widening as he plummets into the tracks, a gasp of surprise smothered by the blare of an air horn and the groan of steel and bone as the train screeches and roars over his body.

17

The sound of screams echoes through the station, and you swallow back your own horror and sprint after the assailant. Up a flight of stairs, the descending throng curses you as you plow onwards, across the uptown platform and onto an idling train. The huddled figure wends through the barrage of oblivious commuters, and when the crowd fails to part fast enough the killer brandishes a straight razor and raises it in a black-gloved hand.

"Look out!" you cry. A man pleads for mercy, but the maniac's blade slashes down at him, his cheek slitting open in a grisly red spray. Chaos erupts as passengers stampede from the train car, and when the assailant glimpses back in your direction a pair of disquieting yellow eyes glints behind the telltale devil mask.

In a rush of bodies the car is emptied. You hurry off yourself, up the final set of station stairs as the killer exits into the open air, with you still very much still in the hunt.

18

You race down the street, the masked figure maneuvering ahead of you through the bustling lunchtime crowd. As you draw closer, the monster seizes the handle of a baby carriage from a passerby, who shrieks as the pram is wrestled from her grasp and thrust into traffic. You dive for the carriage and manage to knock it off its path, preventing certain catastrophe beneath the wheels of a speeding taxicab.

The mother hurries for the carriage as it halts against the curb, and by the time you collect yourself your quarry is across the road. You return your attention to the distraught woman and are startled to discover she is your new patient, the paranoiac mask-maker.

"Don't cry, my sweet baby, don't cry," she coos, and lifts the child into her arms. Only it isn't a child, but rather a yellowed porcelain doll. As she comforts it, the doll stares at you over her shoulder, its round eyes unblinking and accusing.

19

You catch your breath before you take off after the killer again, and you thread through traffic in pursuit, the city a riotous blur of steel and glass, plastic and brick, garbage and asphalt and steam. After some time, you track the masked figure to a crumbling mansion on the outskirts of a residential neighborhood. They disappear up the wide stone steps, and as you cross the threshold you glimpse an uncoiling snake carved into the red marble lintel above.

You creep across decayed floorboards to the darkened parlor, where a fire roars in the hearth. At once you are set upon, the razor-wielding fiend launched from the shadows and knocking you to the threadbare rug. You wrestle before the fire, the heat prickling your skull as the blade threatens to pierce your chest. You seize hold of the black gloves and attempt to push them away, but your hands cannot find a decent grip and they slide off instead, as if your opponent is comprised of rubber.

With all your strength, you kick upwards, and your heels send the maniac headfirst into the dancing yellow flames. Terrible screams, but still you hold tight, and once the room falls silent you haul the prone body free. You use a nearby poker to pry free the smoking devil mask, revealing an unrecognizable mash of pulped and ravaged gore.

20

You go to check the killer's pulse, and rear back: the body is but a writhing mass of teeming snakes, the seething red creatures slithering free from their costume of anonymous black clothing. Exhausted and revulsed, you drop the poker and back away.

Flickering light flares from down the corridor, and you are drawn into an adjoining room, where a battered movie projector is unspooling a filmstrip against the wall. Sepia-toned images of slashings and beatings, of shootings and maimings. Of the black cord tightening around your landlady's throat, the butcher knife carving out the victim's pancreas at the mouth of the crosstown tunnel. The killings you knew of, yes, but also more, far more than you ever dreamed.

Alongside the images an accompanying narration sounds from a connected speaker, the words spoken in a distorted and genderless pitch. What the recording says is this:

I am the killer.

You are the killer.

We share the very same fate, in service of the greater body.

God, the devil, the universe, these idle hands and minds, each and every one.

I am already dead.

You are already dead.

The red serpent is but a path you are destined to walk, just as we have walked it ourselves.

I am the killer.

You are the killer.

We share the very same fate, in service of the greater body.

God, the devil, the universe, these idle hands and minds, each and every one...

21

As the recording loops, you drift back toward the parlor and retrieve the devil mask from beside the deflated black costume, a stray snake wriggling across the rotted floorboards. You take the black gloves as well, and you leave the mansion to wind your way through the coiling avenues, the dark blanket of night descending.

From the shadows of a doorway on the south side of town, you watch a gang of teens throw an elderly priest to the cobblestones and beat him with his own cane. From a pedestrian walkway on the north side, you witness a yellow-toothed junkie lying in her own filth, ignored as she begs passersby for change. At the city center, a rabid dog sets upon an unclothed child, who bites the dog back with a wild and manic yowl. The viciousness you knew of, yes, but also more, far more.

The recording led you to the answer you have always known in your heart to be true, but never dared to utter aloud: the solution to the mystery. It is the city's people—its every resident, even its lowly beasts—all working unwittingly as one. The city itself is the killer, just as surely as if it had opened its gaping maw and swallowed its denizens from below, the serpentine streets running red with blood.

22

After walking and watching all night, you return to your apartment near dawn. You stand before the windows, your tattered coat scored with gouges and stained with dirt, with vomit, with blood. It is more than you ever dreamed. No daylight will change that, and you draw the blinds against the bright rising orb.

You go to the mirror above your desk, where the lurid message written in blood is now dried and faded beneath fingerprint powder, but still at the forefront of your mind.

YOU'RE NEXT

Once, you found these words threatening. Now you glean their true meaning, and reach inside your pocket for the gloves. You slip them on, the black leather straining against your flexing fingers. From your other pocket you retrieve the mask, its contours reeking of seared meat as you slide it over your skull, the face of the devil staring back at you from the mirror. You rummage through the desk drawer and produce a letter opener, the needle-sharp blade glinting in the available light.

The city is inside you. It's always been inside you. And you have a great deal of work to do.

DST (FALL BACK)

I drove down to Milford on a Saturday in late October to see
Martin for myself. I'd heard how much he had changed, but
when I first laid eyes on my one-time romantic rival I almost
failed to recognize him. His face had gone bearded and haggard,
though he still had his paunch, a decade passed since he and Jasper
left the city for the quaint domestic appeal of small-town Pennsylvania. Jasper, however, was prone to callousness (as I myself had
learned the hard way) and I'd wondered how much longer the two
of them would last. I suspected Jasper had, in due course, broken
Martin's heart just as he'd once broken mine, and that I'd been
summoned in the spirit of newfound solidarity. I had nothing better to do, myself.

"I used to work here," Martin said, and cast a baleful look across
the wide porch of the Fauchere, the boutique hotel busy at late
lunchtime before the guests headed back out to catch the last of
the countryside's technicolor array of fall foliage. "Got a bit long
in the tooth for the management's taste, though I could never
prove that was why they let me go. They just kept shortening my
hours until I was forced to leave. I like to come back every once in
a while, just to remind the staff of the decrepit future that awaits
them. A kind of living momento mori, if you will. 'You are now
what I once was. I am what you will one day be.' That sort of
thing."

Martin reached across the table for the ceramic creamer, his shirt cuff divulging a stippling of encrusted sores along the length of his meaty forearm. I was beginning to regret accepting his invitation.

"So, what's this about?" I finally asked. "Is everything alright with you and Jasper?"

"Well, no, actually." He looked down at his coffee, the mug's milky depths as clouded as his eyes. "Jasper's gone missing."

"Missing? What do you mean?"

"It's been over a month now. Nobody knows where he is. The police are aware of the situation, but since Jasper and I are no longer together…" Martin winced as if pained.

"Sorry," I said, and my ears felt hot all of a sudden. "I didn't know."

"We broke up for good in March. But the trouble started before then, a year ago now. I woke up one night and his side of the bed was empty. The next morning, I found him on the front lawn, naked and passed out and nearly frozen; thank God I got him inside before the neighbors called the cops. When I asked him what happened, he told me he'd gone for a walk in the woods. I pointed out that his clothes were missing, but he didn't say anything else, just stared off queerly into the trees behind the house.

"He was never the same after that. Started staying out at night, coming home at dawn, if at all. Well, you know what a horndog Jasper always was, I figured he'd found someone else to hold his attention. But then the cutting started."

Martin exhaled and leaned in close, crossing his mottled arms as if chilled. "Little nicks at first. He'd come home with mud on his boots, so I assumed they were scratches from branches, from trudging through the woods. But then they got bigger, and I started to notice how symmetrical they were. Round marks, in the flesh of his arms and legs. Across his chest, even. He stopped getting undressed in front of me, but every once in a while I would catch a glimpse of some fresh wound. A BDSM thing maybe? Who knows? Either he was letting someone do it to him or he must have been doing it to himself."

"Jesus." It didn't sound like any Jasper I'd ever known. The vain and smooth-skinned dancer, who wouldn't leave the house with so much as a blemish, let alone an open wound. My stomach knotted and I swallowed. I was surprised by how much I missed him. "Suffice it to say, we didn't last much past the winter. He got his own place, a little hovel above a thrift store over on Broad Street. Said he needed to devote more time to a new project. He came around less and less, until he stopped coming around altogether." Martin shook his head. "I suppose in his own way he was shortening my hours as well."

"I'm terribly sorry to hear all this. But I'm not sure what you want me to do about it. I haven't seen Jasper in years."

"I wanted you to come because he spoke of you, not long before he went missing."

"Me? Really?"

Martin nodded. "It was the last time I saw him, over the summer. He was far gone by then. He'd been fired from his studio, arrested around town for trespassing, vagrancy, vandalism, one thing after the next. I suspected it was drugs, but that wasn't it. He was losing his mind. I spotted him wandering beside the road along the highway and pulled over to try to reason with him. But there was no use. He wouldn't even stop walking, just kept staggering along the shoulder as if he were late for something but didn't know where he was going exactly. Like he was in some sort of trance.

"He kept ranting about the date, the weather, how he wasn't going to make it. To wherever he was trying to go, I suppose. Burnt red as a lobster, his clothes filthy, sneakers worn through, toenails yellowed and cracked. I pleaded with him to get in the car so I could take him to the hospital, to see a doctor, *someone*, but he just shrugged me off.

"Jasper claimed I couldn't know what he was going through, that no one could. That's when he mentioned you. He said you were the only one who could see, when it was time. And then something about playing disco in 2000. A disco race? Something."

"*Disco Death Race 2000?*"

"Yes, that's it. What's that mean?"

"It's the name of an old techno album."

I was a late-night DJ at our college station, and when I spun a track from the album on my weekly show I received a rare call from a listener, praising my taste. Jasper and I got to talking, and he popped over from the dance center across the quad. As the end of my shift neared, I was packing up my record crates when the station manager called: it was the end of daylight savings time, and once 3AM fell back to 2AM I'd have to add another hour onto my show. I ended up throwing *Disco Death Race* back on the deck, and Jasper and I let the album play to the end as we fucked in the cramped space beneath the sound board. I'd never felt so happy.

Martin surveyed the porch's outdoor dining area once more. "Look at this place," he muttered, and shook his head again. "They have a twenty-five-year-old maître d' in the main restaurant now. Twenty-five! Some twink from Germany. I asked him where he was from and he said Nuremberg. Then, get this: he asks me if I've ever heard of it. 'Nuremberg? Uh, no, sorry, doesn't ring a bell.' Little twerp. Kind on the eyes though…"

I glanced out the window at the trees between the hotel and the town's main drag, their leaves red, yellow, orange, golden, brown. "Martin," I said, "where do you think Jasper might have gone, exactly?"

"Honestly, I have no idea," He drained his coffee mug and wiped his mouth with the back of a cracked white hand. "But there's something I want you to see."

I followed Martin's pickup through town until we reached a turn-off leading us past a large gatehouse. We drove up a scenic winding drive, and soon a grand and imposing mansion arose before us in a stunning assemblage of turreted towers and bluestone. We pulled around the castle-like building and into a largely empty parking lot in the rear, where we both got out of our respective cars and rejoined beside a slate patio overlooking the impressive property, the rolling lawns a stalwart green despite autumn's onward march toward winter.

"What is this place?"

"Grey Towers. The estate of Gifford Pinchot, who was the governor of Pennsylvania about a hundred years ago. Before that he was the first head of the U.S. Forest Service. His wife was a big suffragette. Fascinating family, the mansion is to die for. But we're not going inside."

"Martin, I'd really like to head back to the city while it's light. And it's starting to get late…"

"Come." He pointed away from the estate, past the parking lot and toward a wide stand of trees where a path snaked its way into the woods. "We're going there."

We hadn't walked for long before the scattered hemlocks and white pines began to thin and we reached a clearing, on the other side of which was an unusual wooden structure. Raised up on iron piping and suspended about twenty feet above the forest floor, it was quite large and resembled a grain silo, or perhaps a water tower you might see atop an apartment building in the city. It was tilted, however, at what appeared to be a forty-five-degree angle.

"What is that thing?" I asked, shielding my eyes from the setting sun as it stole low beneath the weblike tree canopy.

"It's what I wanted to show you. This way."

The air crisped in a swelling breeze, the crunch of dry leaves underfoot its own steady pulse as we made our way across the clearing to the mammoth structure. Peering up at it, I could now see it wasn't barrel-shaped so much as conical. Or perhaps it could be best described as corkscrewed, the wood at its base narrowed like the mouth of a conch but still wide enough for someone to access through a narrow rusted ladder bolted to its frame that led up and inside the occluded interior.

"It's called a cosmoscope," Martin said, and placed a pale hand against the dark wood. "It's a kind of observatory. Conceived long ago by a scientist from New Zealand, a summer visitor at Grey Towers. The cosmoscope was built to his specifications by Yale School of Forestry students, between the world wars. Unfortunately, the damned thing has been in disuse for decades. Sad, really. They haven't had the budget to restore it."

"This is all very interesting, but…"

"But what does it have to do with Jasper? They found him out here. Just last month. In fact, that seems to have been the very last time anyone saw Jasper at all. He'd been living inside the cosmoscope. Not only that, but according to the guide who brought me out here, someone appears to have modified it." He pointed to a length of rubber tubing, one of many fastened to the exterior. They had an oddly intestinal look. "See these things? The guide thinks they're meant to transmit sound. So if you're inside the cosmoscope, they let you hear the noises of the forest without any background noise. Birds, bugs, the wind through the trees, but magnified."

I waited for him to head up the ladder, and eventually he cocked his head and laughed. "Are you kidding? I can't fit up there. I'm not a little guy like Jasper. Or you."

I pushed against the small hatch, which creaked open and hit against the inside with a hard slap, and a musty funk washed over me. Holding my breath as I peered up inside the cosmoscope's wide barrel, I began to ascend, an astronaut climbing into a soon-departing rocket ship. This sense of transition was coupled with an additional nervousness I was hesitant to place at its source: that Martin had brought me out here for some nefarious purpose I had yet to ascertain.

He was right about one thing, though: not only was the entrance too small for him, but the interior of the cosmoscope appeared to be constructed with an almost labyrinthine relay of wooden compartments. What I could see from the small amount of light from the open hatch (though there must have also been an opening in the cosmoscope's roof high above) was a series of inner walls, hard stops that, due to the severity of the structure's tilt, resembled nothing so much as a canted rat maze. How Jasper could have managed to live inside this strange contraption was anyone's guess. I reached into the wooden cavity above me. Below a section of rubber tubing my hand stuck to the curved siding, which was coated in a viscous texture not unlike tree sap; I had the fleeting thought that the cosmoscope itself was somehow alive. It was only once I closed the hatch and started back down the ladder that I could see a small triad of words carved into the structure's base. *George Vernon Hudson.* The name was etched in erratic lines, barely legible in the dying light of day but there nevertheless.

I dizzied, and when I reached the ground again I stared down at my hands and the rust-colored substance that had coagulated upon them, a black and red amalgam of some unknown provenance collected from inside the cosmoscope. *Everybody thinks I'm high*, I thought, and froze. They were the first words of *Disco Death Race 2000*, the song "Sixteen Bit Suicide." Jasper and I would whisper those words to each other once upon a time, apropos of nothing. *Everybody thinks I'm high.* I couldn't help but smile.

I wiped away the angry stains on my trousers, and as I did so the smell of raw meat tinged the air. An olfactory hallucination, perhaps. Martin was watching me closely.

"What was Jasper doing out here?" I asked him. "What did he want with this thing?"

"Observing, I suppose. Though I had hoped that you might know the answer. He said he'd tell you at the right hour."

Martin stared down at the forest floor. For a moment he shook his head as if clearing away an unpleasant thought or memory, then started toward the path back to Grey Towers and the parking lot. I stole one last glance at the cosmoscope before I followed.

Dusk fell in a contusion of purple light and shadow over the distant hills as Martin and I parted ways at the center of town, hands raised in salutation behind windshields as I headed back the way we had come. I was bone tired and wary of the drive home to the city, so I returned instead to the hotel and checked myself into a top-floor suite for the night. I picked at a pink steak in the hotel's chic restaurant, accompanied by a lovely glass of port, but I couldn't bring myself to finish either. Since Martin took me to view the cosmoscope, I had the disagreeable impression that time had begun to slow, that I was walking through the world as if attempting to traverse some kind of jellylike sea, my progress no longer assured. I couldn't remember the last time I felt so drained. Or so very alone.

I returned upstairs to my room, hung the Do Not Disturb sign on the other side of the door, and engaged the safety latch, and as I did so I recalled the name scratched into the base of the cosmoscope. *George Vernon Hudson.* A quick Google search on my phone revealed him as a London-born New Zealander who first drew popular attention to daylight savings time. An ancient concept, yes, but his advocacy was critical to the larger movement and its adoption over the course of the last century.

A peek out the windows—at the tall pines that separated the hotel from the tranquil street beyond—before I drew the heavy curtains against the vast sweep of night that had settled over the town like a black shroud. I fumbled my way out of my loafers, their striated rubber soles encrusted with dried mud, and collapsed upon the bed without so much as undressing. Instead I buried myself beneath the sheets, curled a pillow over my head like a crescent, and descended into sleep's sweet release.

Sometime later I awoke in darkness to a decided chill in the room, as well as a deep feeling of unease. I reached for the bedside lamp on the nightstand, just beyond the digital clock and its LED display that read 2:59AM in bold green bars.

"Don't," a voice said from the corner. I jackknifed to attention and suppressed a startled cry. Of fear, yes, but also one of anticipation, since I recognized the voice at once. It was as if I had only just been dreaming of it.

"Jasper?" I said, rubbing at my eyes. And there he was, his familiar lithe frame visible in the half-light from the now-parted curtains. From what I could tell, he was completely naked. "How did you get in here?"

He raised a finger and pointed it upwards, toward the ceiling; I took it to mean he must have climbed down from the roof. Indeed, the window nearest him was cracked wide, the drapery's lining fluttering and pellucid in night's steady exhalation. Once my eyes adjusted I could see more of him: his pale face colored or flushed or bruised, round black marks along his limbs and concave chest, ribcage protruding as if trying to escape.

"You scared me half to death," I said. "They're looking for you. Martin's looking for you. They have no idea where you are."

"We're all looking for something." The space between us was obscured by a vapor of condensation from between his lips; the room was colder than I'd thought. "But to find it, you have to look in the right place. At the right time."

He pointed his bone-white finger at the ground. "They weren't very nice to him," he said. "They ridiculed him. But he was a visionary. And eventually, he prevailed."

Jasper peered out the window, his face bleached in the moonlight bleeding through the trees. "He was an entomologist, as well as an astronomer. I find that interesting. Because you see, you cannot glimpse the multitude of the heavens without listening to the multitude of the earth. As above, so below."

George Vernon Hudson, I thought, and Jasper smiled. "Yes," he said, and nodded. "Starlight and stridulations. Together, they open windows. But only inside the gifted hour. Otherwise..." He sighed. "Otherwise, they won't let you see. And he was the one who saw, first."

"Jasper," I started, but he shushed me with that white finger pressed to his bloodless lips. In an instant he was beside me, in less than a blink of the eye. I heard the sounds of his movement as a distant afterthought, the crunch of bare feet on dry leaves, as if the floor of the room was carpeted in dead foliage. Always the dancer.

"We fitted together," he said. "You and I. Wore the same clothes, to boot. I remember one time at the theater we were mistaken for each other, do you?"

His breath on my face was beyond stale, beyond rank, the smell of the grave. I took a step away from him, toward the still-locked door. Yet as he reached out and caressed my cheek with the back of a dirty hand, I nevertheless felt the old stirrings within me, my dormant cock roused to new life. It had been so long since I'd been with someone, since I'd been held; it had been since I'd last seen Jasper.

We kissed, and I stung where his tongue touched mine, pins and needles pricking at my mouth, my lips. I tried to ignore the pain. His hand upon the back of my head kept me pressed to him, however, his fingers cupping my skull as if drinking from it, his hardness against mine.

"Manipulation of time," he whispered in my ear, and gooseflesh pebbled my skin. "Their gift is also our key. Only then can we be open wide. Only then can we let it in, during the twice-born hour. Sixteen-bit suicide. All the way down."

I tried turning away but his steadfast fingers held me in place, his expression unreadable. Jasper's lips dropped open, a dark void absent of teeth, and his throat emitted the cry of an injured animal dragging itself across a frosted tundra. Black ooze spilled from his lips and ears, from the small mouths carved up and down his limbs. I couldn't scream, though I tried. I couldn't scream and so I twisted from his grasp, falling back upon the bed. The dark fluid took hold of me there, hardening and pinning me to the sheets. My mouth formed a final cry of anguish as the thrashing tide forced itself down my engorged throat, my teeth cracking one after the next in the black fluid's relentless irruption.

Just before I lost consciousness, my bulging eyes caught sight of the clock on the nightstand. Its alien green digits still read 2:59AM, and they trembled and strained and failed to change over, to a new and other and unknown time.

The main gates at Grey Towers were locked. Once I rolled up my shirtsleeves and trouser cuffs, however, it wasn't difficult to hop the adjoining stone wall, and I kept low to the ground as I circumnavigated the rolling lawn on my way up to the woods behind the Gilded Age mansion. I waited until I reached the path to turn on the penlight retrieved from my glove compartment, no sound but the soughing of the wind in the trees, a distant or perhaps imagined scent of cedar smoke on the air as I hurried into the dark heart of the night forest. I checked my watch: 2:37AM. It was still within the gifted hour, the end of saving daylight that Jasper had spoken of, in the dream that was not a dream. I still had time to see for myself.

I reached the base of the cosmoscope. Clasping the penlight between my teeth, I climbed the rickety ladder and hauled myself into the first compartment within the immense wooden cavity. I could just fit inside. Jasper had known that, of course. We were the same size, on balance, and really had been mistaken for each other, not just that one time at the theater but so very often.

We always fitted together, it was true. Jasper had wanted me here, in the end and after all these years. I'd been needed after all.

I forged my way deeper inside, crawling and stretching and compressing my form, and it soon became clear I was traveling in spoked circles. It was as if I were traversing the interior of a gargantuan wagon wheel, a narrow course designed for another age of man, now past. My palms were slicked in sweat and the strange viscous substance I'd encountered earlier, only now I could sense that the whole of the cosmoscope was coated in it, rust-red ooze atop ocher lumber, sudden flashes of ragged scratch marks against the damp siding in the penlight's erratic beam.

After some time, I reached the center. It was a coffin-sized recess, puckered out from the rest of the cosmoscope to comprise its highest elevation. I pulled myself up and inside, and laid myself out against what should have been hard wood but was in fact pulp, with the moldable consistency of sponge. I turned off the penlight and waited for my eyes to adjust, all alone in the dark. And then, I saw.

High above me—above the tilted round face of the cosmoscope and the vaulted tree canopy, branches bending away from the clearing in a wide and deferential circle as if woven by a godlike hand—was the wide and starlit sky. It was as clear as I'd ever seen it. As clear, I knew, as it could ever be seen. The stars were closer to Earth than would seem possible, smoldering crystalline globules of fire that appeared to hang no higher than the thermosphere. The celestial heavens rattled and hissed as if threatened, trembling and straining, the firmament awakened to new life. And now Jasper was on his way.

A rustling noise, the uneven lurch of something crawling over dry leaves, and I became aware of the perimeter of dark holes lining the small chamber around me, making themselves known by a rising susurration of whispered breath through their mouths. It was the sound of the forest, called forth and issued from the rubber tubing threaded through the cosmoscope. A droning buzz and the frenzied communications of insects flared, hungry and watchful, a piercing hosanna that refused to end, even as the wind from the holes began to take a shape all its own.

My skin. It hummed with a thirst for communion, for the total unity of matter that only oblivion could provide. Jasper, he wanted me to see what he had seen, to feel what he felt. He wanted us to be the same. Not just us, but all things, if only we could find our way together. And now I could really see.

The nebular sky ripped open, the pinpricked curtain thrust wide at last, and in a heaving of rent wood and bone the cosmoscope undulated and spun, expanded and contracted, suspended in air, in darkness, in light, tremulous, wild. The thing that Jasper had become a part of took hold of me, slender black coils lashing and sucking with a thousand hungry mouths, an anarchic rattle of spurned life crying out in pain, in rage, in exaltation, transmutation, ecstasy.

I bled into it, into dark light, into sound. I became part of the greater whole. Because we were the same, Jasper and I, just the same, and we would never be apart again. In this hour, we could see what we were made of, and we were insects, we were dust, we were light, everything in the brightest of high color and made of stars.

I saw his face. His wry smile, Jasper here beside me once more, joined as one in yet another cramped space among many, as we were meant to be. Together, we gave ourselves away, and what remained of the structure's provisional contents splashed against the internal walls as wet gristle in a mighty centrifuge. We were elsewhere now.

Silence. The cosmoscope was still. A withdrawal, that of a hypodermic syringe, its plunger pulled back from its barrel. A slowing, a swallowing, a satiety, the clearing hushed, the forest hushed, time beginning anew, and what was left of that bodily cage dripped down to the roughhewn wood flooring. The crunch of dry leaves, a skittering through the quieted underbrush, as night continued its slow and glutted retreat until morning.

THE VAULT OF THE SKY, THE FACE OF THE DEEP

They left me here during the evacuation. Old shrunken and childless widow with broken hips and no one to check on her, knees that lock beneath soiled nightgown and sheets, I listened as it all played out on my now-dead transistor radio. "Only three days," my wageless nursemaid Natalia said, "I'll be back in three days," and she never returned. No food for a week, well-drawn water long emptied from the bottles at my bedside in this patchwork cottage with the windows covered in newsprint since the light hurts my eyes, the same way it hurts to look at you. So blindingly blue. Now they're gone, from Pripyat to Chernobyl, all of them gone, eighteen miles in every direction around the plant. Such a waste. And I'm reaching the end.

Fitting fate to die alone, but then you came. Part of me hoped you would. And now you're here. Just as you were then, so very long ago.

Come closer. No, closer still, for you and I must speak on what I pray will be my last night on this godless earth. I might have had a few more days or weeks if someone else had come for me, but no matter. One day is just as good as another.

Tell me your name. I've always wanted to know.

No?

So then you came to listen. In that case I'll talk, and tell you what you want to hear. If only you'll do me one favor.

Yes?

Then I'll tell it.

I was born at the turn of the century as Irina Aleksandrovna Semonenko, named after the Grand Duke's daughter. Our only royalty, though, was my father, who was indeed a king but only of the local tavern, where he would rule over his court of drunken loyalists. Member of the Black Hundred through and through, and I remember his second pair of workboots lined up against the wall in the hallway, wondering when the first would walk home from the fields, his swollen feet inside. He was not a bad man, as far as fathers go: as a breed they are largely absent. The worst kind are the ones who are always hovering about, and he was a mercifully empty space in my childhood.

My mother, however, took great joy in her children, the four that lasted through infancy. We would dance around her dress hems, making mischief which might earn a hard slap on the head; that didn't mean the same thing then as it does now.

There was no school in those days, certainly not when this place was called Lokachkiv, so family was everything; my oldest brother Ivan was the one who taught me how to read. There was no going to Kiev then, no modern means of transport or pleasure to occupy our time, and when there wasn't work there was boredom, which hung heavy over all of us. Especially the men, who would drink and drink more until their thoughts turned to either hatred or lust.

Now that I think on it, that's why we're talking now.

When was it? Was I six years old? Or was I seven? It's hard for me to put it in place, all that time before the revolution we were supposed to forget. My strongest memory from that time is of you; that's how I knew you'd return to me, once the accident happened at the plant. I said before I had hoped it, but actually I knew. I knew.

You ruined my wedding night, did you know that? The night I

became a Petrova. You came to me in a dream and gave me a horrible scare. Sergei had to stay up with me until morning. I was so afraid, over nothing. I tried to talk with my friend Elizaveta about you years later but she just laughed, as she did the night it happened. I never mentioned you again.

Where was I? Pardon me. I keep thinking I hear someone calling me. My mother perhaps, crying "Irinotchka" with anger from the kitchen, for I've done something wrong. But she's dead now.

Then again, so are you.

This has become a village of ghosts, and in a way, it's your fault, your people's fault, I mean. They're the ones who invented this way of turning energy into destruction. And now you've gotten your revenge on us, made us flee our homes as we once made you flee, and I suppose I can't really blame you for that. For there was a time when some of the men of this province wouldn't think much more about slitting one of your children's throats than they would peeling an apple; it was almost their national duty. So try not to judge us too harshly, if you can. Especially Ivan, God rest his soul, may he live on in heaven's embrace. He of the three of them was the drunkest, and if I hadn't gotten him from the tavern that night, then they might never have done what they did. But maybe that's just the wishful thoughts of a dying old woman.

And you. Come even closer, sit on the edge of the bed. Right here. Take my hand. I know you came to hear about yourself, not me. All young men are that way. You're more handsome than I remember, especially for what you are. And so young. So very young. How old are you, sixteen years? Seventeen?

I can feel pins and needles on my face, pricking at me. Is that you?

Your skin is the color of the sky that first night after the accident, has the same radiant bluish glow that there was in the clouds over the plant, one month gone now. Natalia propped me up in bed before running off with everyone else to the hills and rooftops to watch. So bright.

Is the accident what brought you back? I heard a program on the radio once, regarding some foreigners, from the Orient, I believe, who could think something so strongly that they could will it to life, so that it walked free in the world. Is that what you are? Or perhaps you were here all along, watching me, and the radiation just illuminated you, made you visible to the eye. I don't know about such things, the old superstitions weaned from us by the state, only what I hear on the now-dead transistor, or what I might hear from Natalia, who is a gossipmonger; she talks a lot, and never listens. You're a good listener.

So you want to hear a story you already know? But why?

Are you my confessor?

If you insist, then, I'll tell it. It will be my last tale.

That night Alexander and Yuri found you, our mother had sent me to bring them home; your cries hurried me along the rain-slicked streets and that's when I found the three of you at the corner, my brothers bent over you, taking turns kicking you in your sides. Your skullcap had fallen off, and Yuri ground it into the mud with his heel. I ran inside the tavern and screamed, "Ivan, Ivan, they're beating a Jew in the gutter," and the whole town seemed to spill outside to watch as your blood started soaking into the dirt. It was Ivan who stumbled forward and shouted for them to stop, and a grumble of disappointment passed through the crowd.

You got up, or at least on one knee, and Ivan reached out his hand. You looked so peaceful then, not afraid, peering with wonder between the curls on the sides of your head as if looking up into the face of God himself. When you went to take his hand he grabbed you by your wrist instead and dragged you through the crowd, which roared its approval and trailed after him. I ran alongside you, watching as you tried to keep your head from hitting the stones; maybe it would have been better for you if you had managed to concuss yourself, I don't know.

The alley behind the tavern reeked of urine and sick, and there was a wooden barrel there against the wall, high as Ivan's waist and nearly full with rainwater and vomit. He pulled you forward as he held your hands behind your back, tipped your head into the barrel as Alexander and Yuri lifted you from your feet. The crowd cheered.

Our father stepped out of the back door of the tavern then, and when he saw what was happening his face lit up with pride, radiant. He began to clap his hands above his head and started the crowd in a Black Hundred rhyme. Oh, let me see if I can remember it...

"Remember the crown, for the good of Russia,

Strike out at the heart of thieves,

Take up the sword, and make it prosper

May it bloody our enemies."

Something of the sort.

I watched you begin to drown, your body convulsing like a fish on the floor of a boat, and then your legs twisted so hard that my brothers, laughing, dropped you into the barrel before lifting you again so that only your head was beneath the water's surface. I turned to the crowd then, everyone so much taller than me I could barely see their faces, though I do remember seeing young Elizaveta Baranskaia—Natalia's mother, she died just last year, God rest her soul, may she live on in heaven's embrace—with a great smile on her lips. How much fun they were all having. I laughed along with the rest of them, clapping my hands and stamping my feet into the mud. But part of me felt for you, it really did, for I didn't know how to swim and I have always feared the water so.

Maybe that's because of you.

I started to turn away but there was a strong hand on my shoulder and I was made to face forward, your legs just twitching now, barely struggling at all. "Irinochka, what are you doing?" my mother said at my side, holding me. "You must watch." And I did.

After a few minutes my brothers lifted you out of the barrel, and your dead face had gone blue. But not the blue of you now, the steady blue glow of a toxic cloud, but rather a face mottled with white and red blotches. The crowd continued to carry on, and my mother abruptly scooped me into her arms as she made her way through the crowd. "Okay, time for bed now, sweet one. All good little girls should be in bed."

All good little girls should be in bed. And now I can't get out of mine.

And now I'm done. Eighty more years gone, and I'm done. Over there on the wall is a portrait of my husband Sergei, God rest his soul, may he live on in heaven's embrace. Everyone loved him so. When I met him I was nearly your age, and he reminded me so much of my father. So loved.

How does it feel, then, to be hated? To be despised, hounded from your homes and hunted down in the streets like dogs until you're driven out or dead? Of course, your people have their own land now; the world should have thought of that sooner. Such a waste.

Oh, it's time, it's time, I must leave my bed for the very last time. Won't you help me, so I can see the midnight sky once more? I've told you the story, so that you might be free of it, if that is why you came. But now it's time. And you promised.

That's it. Slip your hands beneath me. Oh, pins and needles, pricking everywhere. It's your skin, you unholy thing, it's on fire with power like sunlight, penetrating me. That's it. Lift me up. Not too roughly, I'm all bones and loosened flesh. Only a monster like you would hold me now.

Carry me to the front door. That's it. Careful. I'll help keep your skullcap upon your head, if you'll let me. Now, over the threshold, like a bridegroom from the cinema. Look, there's my cat Misha. So skinny, what have you been eating, my dear, nothing but weeds? Oh, my garden, my once-beautiful garden, who will tend you now?

One moment. There. Look around, do you see them? There. Right there. And there. What are those things, glowing blue in the darkness at the edges of the field, watching us as we pass through the garden gates? Are they your people? They frighten me. So many of them. So many of them so young. Look at her, that child there, her face is familiar to me. Perhaps she and I passed one another on the street one summer's day, when I too was a girl. So bright, blinding radiance, it hurts to look. I'll close my eyes, and never open them again.

Is that the sound of my mother, calling me from the kitchen? It's too late for that.

Now, do as you promised, monster Jew. I can't do it myself, for that would be a sin. Help this old woman down to the well and throw her in, so that I too may see the true face of God.

ANAÏS NIN AT THE GRAND GUIGNOL

Before I go to bed, I look under my bed with fear. I fear the dark, the storms, the sea, the unknown and my own darkness.

— Paula Maxa

PARIS, 1933

While Hugo is in London, Henry comes to see me at Louveciennes. Emilia serves us a lovely lunch of steamed clams and a salade niçoise, as well as the festive carrot soufflé from my aunt's recipe, all of which Henry takes to with his usual lustful brio. He drinks and I smoke, and we play with the dogs in the garden while we wait for Emilia to clear away the dishes. I watch as Henry tosses the ball out for Banquo, who brings it back for another go, just one more, one more, more. I retain a smile, but this surface contentment is an inaccurate reflection of what lies beneath, a mask I wear so that I might be found respectable and worthy of companionship. In truth, I am adrift.

I give Emilia the afternoon off and send her home early. No sooner is she out and past the green garden gate than Henry and I set upon each other, hungry and wild, and we caress with an unmoored enthusiasm.

"How long do we have?" he says, as we make our way up the stairs. "Tell me I can stay the night."

"Another night, but not this one. I have too many errands to tend to in advance of Hugo's return. Then he is back here through the end of April."

"Damn it to hell. I did hear somewhere that April was the cruelest month." Henry hikes my dress up and around my waist. "'Breeding lilacs out of the dead land...'"

"'Mixing memory and desire, stirring dull roots with spring rain....'"

"Hey, you know your Waste Land," he says, and he presses himself against me, no time to disrobe before I feel him hard against my thigh. "I'm impressed."

"I know a great many things besides Eliot." I smile, with a wicked knowledge born of experience. "Allow me to show them to you."

I move toward the bed, but "No," he whispers in my ear, "right here," and he takes hold of my buttocks in his rough tailor's hands and seats me upon the windowsill.

I fumble with his belt buckle, release him from the confines of his trousers and worn-out underwear. I help him from the remainder of his clothing, as he helps me from mine, our costumes shed so that we may be free from the staged production of our ordinary lives. We cross over as one into the more real world of fantasy, undiminished and undisguised, my native country above all others. For it is only in the act of pleasure that I can find myself, my true self. There, and in this diary.

Henry thrusts himself inside me, and the whole of my body spasms, his iron embrace all that keeps me from crashing through the leaded glass at my back. I grasp him closer, tilt my pelvis so that the small core at my opening bears down upon his firmness. I squeeze my eyes shut and ride him faster, my panting breath unfurling into a quiet and steady prayer.

"Please," I whisper, "please," not so much to Henry as to a distant god of mercy. This is the only way I know how to heal what has been broken.

"Oh, Christ, Anaïs," he mutters, and I scramble for leverage against the walls of the window casing, fingernails scarring the plaster with crescent-shaped marks, lest they find a softer target and draw blood. "You make me crazy," he says. "There's no one else but you. You know that. There's no one else in the world." The animal sounds of our lovemaking echo in my ears, ring out across the bedroom and through the open door, and we fall into a dance of wordlessness, into the language of movement, the divine alchemy of the physical.

The wordlessness is just as well, since I cannot respond to Henry in kind. I cannot tell him there is no one else, because unlike him I am not so quick to lie. I know he believes these words as he speaks them, however, just as I know that, in another moment or five moments or ten, his imagination will steer toward one of his many whores. Or perhaps toward June, glittering and regal and imperious. The billowing curves of her hips and breasts, her severe face that captures the female and the male in its own golden ratio, she who commands the beauty of both sexes at once. Since she left for New York, a whirlpool of loss has opened inside me, one capable of swallowing me whole. My longing for her is so powerful it disturbs me.

As Henry spends himself inside me, I wonder if he thinks of her now, and the affair that sent her away. The one that Henry and I have carried on for all these many months, that drove his wife from his arms. I wonder because I cannot help but think of June myself.

I go into the city for my session with Dr. Allendy. The small office he keeps at his home address is uncomfortably warm, a strange humidity laced with pipe smoke that narcotizes me as soon as I enter.

"Close your eyes," he says. "Relax, and simply talk." I lie upon the couch, and he steers me down the usual paths of analysis: my dissatisfactions with domesticity and my role as a wife; the highs and inevitable lows brought on by my various love affairs; the loss of June, and what it means for both Henry and myself. As the session progresses, I find myself unable to concentrate on the task at hand, to draw upon the usual connections and associations crucial to therapeutic success. Somewhere along the dance of my life, I have lost my footing, and I can no longer disguise it when I drop a step.

"Anaïs? What is the matter?" Allendy strokes his beard as he stares down at me with his typical air of avuncular concern. "You do not seem quite yourself today."

"It is nothing," I say, though neither of us is fooled by these empty words. "It is just…" I shake my head. "I am beginning to feel I am not present in my own life. That I have taken on the role of an observer. It is as if I am somehow outside of my skin, cursed to look on as I go about my daily business. I worry that I am becoming a stranger to myself."

"Perhaps this sense of separation is due to your work," Allendy says. "Is it not possible that this secondary life on the page—your mirror life—is actually subsuming your everyday existence? Nowhere is this more acute than in the case of your obsessive diary writing." I feel my journal from the corner of the room, where it burns inside my bag like a fiery cinder, an irrepressible itch in need of scratching. It begs to be written inside of, page after page and cover to cover. I am an addict, it is true, the diary my opium.

"Normally, I would be inclined to agree," I say. "But it is not my writing that has caused me to feel this way. It is as if I have become my own ghost."

"Do you have any thoughts about what might be causing this sense of dissociation?" Allendy crosses and uncrosses his legs, brings his pipe to his mouth. I exhale, and contemplate how best to answer.

"You want me to say it is because of June," I say. "It is true that I wanted to save her from the pallid existence she had made for herself, and the ruins of her marriage to Henry. But June is the death drive that counterbalances Henry's vitality, his love of life. And now? Now, she is gone. Her choice, of course. She proved once and for all that she did not desire saving in the first place. Least of all by me."

"Then perhaps it is time for you to find someone else on which to focus." He bites at the lip of his pipe before slipping it from his mouth. "Perhaps it is time for you find someone else to save."

"Perhaps it is."

I stare out the window, at the tops of the honey locust trees in Allendy's garden, their flowers just beginning to blossom on the far side of the glass. "At Louveciennes," I say, "behind the wide wooden trellis covered in thick ivy, the front of the house is faced with shutters. There are eleven of them: five windows onto the west rooms, and five onto the east, with a single closed shutter at its center. That center shutter is always closed, you see, because it is only there for symmetry. There is nothing behind it, no window or room whatsoever. Yet I often find myself dreaming that there is in fact a room, a place I call the sealed room. I imagine that if only I can locate the door and manage to unlock it, then what lies inside will prove the missing element that is destined to complete me at last."

"This sealed room," Allendy says. "It is where your unknown self is kept from you, yes? Your own private mysteries, hidden away. The essence of your repressed desires."

I nod. "And so I am unmoored, and doomed to continue searching for what I have lost, the way I search for the room in my dreams. Unmoored more than usual, it must be said, in June's wake."

"Yet she is not the primal cause of your malaise." Allendy taps out his pipe in the ashtray, though his dark eyes remain fixed upon me, pinning me to the couch like a specimen. "Your feelings about her absence are but an echo of the original and formative event: the abandonment you suffered at the hands your father."

"Maybe so," I say, and shift uncomfortably upon the couch, the room growing hotter. "I feel betrayed by her. An echo of the loss, as you say, that I felt as a child. The difference, however, is that

June left because of Henry and me. She claimed I was the source of the entire rupture."

"You said Henry and June's marriage was foundering long before they moved to Paris and crossed your path. In truth, your guilt is precisely the same self-blame you bore in the aftermath of your father's abandonment. It stems from your unconscious conviction that if only you had managed to be a better daughter, then your father would never have left."

He smiles. "This desire for self-flagellation is a knot at the center of your resistant mind, Anaïs, one that is in desperate need of untying. Your shame is also the cause of your masochistic dreams, those in which you desire to be dominated. Indeed, to be punished, humiliated. Your intense desire for your father's affections is coupled with your allegiance to your betrayed mother, aligned as you are with her sense of outrage. You find it easy to place yourself in her position, that of an abandoned lover, yes? This naturally lends itself to feelings of inadequacy. Have you had any erotic dreams about your father?"

I smooth my dress over my knees, and look up to find him watching me. "How do you suggest I free myself from this cycle of self-punishment?"

He puts down his pipe and stands. "I want to show you something."

I follow him out of his office and into the adjoining parlor. Against the far wall is a square slatted box the size of a wardrobe, the dark brown wood out of place amid the room's black-and-white decor.

"This is called an isolation accumulator." He opens the door to the structure to reveal its metal interior. "It is a prototype created by a former colleague at the Vienna Ambulatorium, designed to stimulate the production of positive flow through the lessening of distractibility. I would like you to try it, to better open yourself to that which keeps you from healthful integration."

"And… how do I go about using it, exactly?"

"You sit inside, and I shut the door." Allendy slides a chair from the nearby table and places it in the box. "Then, you close your eyes, and you breathe. Consider your feelings of guilt and shame, and how these repressive emotions are ultimately of your own making. Picture them as particles of negativity among a sea of energy, energy that you are able to disperse, until you are awash in positive light alone."

Allendy steps away from the box. "I will open the door in twenty minutes, with time to share and evaluate your experience. That is all you have to do."

I enter the small chamber and settle into the chair, and he swings the door closed. I am sealed inside, with only the darkness as my companion. At first, the totality of silence is unnerving. There is a dull throbbing in my ears, though I soon recognize it as the sound of my heart beating, the blood as it pumps through my veins.

I begin to relax into my seat. My mind wanders, and my thoughts drift from Allendy to my husband, from Hugo to Henry to June, a rotating cast of characters whose features blur together until I am faced with a single mask-like face. Or perhaps it is a mixture of faces, the skin there smooth and colorless and without any discernible attributes, unformed as a lump of clay. I attempt to shape the features into those of my father, but I find a stubborn resistance there, an unwillingness to summon him from the ether of my imagination.

The smell of the sea, the touch of silt and sand and rock beneath my toes, and I am naked and stretched out upon a strangely familiar shore. The seaside of my youth in New York, perhaps, or maybe Cuba, I cannot say for certain. The waves make a gentle slapping sound, and a lone gull wheels overhead. The sun is low to the earth, a swollen and bloody ball in the process of sinking beneath the horizon. *Red sky at night, sailor's delight.* The words taught to me by my father, just before he left us for good.

How I prayed to God that he would return to me, that he would love me and possess me completely. The way a devoted husband loves a wife, with every fiber of his being. God never answered, however, and so I stopped praying. I began the diary instead.

I sit up inside my reverie, and shield my eyes from the harsh glare. There is someone in the water, up to his or her neck and backlit by the blurred red orb of sun that hovers over the ocean like a glutted leech. Silver-yellow eyes gleam from their skull, twin flames flickering as they watch from the waves.

The figure wades toward me, toward the shore, and now I can see that it is a man. He is tall and broad-shouldered, his face obscured as he approaches. At once, the sky blackens and a storm front rolls over the beach, angry clouds blotting out the sun and plunging the world into darkness. The tide rushes across the shore to drench my limbs, and a furious wind whips my hair about me, a conjured chaos descending everywhere at once as I stand and begin to run.

A talon grip takes hold of my ankle and pulls me to the ground. A human hand, yet unlike any I have ever seen or felt, its strength icy and elemental. I struggle to free myself, my fingers raking across sand and rock. It is no use, however, and I am dragged back across the remainder of the shore and into the sea's cold embrace. The weight of the ocean bears down upon me, saltwater stinging my eyes, my throat, filling my lungs with its unyielding pressure, and as I drown I attempt to scream.

I know that I must rouse myself from this waking nightmare. And yet a strange comfort passes over me, a dark knowledge that it will all be over soon, if only I surrender to it. I must fight this impulse as well.

I flail my arms, my palms smacking against smooth walls on either side of me, and I am back inside the strange box in Allendy's office. Only the box is filled to the brim with seawater, and I am drowning here as well, still caught in the ocean's relentless whirlpool. And all the while, the cold hand grasps my ankle, fingers stroking my calf and lengthening and extending like a tangle of hungry eels to coil about my thigh. A slender and viscous digit finds its way up and inside me, filling me as the brine fills my eyes and mouth, my ears and nose. I am consumed.

A brightness flares in the dark, and I wince. Allendy stands before me, framed in the entry to the slatted box, the light of day animating motes of dust winking in the air around him. I leap up and hurry from the box, my hands clamped to my arms to keep from trembling as I move past him and down the hall.

"Anaïs?" Allendy calls after me. "Are you all right? You cried out."

"So sorry, Doctor, but I forgot that I am due at home earlier than usual." I calm my breath as I meet his watchful eyes. "We will continue this next week, yes?"

"Of course," he says, his expression tightening with unspoken concern. "We will pick up where we left off."

I thank him and head out onto Rue de l'Assomption. As I glance over my shoulder, I notice for the first time the resemblance between Allendy's quaint townhouse and the house where we lived in Brussels when I was a child. How the whole of my existence becomes a vast echo over time and space, from which there is never any escape. I shake away the observation, just as I negate the conjured image of the predatory yellow eyes staring out from the dark ocean's unsettled waters.

I continue down the street, and give myself over to the dirty swirl of the city, allow its anonymous embrace to erase my panicked state. Still, the fear refuses to let me go. I conjured a horrible fate inside the box, it is true, one of a mysterious and unearthly creature drowning me, penetrating me, more. Another manifested daydream of submission, as Allendy would surely have noted if I had summoned the courage to reveal this disturbing product of my fragmented imagination.

My dark desires, they have long carried a vast and primitive voluptuousness capable of opening doors between places I once thought locked forever, a rising tide of sensual oblivion I had hoped to bury for good. Forbidden pleasures rooted in taboo desire, transmuted by my imagination in much the same way I transform my intimacies into art. And who can say for certain where it is these desires might take me? Perhaps I will discover the door to my sealed room after all.

Hugo has returned from his business trip. Following dinner, we retire to the living room, where we sit in front of the hearth. He is hard at work on his latest hobby, a detailed series of astrology charts, while I write in my diary, the dogs curled up together on the floor between us. After some time, I look up to find Hugo watching me, and any sense of focus or resolve dissipates like the early morning fog over the village. His gaze is soft, but it penetrates nevertheless.

"What is it?" I ask. "Is there something the matter?"

"I was just thinking how very lucky I am," he says. "Not only to have a wife of such exquisite beauty, but one so devoted to her art. You are in every way an inspiration to me."

I laugh, and the effort feels false, an attempt to conceal an essential dissatisfaction behind a veil of mirth. "If I am able to brighten your mood in this way, and after all this time," I say, "then I shall consider it an accomplishment. You know how important my writing is to me, that I cannot live in the real world alone. As for your admiration of my appearance, that says more about the kindness of your eye that it does about my looks. Paris has many ladies who are far more alluring."

"You do yourself an injustice, Anaïs. You are the most ravishing woman I know."

"All this?" I gesture with lacquered nails at my painted face, my silk dressing gown. "It is but an illusion. Feminine inventiveness, if you will. As for my art, well…" I smooth the pulped pages of my journal. "I believe in myself, and what I do. But as there are greater beauties, there are greater writers as well. Important ones, whose work will one day change the world."

"Like Henry." The hint of betrayal is plain in Hugo's voice. It is a strange relief to hear Henry's name, since in a sense he was already here with us, a vaporous phantom lingering smoke-like between us. It is to Hugo's great credit that he can acknowledge my needs outside our union, that in his own quiet way he allows me the freedoms I find necessary to live a life of bohemianism, of excitement. But what good can come of these liaisons, when the anguish they inevitably yield proves as robust as the passion itself?

"You know how much I respect Henry's dedication and talent," I say. "I have no need to compare myself to him. Not when there is so much more for us both to accomplish."

"You have great faith in him."

"I do." I close the cover of my diary, press it hard to my chest like a holy object. "I understand Henry on that level, and he understands me in the same manner. We recognize the artist in each other, and see ourselves for what we are."

"He may see the artist inside you, but I see the woman." Hugo kneels beside my chair, his spectacles catching the amber light from the fire. "Let us do something special together this evening. Something gay, just the two of us."

"Wouldn't you prefer to spend the evening at home?" I cup his eager face in my hands. "You have been gone the better part of a week."

"First a night out, and then the whole of the day tomorrow lazing in bed. I want to show you off to the world."

We kiss, tenderly. "How can I refuse such flattery?"

"Wonderful. So. Where is it you would most like to go?"

I inhale, and in an instant I find myself startled to return to a certain cold December night. It was my first outing with June, not so very long ago but still part of some other era, another age. Dinner at Louveciennes, and then a car into the city to the theatre. Hugo and Henry discussed politics, while June and I nestled together in the back, huddled close and whispering shared secrets like schoolgirls. When we reached the theatre, she extended her hand, beckoning me from the car like a siren to my own shipwreck.

I knew in that moment that I would do anything she asked. That perhaps I always would, no matter where her destructive spirit took me. She is Thanatos, braided through Eros in a tightly knotted rope.

How appropriate, then, that we had decided that evening to visit the holy palace of such matters. That night in the theatre, I was so taken with her I had barely paid attention to the show. Seated between her and Hugo, it was only June that I watched out of the corner of my eye. Her face contorted in skeptical bemusement as ghastly scenarios of bloodletting and torture unfolded before us, only to roll her eyes once the act ended and shifted into the next. Even in my state of distraction, I laughed and cried out in revulsion along with the rest of the audience, swept away in a tide of emotion that June seemed unable to access. My heart near bursting with feeling, with a rapidly unfolding desire for her that was so overwhelming it threatened to engulf the world. In that perverse theatre and under the cover of its luxuriant darkness, I had felt more alive than ever.

"Darling man." I smile at Hugo, and take his hands in mine. "I want to go to the Grand Guignol."

I stand in front of the theatre and smoke as Hugo waits on line at the box office to retrieve our tickets. The dark and narrow street outside 20bis Rue Chaptal is bustling, the cobbled court glutted with preening couples, high-heeled women on the arms of their companions to steady them as they negotiate the uneven stones. The Theatre du Grand-Guignol is nothing if not an ideal night out for the amorous, lovers who innocently enter the small Pigalle black box only to cling to each other in paroxysms of laughter or fright, the emotionally heightened scenarios blossoming like poisonous flowers upon the stage.

"Shall we go inside?" Hugo says, returned to my side.

We file through the heavy oak doors alongside the other patrons, traverse the crowded foyer and stop at the bar for a drink. As we enter the theatre proper, we are handed our programs, and I inhale the room's heady and contradictory scents, what D.H. Lawrence might refer to as *fug*: perfume and cigarette smoke, must and alcohol, greasepaint and dry ice. The building was once a chapel, and the space still carries something of the sacred, tapestries hung from the baroque wood paneling and arched beams decorated with carved gods and monsters, angels and demons, the vaulted ceiling thatched with fleur-de-lis and pierced by iron chandeliers. Special patrons watch the performances from the row of confessional boxes at the rear of the theatre, where the amorous are free to hide behind ornate mesh screens and carry on their dalliances unseen.

We pass beneath the balcony's low overhang, make our way to our seats in the pew-like rows at the middle of the house. We wait, and soon the lights dim, as a backstage accordionist squeezes out a jaunty tune upon a weathered concertina. A portly master of ceremonies appears in front of the red velvet curtain. He is dressed in formal evening wear, top hat and all, though the attire is shabby, a worn pose from the hazy past. He walks the half-dozen steps to the foot of the small stage, where he clears his throat, rocking on his scuffed heels until the accordionist ceases to play.

"Ladies and gentlemen," he says with great portent, "thank you for joining us this evening in the bastion of pleasure and terror, virtue and vice. Tonight, your most hidden desires and private fears will be conjured upon our humble stage, so that you may delight and despair in the darkest corners of your imagination. Welcome to the Grand Guignol!"

A renewed squeal of song, and the curtain rises upon a pastoral scene, a busty shepherdess standing in front of a backdrop depicting an alpine idyll of rolling hills beneath a bright blue sky. She wears a traditional taffeta dress and bears an oversized crook, and she glides across the stage while singing a sprightly little song, an echo of the accordionist's opening number.

"Oh, how lonely is the life of a shepherdess," she bemoans in a girlish falsetto, a lace-gloved hand pressed to her brow. "If only I had a handsome man with me as I tend to my flock."

A broad-shouldered herder in lederhosen and a feathered cap enters to boisterous appreciation from the audience. "Oh, how lonely is the life of a goat herder," he calls out. "If only I had a fair maiden for company as I see to my goats."

Hugo strokes my hand, and he smiles over at me, a smile I am only too happy to return. He laughs when I laugh, I whistle when he whistles, the both of us taking care to ensure the other is enjoying themselves, engaging in the playful camaraderie that Henry disparagingly calls our love antics. But inside me, the swirling question makes itself known, the one that says:

How can you pretend to be fulfilled, Anaïs, when the aching emptiness still lurks inside you? The void that took shape when you were a young girl and first drank of the deep well of loneliness, it remains, and will stay with you until your life is finally over. Only then will the pain cease at last.

I twist in my seat, as if upon an instrument of slow torture.

Not three minutes pass before the goat herder has the shepherdess stripped to her undergarments. He thrusts himself upon her, their interlocking bodies only somewhat obscured by stuffed goats and sheep rolled in by stagehands on poorly disguised casters, tufts of cotton and fur billowing out into the pews as the audience hollers and cheers their approval. This is the light, before the darkness takes over.

I allow myself to fall into the familiar rhythm of the Guignol. The ludicrous machinations of the sex farce giving way to the degradations of a *rosse* play depicting a cruel soldier as he menaces a negligee-clad prostitute, and then a return to broad comedy again, the jarring dissonance leaving the audience delirious and hungry for more. It is the theatre's signature method of alternating between extremes, the acts vacillating so that we are taken from hilarity to terror, from sexual libertinism to sexualized violence. The audience is provided with the effect of *une douche écossaise*, and indeed I blush with the force of each novel sensation, blood rushing to the surface of my newly awakened skin.

After a brief interval, the curtain opens once more, onto an ominous and candlelit stage. The scene is that of an off-kilter hospital, the sharp angles of the spare black-and-white set pieces jutting out at irregular angles akin to a small-scale reproduction of *The Cabinet of Dr. Caligari*. An operating table and surgical stand are positioned at center stage, and a murmur of appreciation passes over the crowd. This is what we came for.

Two uniformed attendants enter with a straitjacketed woman between them, the patient struggling against her restraints to no avail. They strap her down screaming upon the table, her hair a nest of unkempt blond curls, face gaunt with bulging and haunted eyes. In the flickering candlelight, she is odd-looking, but in her own way she is beautiful, with an air of the familiar. I suspect I may have seen her before.

A moment later a doctor emerges from the wings. Balding and extremely thin, he appears almost skeletal beneath his white apron and surgical clothes. "I see the nymphomania treatments have failed to yield the desired results," he says over her cries, his tone disturbingly cool. "I will have to take more drastic measures to relieve our patient of her unquenchable cravings. Thank you, gentlemen, that will be all. I shall call for you again once the procedure is complete."

The aides depart, and the doctor bends over the patient's supine form. His hands roam her body, undoing the laces of her straitjacket and reaching inside the loose cotton nightgown beneath. He frees her breasts, which are fuller and less firm than my own, and he squeezes one of them, pinches the large brown nipple so that it hardens like a raisin. The woman stifles a cry, her eyes widening into round white circles. I am transfixed.

"You've given us all a great deal of trouble, Christine." The doctor plucks a scalpel from the tray upon the surgical stand. "But now it is time for us to bring a halt to the hysteria, for your tragic condition to come to an end. It is time for you to find your relief at last."

He brings the knife to the edge of her nipple and begins to cut into her flesh. She shrieks with wild intensity, bucking against the leather straps that bind her to the table. Blood trickles fast from her breast, her alabaster skin running red in a dark wet current. Stagecraft, yes, but with the illusion of sickening realism all the same. Hugo and I squeeze each other's hands as the patient's agonized face shifts in the candle flame. Beneath her powder and paint, past a damp sweep of tangled hair draped across her brow, the bloodied victim wears a new face. June's face.

I gasp. A woman screams behind me, just as the stage lights blare brightly in unsettling patches of green and yellow. I dare not take my eyes from the stage, from the bleeding patient and her tortured expression, June's eyes pleading for release from her perdition. As the blood-soaked nipple is sliced away and delivered as a delicacy to the doctor's eager lips, all I can see is that it is June who is defiled. In this conjured vision of her degradation upon the stage, I feel only abandon, for the first time in far too long. In a most unexpected way, I feel alive again.

The doctor chews the nipple with noticeable relish, and the audience roars in disgusted horror, the balcony loudest of all, with the greatest vantage point of this particular carnage. The maniac physician swallows and laughs and sets to work on the other nipple, severing the brown tip with great gusto. A man rises from a nearby seat and stumbles into the aisle, where he falls in a dead faint, an usher rushing to assist him.

With a final cry of terror, June's body slackens, and her head lolls to the side. For one brief moment our gazes lock, until her eyes close and the actress succumbs to a feigned unconsciousness.

"Now, my tender and delicious Christine," the doctor says, "let us see what you have down between your legs, shall we?" He lowers the scalpel, and the crowd shrieks as the curtain comes down, Hugo squirming next to me as we applaud the sordid play's appalling conclusion.

I bring his hand to my lips and kiss his knuckles, the room electrified with murmurs and movement as the patrons resettle in their seats. Like me, they are unsure how to feel, how best to absorb and respond to what has just taken place before them. Did they see their own objects of desire and longing in the patient, the way that I saw June? Did it make them feel the same exquisite satisfaction, the first twinge of a new and awakening pleasure inside?

The curtain rises upon another ribald comedy. The audience laughs and whistles, Hugo along with them, lulled into another scene of bawdy seduction and innuendo. Yet I am somewhere else now, inside my head. I am back in the operating room, the fiend standing above June as he grasps her breast in one hand and the scalpel in the other, a seam of yellow candlelight gleaming from the blade.

I hunch over in the pew, and in the dark I seek out the soft pebble of one of my nipples. I pinch it until it stiffens, so hard that I am afraid it will burst.

At intermission, Hugo and I hang on each other as if we are drunk. Once we exit the theatre, he immediately leads me through the crowd and raises his hand to flag down a taxi. "The show is not yet over," I say as he opens the door for me, but it does nothing to dissuade him. He need not say why, the lust plain on his face. I recognize it for what it is, almost as well as I am capable of recognizing my own. He provides the driver with directions, and the moment the car pulls away from the theatre he is upon me. His tongue in my mouth, teeth tugging at my earlobe, lips sucking at my neck until he lowers himself onto the floor of the car, his head foraging between my legs.

"Hugo!" I whisper, startled as he slides my underwear down to my ankles. Though a passionate lover, I have never known him to give himself over to such public and impulsive displays, not in all our many years of marriage. He kisses at my thighs, his enthusiastic tongue wriggling inside me, and I tremble and hold tight to the seat's hard and cracked leather.

As I roll my head back in pleasure, I catch the driver's gaze in the rearview mirror. He watches us, watches me with silver-yellow eyes: it is the stare of a carnivorous beast, malevolent and ravenous. It is the animal gaze of the creature from Allendy's box, a macabre fragment I unwittingly carry inside me as a jagged splinter beneath my skin.

Flush with fear and desire, I begin to moan. I force a knuckle into my mouth, squeeze my eyes shut as I shudder and thrill, Hugo's tongue and lips seeking out the softest and most tender parts of me. With a suppressed cry of joy, I convulse as the car rumbles through the cool Paris night, street lamps streaking past in molten waves as we are delivered back to Louveciennes.

Once we are home, Hugo possesses me completely, his ardor undiminished. I wince as he enters me, and this time I find that I welcome the pain of his penetration. Pain, mixed with pleasure, and I think of the actress on the operating table. The way I had imagined June into the scenario as well, the same way a child daydreams those closest to them as figures in a puppet show, in order to make meaning of a world beyond control. The woman's pleading eyes, her face both June's face and not, commingled by some strange trick of the light. I see her as my husband thrusts inside me. Her and the leering eyes in the taxi's rearview mirror that watched me with such hunger, a demoniac lust that helps quiet the seething void within.

I close my legs about Hugo and bite down on my lip until I begin to draw blood.

I meet Henry in the afternoon. We have his flat to ourselves, and we write at the kitchen table and comment on the other's pages, discuss Joyce and Lawrence and Dostoevsky until we are breathless. How pleasant it is to work across from each other at our respective typewriters! Eventually, however, he takes the opportunity of our close proximity to place his hand beneath the table and between my stockinged legs.

"Please, Henry, I am trying to work," I say, and brush his hand away.

"What if we just have a little quickie?" He lowers his glasses down his nose and delivers one of his pleading looks. "Hey, I gotta at least ask, okay? Don't fault me for asking. A man has his needs, after all. You might not understand that, but it's true."

"A man has his needs, but not a woman?" I scowl and cross my arms. "You seem to have forgotten the rest of your Eliot, Mr. Miller. Or at least the source mythology for his poem. Remember the hermaphrodite Tiresias, who was cursed by Hera? And why? For revealing that it is in fact woman, not man, who is the more sensual creature."

"Screw Tiresias," Henry says. "And screw Eliot too. I never liked that guy anyway. So. Maybe just a little hanky-panky after we write a couple more pages?"

"I said no." I make a face, though I cannot help but laugh at his persistence. "That is not what I need from you right now. I need your insight, your raw intellect. Today, I require a different aspect of your potency. I need the attention of your brain, and not your… prick," I say, borrowing one of his favorite words, and now Henry is the one laughing. "Although if I change my mind, I promise you will be the first to know."

"Can't argue with that. You're the boss, after all." He slides up his glasses with a thick finger and returns his gaze to his typewriter. "But don't think I haven't noticed you've lost a little bit of your swing as of late." By which he means since June left.

"Yes, well, so have you. As of late." I begin to type again, and soon enough he does the same. We fall into a familiar, if not altogether comfortable, silence.

For while it is Henry at Louveciennes who plays the role of the invisible specter that hovers between Hugo and myself, here in Clichy we are haunted by June, who has written Henry to announce that she will not be returning to Paris. He has taken his own childish revenge by removing her picture from the wall and replacing it with one of his lovers, a beautiful dancer from the Bal Nègre. Too complicated to unravel our cat's cradle of affections and recriminations, our seductions and our passions and our hurts, though Henry and I are united by more than our fucking (another of his favorite words).

I jolt anew at June's rage when she discovered our affair, her drunken and tearful declarations of betrayal that evening in their flat made all the more painful because I was not just another one of his nameless dalliances. She must despise the very thought of me, if only because she misconstrued the unspoken arrangement in which we all found ourselves. June and I shared our own voluptuous fantasy, of course, our own distinct form of intimacy. I wonder if I will ever manage to find that same closeness again.

After a lunch of sandwiches at Café de la Place Clichy, I leave Henry to browse the shops, the first perfume blush of spring washing over the city in a tide of pink and yellow and green. I wander aimlessly as if ensorcelled, until it dawns on me that I am traveling in a specific direction, one that soon becomes clear the farther I stroll. Eventually, I must admit to myself where I am headed, and find myself drifting up the narrow street that opens onto Rue Chaptal and the Theatre du Grand-Guignol.

A lone woman, small and dark-haired, stands smoking in front of the shuttered entrance. It is only once I get close enough that I realize it is the actress from Friday evening. In the light of day, she looks nothing like June, and must have been wearing a blond wig as she lay captive and mutilated upon the mad doctor's operating table. Reflexively, my nipples begin to tingle, the mere sight of her enough to trigger a commingled sensation of pleasure and pain. I do not want her to catch me staring, and so I lower my head as I move to cross the street.

"You," the actress calls out. She steps from the shelter of the entryway, her brown eyes searching my face. She appears roughly my age, a few years older perhaps, her face less full without the benefit of stage lighting and theatrical makeup. "You were in the audience here this past weekend."

"What? Oh. Yes. I was." Apropos of nothing, I giggle like a fool, my cheeks flushing. "I enjoyed it very much. The hospital play especially. It was quite disturbing. Gruesome, even. The depravity of the doctor's cannibalism was astounding."

"That?" she scoffs. "That was nothing. A common and sensationalist trifle at best." She lights another cigarette from her last and flicks the spent stub into the gutter. "It is only when we are able to draw from hidden wells of fear that true fright is made known. Your first time at the Guignol, I take it?"

"Far from it." June beside me in the pew, her bare arm pressed against mine, the dual scents of her perfume and natural musky odor intoxicating. Delirium, darkness, delirium anew. "The Guignol is always a special experience, no matter how often I attend."

"Then you have seen your fair share of horrors. What is cannibalism, then, when compared to uncontrollable lust? Or compared to wanton betrayal? Next to that, eating human flesh is nothing." She exhales in a scattered burst of smoke. "My name is Paula," she says, "but everyone calls me Maxa. Also known as The Maddest Woman in the World. If you've been to the Guignol before, then you've also seen your fair share of me."

"I am sure that I have. Only this was the first time that I…" I shake my head and glance at a poster on the theatre's façade, its image that of a lingerie-clad woman on her knees as she cradles a man's severed head, a coy smile stretched across her blood-red lips.

"Tell me." Maxa's eyes narrow, intrigued and wary in equal measure. "Go on."

I search for the proper words. "It was the first time I found my own story intermingled with that of the proceedings. I saw a friend of mine, violated upon the stage during the hospital scene. I saw her, in your face."

She smiles. "To many patrons, the Guignol functions as a mirror onto their secret desires. *I* function as a mirror, especially for women of a peculiar disposition. The passionate. The artistic.

The… conflicted." A coil of smoke slithers out from between her lips. "And how did it make you feel, then, to look upon your friend in such a horrifying predicament? To see her violated like that. Used as chattel is used, treated as if she were but a plaything for a madman. Such demonstrations of sadism and perversion, did they cause you to realize they are mere reflections of what is already inside of you?"

"Yes. Yes, they did." My throat goes dry, and I swallow. A wave of displacement overtakes me, as if I should be back in Allendy's office, answering these invasive questions upon his couch. Only I find that it is here and with this bold actress that I can fully answer from my heart. "It also made me… excited. And it made me feel wholly alive, for the first time in far too long."

Maxa smiles, a blush of evident delight coloring her face. "If you want to feel more alive yet, come back and attend the show this Saturday night. I'll ensure you have an excellent view of the proceedings."

"Wonderful," I answer at once. "I will be here."

"I will see you on Saturday, then. Mademoiselle…?"

A fleeting scent of spice, her perfume perhaps, and my eyelids flutter before I force myself to maintain her gaze. "You may call me Anaïs."

"Until then, Anaïs." Maxa drops her cigarette and crushes it beneath her heel. "Stay safe," she says, and with that, she turns and retreats through a side door. I am left alone on the street, the yellow sun beginning to lower over the distant rooftops.

Even now as I write these words—Hugo lying asleep beside me, with the dogs huddled in the corner upon their pillows, the fire crackling in the hearth—I cannot escape the fathomless pools of her brown eyes. Flecked with swirling amber, they threaten to reduce and absorb me beneath their mystical gaze. Surely I am coping with June's absence by forming a schoolgirl fascination with another woman, what Dr. Allendy might refer to as sublimation. Regardless, the thought of Maxa and her enveloping attraction is too alluring and powerful to repudiate.

My hand travels down my chest, across my belly and to the inside of my thigh, and I touch myself there. My fingers seek out the wet folds, the sacred core of my being. I count the days until my return to the theatre, the holy temple of nightmares and lust that awaits me as its own breathless lover. I count the hours and minutes as well.

On Saturday night, I return to the Grand Guignol. There is a single ticket waiting for me at the box office, as if Maxa knew I would be alone, sensed my need to open myself to her without the distraction of a companion. Either that, or she wanted me all to herself.

I settle into my third-row seat and leaf through the evening's bill; last week I had left my program behind thinking I would be returning from the intermission, only to be swept away by Hugo and his abrupt and demanding amorousness. This time I find her picture, the size of a half-page with her face in profile as she peers over a pale and exposed shoulder. Examining the image leads me to believe I may indeed have seen her on the stage in the past, though I have no specific memory of it. No wonder, really, as everything inside the theatre seems so very different now, as if I am glimpsing it all through new eyes. The house lights lower, the audience applauds before hushing, and I once again fall under the spell of the Guignol.

After three preliminary productions—a comedy of mistaken identity that takes place at a nunnery, followed by a harshly realist play on police corruption and an elderly couple evicted and thrown into the street, as well as a sex farce in an overgrown greenhouse in Marseilles—it is time for the bill's featured attraction. *La Famille du Péché*, the title printed in the program's largest lettering. The Family of Sin.

The curtain opens onto a dimly lit stage, where a girl of perhaps eighteen is asleep in bed. She rolls back and forth in the sheets, and as she does so a bespectacled and middle-aged man enters. He approaches on the tips of his slippered toes, a flickering candelabra in his outstretched hand, and he slowly circles the bed. He peers down admiringly at the sleeping girl's figure, and reaches across the bed to stroke her long hair upon the pillow. At last she rouses, and she stares at him in wonder and doe-eyed confusion.

"Father?" she says, and sits up with the bedsheets clutched to her chest. "What are you doing in my room at this late hour?"

"I came to check on you, my darling. To make sure you're not suffering too much on this cold winter's night, what with the stove heatless and in need of repair."

"I am quite cold in here, it is true. Would you lay with me, and help make me warm?"

"Oh yes, of course. I will lie with you all night, if that is your wish."

The father rests the candelabra on the nightstand and pulls back the sheets, climbing into bed beside his daughter. He presses himself against her back, runs his hands up and down her arms, along her sides and her narrow frame, until he starts to undo the buttons at the front of her nightgown. Is it a trick of the imagination that, for a fleeting moment, the man resembles my own father Joaquín? That the daughter he touches in such a seductive manner might also pass as a younger version of myself? I shift in my seat, newly unnerved.

"Father!" the daughter whispers, aghast. "What are you doing? This is against God's will!"

"Come now, my pet. You know what it is I am doing, why I came to your room this evening. Just as you are aware that you have matured into an exquisite womanhood, and have blossoming desires of your own. You know what it is I want, because you want the very same thing yourself."

"But… But what if Mother should hear us?"

"That old cow? She was in the wine all night, and fell fast asleep long ago. We have nothing to be afraid of, nothing in the world.

Believe me, dear daughter, this is just as God intended. Now, lie down on your stomach. Go on."

He finishes undressing her. Soon, he enters her from behind, his trousers dropping to the floor as he thrusts against her. "I have never felt this wonderful before!" the daughter cries, her bared breasts dangling from the foot of the bed as he continues rutting away. "Is this what love is meant to be, at last? If so, may this cold winter's night never end!"

A square of dim light materializes on the wall, upstage from the bed and the incestuous pair. An opened doorway, filled at once by a shadowy figure, and the audience murmurs in equal parts trepidation and excitement. From the wings steps Maxa, barefooted and clad in a silk robe. Wild-eyed and crazed, she gazes cursed upon this scene of perverse and unspeakable horror, one beyond any real mother's sane comprehension. She slowly approaches the bed, as father and daughter proceed heedlessly in their dance of lust and forbidden desire, oblivious to her ghastly presence.

"Are you warm yet, my little darling?" the father pants, bent over his daughter and grasping hold of her breasts in his large hands. "Can you feel me hot inside you?"

"Oh, yes," she answers, "yes," and she arches high her body, the carved figurehead of a mermaid rendered upon the prow of a ship. "Keep warming me, Father. Keep warming me! And promise that you'll never stop."

"I promise, sweet daughter," he says, his eyes rolling back in his head as he approaches orgasm. "I promise…"

"You dare!" Maxa thunders. The blaspheming pair separate and scramble away from each other, toward opposite sides of the bed. "Such flagrant sin and depravity, under my roof? The only warmth you'll know is from the infernal pits of hell itself!"

She takes the candelabra from the nightstand and dashes it to the ground. In a loud rush of wind, a blast of heat and light explodes from the front of the stage, and the crowd gasps as a scrim of fire leaps along the footlights in a barbed circle. The vindictive mother throws her head back and laughs a damned laugh, while father and daughter shriek in terror as the bed appears to go up in flames. I lean back in my seat, amazed by the effect, another of the Guignol's astonishing stage illusions.

Maxa lowers her head, her contorted grimace dancing in the bright flames. Her righteous gaze falls upon mine, and our eyes meet through the wall of fire, her stare so piercing I am forced to shut my eyes from the sight of it. When I open them again, however, it is my own mother who stares down at me, just as surely as it was June that I saw upon the operating table last week. Only this time, I do not peer out from the audience, but rather from the stage itself. Now, I am looking out from inside the terrified daughter's burning body, my mother beside the bed and laughing at my well-earned pain.

Panicked, I turn to face the audience. I glimpse myself seated in the pew, where I smile back through the wall of fire. Or is it Maxa who smiles from behind my eyes, using my very own lips? I lean forward, but the heat from the flames causes me to retreat, and I hold my breath in abject terror.

The curtain closes, and with a sudden snap of heat and light, I am back. Returned to my seat and to my body, in time to see the curtain shut from the audience, my view of the stage occluded as if by storm clouds shuddering across the moon. The crowd cheers all around me, and I clench my hands together, palms wet with perspiration. I cough and struggle for breath, and swallow at the air as if I am drowning.

After the show is over, I wait nearly an hour for her to appear outside the theatre. Finally, the stage door groans open and Maxa emerges, accompanied by her fellow actors, two men and a woman. I recognize them from the cast, the father and daughter from *La Famille du Péché* as well as a gentleman from the greenhouse scenario, who also had the role of the lascivious goat herder during my last visit to the Guignol. I stand stiffly nearby as they bid one another goodnight, and the younger gentleman, the goat herder, offers to walk Maxa home.

"That will not be necessary." She points her chin in my direction. "I have somebody waiting."

The other actors disperse, and Maxa approaches. She puts a cigarette to her dark red lips, which I light before lighting my own. "Thank you," she says with an air of nonchalance I first mistake for superiority, but soon recognize as being closer to inevitability.

"How do you do it?" I say, no longer sure who or what it is I am dealing with, be it woman or something else altogether. "How did you capture me in the performance tonight? Draw upon my private thoughts, so that you were able to craft that deviant scenario to begin with?"

Maxa exhales in a whistle between her teeth, smoke dispersed in the dim shine from a nearby street lamp. "Everyone sees what they want to see," she answers at last. "Especially the lonely, and the self-consumed."

"You play at knowing me. My hopes, my dreams? My passions. You seem so very sure of yourself."

"If only that was the case." She smiles. "Perhaps everything you saw tonight was a fantasy of your own making. You, who wants so desperately to be a part of something larger than yourself that you forced a connection to the piece, one in which you could live out your darkest desires. The association between you and the performance was only in your imagination. A simple delusion."

"That was no delusion." A drunkard staggers across the street, bleating out a tuneless rendition of "Parlez-Moi D'Amour," and I wait until he is out of earshot before I continue. "I could feel the flames upon my skin, the starchy touch of the bedsheets upon my bare flesh. Not only that…" I swallow hard, draw deeply off my cigarette while I wait for the words to order themselves, for their meaning to become clear. "I could feel a once-empty space shift inside me. It was as if I were making room for you, as if we became undifferentiated, two individual souls fused together as a single spirit. I feel it even now."

"Go home," Maxa says. She stares down the block, in the direction of the drunkard stumbling his way around the corner. "While you still have a chance for it all to make a strange kind of sense, so that you may pack it deep down in a solitary corner of your memory and forget we ever met. Tell yourself that you were simply tired, or anxious, that you were enthralled by the great horrid spectacle of the Guignol to such an extent that it overwhelmed you. Perhaps you drank too much, or you fell faint, like so many others before you. Make a story of it for yourself, one satisfying enough to put it all out of your mind. Just go. Now."

Her words resound in my ears like a pagan incantation. Instead of repelling me, they have the effect of a soothing balm, patching over the prickled shock of experiencing the unexplainable. An offer to forget, to smooth my harsh edges as one would polish an unearthed gemstone. I shake away the sedating effect, however, and focus with a renewed sense of purpose. This offer, it is for her benefit, not mine. If she rids herself of me, then she will no longer have to submit to human connection, to her own raw vulnerability. I know this kind of woman all too well.

"I shall do no such thing." I take another step closer to her, near enough to kiss. "Not until you tell me who you really are, and how you were able to entrance me with whatever strange magic you are capable of conjuring. And I will not leave you be until you do so."

Maxa shakes her head, dark curls grazing the collar of her coat. "Some secrets, once fully excavated, can never be reburied. Once you cross certain thresholds, the journey cannot be unwound." Unmoved, I fold my arms across my chest and we stand in silence. Finally she sighs, a smoky laugh hissed between her lips like steam from a boiling kettle.

She flings her cigarette into the path of a passing motorcar. "Walk with me," she says, and juts out her elbow, offers me the crook of her arm. Another woman once offered me her arm here for the first time: June, who slipped her hand over mine as we made our way to a café in Montmartre. More than a year past, a frosty winter's night that kept the pair of us pressed close to each other. June proved an enchantress herself, though one of an altogether different nature.

I lock my arm in hers, and Maxa and I proceed together down the rough cobbled court, walking as one into the chiaroscuro labyrinth cast over the crisp spring night.

Her apartment is only a few blocks from the theatre, and we walk at a brisk pace. Maxa often looks over her shoulder, or stops to peer into the faces of passing strangers, as if she is attempting to glean some hidden meaning from their features. We soon reach her building, the last of a succession of severe tenements, and climb the stairs to her top floor flat.

Once inside, I take in the dark living space, an eerie reflection of the Guignol's sensual morbidity: black velvet draped in heavy folds along the walls and ceiling; all the upholstery blood red, from the tattered divans to the throw pillows atop rugs in teetering piles; elaborate oversized candelabras, whose immense pillar candles Maxa lights one after the next, dried wax suspended in hardened pools across the scored wooden floorboards. She pours us two tumblers of pastis, kicks off her boots, and drops down onto one of the couches.

"Sit, please." She hands me a glass, and I lower myself across from her, nestling upon a pillow beside the tiled hexagonal table at the center of the room. She gulps at her drink, lights a little brass lamp, and fishes a strangely shaped pipe from among the unseemly items splayed across the table. "Would you like to smoke opium with me?"

"I… I never have before."

"Then pay close attention." I watch fascinated as she leans over the lamp and inhales the dark brown tar, sweet blue smoke emerging from her lips and floating upwards, restless spirits made visible. Her eyes close in rapt pleasure, and I feel that I have become vestigial, someone who has seen her safely home to the sheltering arms of her true lover, one capable of meeting all her needs.

I take the pipe from her and inhale, the smoke floral and spiced as it invades my lungs. I hold it in, then exhale it in a wide arc. "And now you have smoked opium," she says. "I did warn you that you were crossing a threshold."

She sighs, her heavy eyelids drooping upon their beds of powder and kohl. "You asked me to tell you how I was able to access your mind, to commingle our essences on the boards at the Guignol. You asked how it was possible to see out from the eyes of another. But in doing so, you ask the wrong questions. If you really want to know how I am gifted with such talents, then you must learn how it is that I reached this twilit pass."

Maxa pours herself another pastis, the glass clouded the way her eyes are clouded, murky and unforthcoming. "In more than fifteen years at the Guignol, I have died thousands of deaths upon its stage. I have been stabbed, strangled, poisoned, hanged, scalped, burned alive, buried alive, and more. An impressive achievement as far as such things go, no one can deny that fact, and believe me when I say that each death has been felt deep inside me. Every one of them, from the first to the last."

She sets the opium alight, draws in the thin line of smoke, and hands me the pipe so that I may do the same. This time I become lightheaded, and try not to cough as I exhale.

"These little deaths, they take their toll," she says. "Upon my body and mind, my very soul. No part of me left untouched or uncorrupted, nothing left of me pure. So it is that in turn, I myself have killed. Murdered, as I have been murdered. For lust, for revenge, in defense of my womanhood: varying forms of rightness or injustice, meted out however the Guignol playwrights see fit. These killings do their own type of damage, and I dwell in a dual darkness of my own making, trapped in a tangled web of violence as both spider and prey. In doing so, I have become the very bride of death itself. There is no escape. Not any longer."

She casts her eyes about the room, as if seeing it for the first time. The mutable shadows and flickering candle flames, the dense fabrics womblike and suffocating, all of it a haze through the dense scrim of smoke. "This apartment was once my safe haven," she whispers. "It was filled with sunlight, with laughter. With the sweet smell of fresh flowers threaded through the air, a home suffused with hope. But then a man came along, and he changed everything. He led me away from the sun, and soon all my hope was gone." Maxa shrugs. "These days, I am a reflection of the world itself, from which hope fast departs just the same. You feel it as well, do you not? The entire globe will be drenched in blood soon enough."

"Surely you can find your way out of this," I say, taken aback by the unending depths of her despair. "Surely there are other theatres who would consider themselves lucky to have an actress of your obvious abilities. Or there are other lines of work to pursue. You needn't be tied to the Guignol and its perverse charms. It is not as if you are some kind of indentured servant."

"But that is exactly what I am." She smiles, though there is no joy in it. "Only it is not to the Guignol that I am enslaved."

Maxa lights a cigarette before her eyes settle on mine once more. "There is a man who walks these streets, the one who stole me away from the light and brought me into darkness. A most dangerous man, cruel and unyielding. He wears black from head to toe, so that he may go unnoticed, until it is time for him to reveal his true face. He goes by many names, and also by no name at all. To some, he is the Dark Angel of Music, whereas to others he is known as Crocell, Lord of the Great Deep. But I know him as Monsieur Guillard."

She glances behind me, into the heavy velvet folds draping the walls, as if expecting to see someone there. "I called upon him once, when I was younger and reckless, and he came to me, as a midnight lover arrives. With a snap of his fingers, he made all my troubles vanish. My profound pain, my loneliness, my hunger? All of it was lifted from me, in a whirlwind of lightning and rain. I never felt so happy, not in all my life. I became Maxa, High Priestess of Sin and Horror, the Crown Princess of Blood.

"I'd found my purpose at last, and my ascent at the Guignol soon followed. As my talents blossomed, I grew capable of casting glamours and charms, like the fairies of legend. I learned to make my face beautiful one instant, and hideous the next. I could even cast a spell to cause a crowd to feel what I felt in that very moment, to look out from behind my eyes. Draw on the audience's hidden fantasies and perversions, to make each role a revelation both personal and profound."

"That is how I witnessed my friend in you the other night."

She nods. "Another gift, from the Dark Angel."

"That is how tonight, during *La Famille du Péché*, that I saw my own…" I do not say more. Though she must already know what dark thoughts stir inside me, what forbidden passions loom behind my mask of propriety. She must know me, now.

"At first, it felt as if they were gifts given freely," Maxa says. "It was a golden time. One in which I made my own name, and was freed at last from the shackles of my childhood and the rest of my unhappy past. Then one gloomy spring night not so very long ago, a night very much like this, Godfather Death finally showed me his true face. I had almost forgotten about him, which made it all the worse when he darkened my door once more. He came to collect his payment, and I could not refuse. Now, I fear I do not have very much time left at all. That is the nature of such bargains, I'm afraid."

"What is it you owe this man? Perhaps I can secure you the necessary funds to help ease your debt."

"Money." She chuckles, her eyes receding into her skull as she slides further into the opium's poppy embrace. "You do not understand. He has no interest in such concerns." She holds her cigarette to her lips, the smoke bisecting her face. "He only desires flesh, in all its many forms. He is the demon lover, and what isn't given to him freely will be taken by force. I attempt to appease him. To sate him, the very best that I can." She glances at the pipe upon the table. "Still, it is never enough."

A firm rap jolts the apartment door. Once, twice, three times, and her face goes ashen pale. "No," she whispers. "Jesus in heaven, no."

"What is it? Is it him?"

"Not tonight, please, not tonight." She rises from the couch and stumbles over the corner of the table as she falls moaning to the carpet. "Please, no, not now. Not now."

"I will protect you." I help her back to her feet, my mind soupy and swimming with the drug. "I will not let him bring you any harm."

"There's no protecting me from him. Not now, and not ever."

Another three knocks, louder this time, more insistent, with the fraught menace heralding the arrival of a villain from the wings. And how we seem to have found ourselves cast in just such a scenario, as if written for the Guignol stage itself! Whether I prove heroine or victim, it is still too soon to tell.

"Quick," Maxa says, and hands me my bag. She shoves me toward the wall, inside a parting in the dense black curtains. "Hide behind here. Once I lead him to the bedroom, you must depart immediately, and hurry straight home. Whatever you do, do not look behind you. Do not see him for what he truly is. Promise me that."

"I promise." I slip between the dark folds. "Do not worry. I will go straight to the police."

"The police can do nothing to help." Her haunted eyes fix me in place. "If he finds out you are here, that will be the last of me on this earth. And it won't end there. It never does." She closes the drapes, and I am left entombed inside the black walls.

The stutter of Maxa's footsteps as she makes her way across the room. The clatter of the latch as it is undone. The creak of the door as it opens. After an excruciating silence, footfall as the threshold is crossed, one deliberate thump, followed by a second. The door groans closed, and I hold my breath, the velvet lapping against me in black liquid waves.

"Maxa?" The unfamiliar voice is a nighttime invocation, a multi-layered harmony that is both young and old, masculine and feminine, and my skin prickles with gooseflesh. "Is there someone here with you?"

"No," she answers quickly, too quickly. Heavy footsteps proceed into the room, steady and precise, a soldier amidst his marching drills as the stranger opens and closes a door somewhere across the room. This is followed by a second door, and a cabinet or wardrobe door. As he navigates the room, it becomes apparent he is searching out a potential interloper, searching for *me*, and I am sure my pounding heart will give me away. All this I hear from the cocoon of lush darkness in which I have found myself, so close to detection and stiff with fright, and utterly unable to act.

I smell him on the other side of the curtain. A man's scent, musky and ripe, but also the smell of the sea, salt and semen and sweat, the aroma brutal and intoxicating in equal measure. I list, and I am flooded, returned to Allendy's strange box and the conjured man that walked from the waves, the ocean rushing over me in a relentless tide.

The black material flutters, and though frozen with fear I force myself to one side as the curtains are parted. A sliver of light against the wall, and the cracked plaster is illumined in a gash of bright yellow. His breath is hungry and rasping and wet, that of a ferocious animal on the prowl. Gloved hands hold open the velvet folds, fingers startlingly long and thin and deathly black. I am unable to breathe.

"There's no one here," Maxa says from the other side, her voice tremulous, so much so that I am sure she has given me away. Yet the hands withdraw, the curtains fall back into place, and the firm thudding of his feet reverberates as he retreats, followed by Maxa's own reluctant steps.

A door opens deeper inside the apartment, and I wait for some time before I dare to peer from my hiding place. The living space is abandoned, and I clench my bag to my chest and tiptoe across the room to the front door. I take hold of the tarnished brass knob, an array of photographs and clippings pinned to the wood: a prayer card of a female saint on her knees, a pamphlet for a perfumery advertising various discounted scents, a portrait of a voluptuous young woman seductively posed on her back, this last image affixed to a ragged shred of wallpaper, the pattern a field of blood-red anemones.

From down the hall, the primal cadences of great abandon issue forth: grunting and slapping and whinnying, the moist sounds of lips and hips and coaxed flesh. I remove my hand from the knob, and turn to face the corridor and the gaping darkness beyond. Down the passageway, the animalistic noises surge in strength and severity, uneven walls panting and undulating in their own heaving breath, in, out, in. I start down the passage in a somnambulant daze, my mind fogged as I look up to find I have reached the end of the hall, the door here ajar. I peer through the breach, a narrow seam of light slashing across the rumpled bed. I should never have come here in the first place. I know this, and still I cannot obey.

It lies atop her, the thing I mistook for a man. Naked and bestial, its shoulders are impossibly broad, tapering down to a narrow waist and meaty buttocks. The whole of its oil-slick skin is coated in a wet down, almost milky in the diffuse light from the tapestry-covered window. Its crown carries a faint suggestion of a ridged skull, hanks of long black hair strewn from its head across the stained silk pillows in a cascade of seaweed-like strands.

I step further into the room. Beneath the beast, Maxa squeezes her eyes shut, her hands grasped tight to its sweat-slicked hide, clinging fast for dear life. Her mouth is slit open the way the door is slit open, her upper lip bloodied at its corner as if chewed at or otherwise bitten. I creep toward the bed on a wave of devouring intensity and hover above their wild and rutting forms. I reach for them, fingers extended to take hold of the beast's heaving back. To what, intercede? To free Maxa from its brutal embrace? To join them? I cannot say for sure.

Before I make contact, Maxa startles to attention. Her eyes go wide as they settle on me, her expression animating with surprise but also with a savage fury. At once, she propels naked from beneath her possessor and cries out in a banshee wail. "Get out!" she screams at me, manic as she beats at my face with her fists. "Get out, get out, get out!"

I sink against the wall, attempt to shield myself as she batters about my head with a series of kicks and punches, until I manage to stand once more. I thrust her to the floor and scramble over her prone form and back toward the door. As I move past the bed, the beast atop it raises its head, snout to the air as if searching out a scent. Though its features are obscured by its damp sweep of hair, I glimpse two small knots of coiled bone upon its scalp, and my blood turns to ice.

With a languid and elegant gesture, the creature extends a long arm in my direction. It is as if it means to beckon me closer, or perhaps impede my escape. I force my way to the door, staggering out into the dim light of the hallway. In my opium haze, I am left to wonder what it is I have truly seen, whether the drug has made falsehoods of the observable world.

The harsh squeal of bedsprings, and I race to the front door and fumble with the knob, my hands no longer functioning as they should. A blur of movement down the hall casts violent shadows at the edge of my vision, and I finally manage to fling the door wide. I slam it fast behind me, and stumble down the stairs and across the landing as the door creaks open above. I don't look back, and descend the next flight and the next, spiraling down into the dark pool of night. When I reach the bottom, I pause to glance back toward the stairwell, into the constricted throat that winds upwards like the contours of an ammonite shell, like the corkscrewed horns growing from the heavy crown of the beast's skull, savage and impossible.

From the very top of the twisting stairs, someone or something stares down from above. I cannot see well in the dim, only a silver-yellow glint from two gleaming eyes as the figure retreats further into the shadows. I stifle a cry and hurry through the vestibule and out of the building, and rush into the street to hail a taxi. Soon, I am on my way back home. To Louveciennes, and my husband, my garden, my life of safety and comfort, and even my own quiet kind of happiness I seem so determined to destroy. I sink my heavy head in my hands, and breathe in, out, in, willing myself into logic and reasonableness. But logic and reasonableness never helped anyone before. They certainly never helped me.

Though the effect of the opium has already started to fade, my perception of the world around me has altered nevertheless. As I write in this diary and dawn breaks on the other side of the drawn shutters, these once-smooth pages have coarsened and become less pure. Even my handwriting is unrecognizable to me, as if penned by a different hand, this skin worn by a different person altogether. Now, as it begins to rain over Paris and its outskirts, I watch Hugo as he shifts and turns in bed beside me, his sleep troubled. Who is to say what has become of him in my absence? Maybe he has suddenly changed forever, and is no longer the man I once knew. Who, indeed, have I become to him? Or even to myself?

I am haunted by Maxa. Her wild cries as she battered me, yes, but also her frozen face as she lay beneath the beast, eyes shut tight and unseeing. I am desperate to free her of her burdens. To endure them as my own, no matter her refusals or refutations. If only I was innocent enough to bear them, noble enough to claim I only want to save Maxa from herself, the way I once tried and failed to save June.

In truth, I must admit there is more to my desire to take on the weight of her debt. For my dark and shameful secret is this:

I want to be the one beneath the savage beast.

A few days later, a letter from Maxa arrives at Louveciennes:

Anaïs,

I am writing to thank you for the kind note you sent to the theatre asking after me and inquiring about my wellbeing. I also wish to extend my deepest apologies to you, in the hope that you will forgive me for what transpired the other night. I was not in my right mind, and never should have exposed you to such illicit matters. It was never my intention to corrupt you, and for that I am most sorry. Allow me to explain myself just a little further, after which we must cease all communication, despite (or perhaps because of) your obvious and heartfelt concern.

I am a very closed person, and indeed you are the only soul of late who has so much as glimpsed behind the heavy veil that obscures my defective heart. Since early in life, I have associated pleasure and pain, and it is this truth that has brought me to the place I am today. The games of doctor and patient as a little girl, in which my flesh would be pierced with needles as we played at inoculation? The summer trip into the mountains that culminated in the loss of my innocence, by means of a brutal attack by the young man I had called my closest friend? It was only natural that I would eventually find my way to the sinister side, called to worship by the midnight muse himself. He who walks at night, who traverses the lamplit streets of this city, under cover of darkness and always on the prowl for his next conquest. Is he not the very same phantom rumored to haunt the Palais Garner, the one who inspired Leroux's novel?

The demon lover is no fiction, however. He is as real as we are, a creature of supernatural attraction that beckons to women who are lonely and artistic and most of all passionate, women who radiate the energy he feeds upon until glutted. Woman like ourselves. While I myself am a lost cause, you still have a chance to find your way free, and I pray that you will choose a different path, and allow yourself to feel worthy. You, who have so many admirers, none of whom will ever fill the void within. I recognized the emptiness inside you, the way only someone with the very same absence could see it. Only you can fill that void, Anaïs. It took me much too long to understand this truth. I cannot deny I see myself in you as well. We are parallel souls, rooted in a sensuous attraction to the forbidden. You have kept your urges largely hidden, however, from yourself as much as anyone. Do not forget, I am able to pull back the veil that obscures your private desires, just as readily as I can remove an evening glove. And what I see in you is a past rooted in perversion and degeneracy, regardless of how much of it you mask in the trappings of polite society.

The absent friend you glimpsed in my face that night at the Guignol, the woman who holds your heart in her hand? The father who came to you as a child, the one whose attentions you still crave, no matter how far you go to bury it beneath the hard and cracked ground of denial? You need to be possessed by another, in order to feel anything whatsoever. That, and more.

I had hoped to take comfort in your welcoming arms, but instead I must entreat that you never think of me again. To dwell upon the darkness is to open a door through which it can enter at any time. Eradicate me from your memory, lest you meet a danger you are unprepared to face. And should you ever cross paths with my tormentor, make certain that he never learns your name. Names have great power, in our world as well as his. You must remember this above all else.

Now I must bid you farewell, sweet Anaïs. Thank you for your kindness, and know that I will hold you in my heart as Persephone did Orpheus, no matter my moonless destination. Light a candle for me, and pray to all that you hold holy.

I remain yours,
Maxa

I read the letter once more before I refold the pages and tuck them inside my diary, smooth the creased paper until it is sharp enough to draw blood. Maxa is done with me. Regardless of the circumstance, I cannot help but sense an echo, a recurrence, as if June is abandoning me all over again. My father as well, as Dr. Allendy would no doubt remind me had I returned to him for further analysis. My life, it is a wide spiral, made up of alluring figures that emerge from the darkness to penetrate my orbit before they are flung out to distant shores, distant dreams. The same story told over and again, until the spiral completes another circuit and a new face emerges from the gloom.

The brightness of the noonday sun bears down upon Les Puces, where Hugo and I walk through the marketplace's labyrinthine assortment of stalls, the smell of fresh lavender and saffron thread-ed through the air. Porte de Clignancourt and the surrounding neighborhood is swollen with shoppers, and I wait in the shade beneath a canvas awning while Hugo tries on carnival masks for a masquerade his supervisor is throwing in a few days' time. At-tendance, unfortunately, is compulsory.

Weeks past now since the disturbing events at Maxa's apartment, and though I have heeded her appeal to leave her be I cannot help but feel a coward, unable to put any of it out of my mind as she asked. How can I rid myself of the image of those cruel eyes as they stared down at me through the darkness? The same yellow eyes from Allendy's box, and the taxi outside the Guignol, watching with hunger as a hawk watches for quarry. The eyes of a demon.

Worst of all is when I look into the mirror, where I am terrified I will find those slick yellow orbs staring back at me in place of my own. Perhaps this inscrutable creature has been watching me all along and it is only now that I am aware, its gaze penetrating me to my hidden recesses, the core of me. Or perhaps the truth is something more alarming altogether.

"Anaïs? Darling?" Hugo waves me over to the booth, the beaked white mask of a plague doctor held to his face. "What do you think of this one? Is it too garish?"

"If anything, too respectable." I scan the rest of the mask-maker's offerings and select a more colorful option, that of a damask joker done in flamboyant points of gilded crimson and gold. I help Hugo fasten it behind his head. "Now, you look fit for a proper night on the town. Still elegant, yes, but not so dour."

"You mean, I no longer appear quite such a bore." He returns the plague doctor mask to its peg. "Would that I had the ease you seem to have, the ability to travel between worlds. You have a keen talent for moving freely through various social milieus, and seemingly without care."

"Is that how you see me, as a chameleon? Someone who changes their face in order to adapt?" I cannot help but feel as if he is mincing words. That he means to call me Janus-faced, willing to alter myself to meet the expectations of others.

"Do not take umbrage, my love. I was trying to pay you a compliment." He smiles and takes me by the hand, and we continue to wend our way through the market. "I was speaking of your generosity of spirit, and the interest you show in those you encounter. I see it in the way you make conversation, as readily with street performers as you do with the wives of my colleagues."

"The wives of bankers bore me, though. Never mind the fact that I am one myself."

"But you never let your boredom show. Through it all, the essential Anaïs is ever-present, thrilling and excitable and attentive. That is why others are drawn to you, no matter their circumstance. You are independent, and alive. Another reason why I am so proud to call myself your husband, why I love you and you alone."

He pulls me into his arms, and we kiss. "And I love only you, Hugo."

And now I have told the lie. However much I admire my husband, there is always someone else. Always.

Hugo wears a wide smile upon his face, and I attempt to mimic his aura of insouciance as we near the far side of the market. A strange niggling sensation pricks at me, however, and I feel as if I have forgotten something, or someone. I glance behind me, back toward the mask-maker's booth and the canopied stalls beyond. Someone is out there, watching.

From some distance away, a dark-haired woman gazes at me through the bustling throng, and I slow my pace. Dressed in black and awash in radium sunlight on the periphery of the market, pale and thin and birdlike in her delicate pose, my first thought is that she appears lost, and perhaps afraid, a solitary figure beside a meat vendor's display. It is only when I cease walking altogether that I realize I am looking upon myself. Into a standing mirror, of which there are many set out for trying on items of clothing or jewelry. But no. The woman that is me reaches a slow hand to her brow, long pale fingers raking through her corona of black hair. Yet here I am, holding Hugo's arm with one hand and my market bag in the other. There is no mirror there after all.

"Anaïs?" Hugo peers over at me in concern. "Is something wrong?"

"That woman," I sputter. I take my hand from his arm and point in her direction. "Do you see her? There. Just past the meat counter."

"What woman?"

"Her! Right there!" I gesture all the more frantically. "The one there, in the black dress."

"I don't see her," he says, and shields his eyes from the sun as he scans the crowd. "Who are you talking about?"

"For God's sake, Hugo." I drop the market bag, a cascade of oranges toppling out and across the dirt. "She looks just like me."

The woman turns, and I follow. I push my way through the throng and past the mask-maker's booth, where in my haste I knock a red leather harlequin mask from its peg. Hugo calls out to me but I don't stop, hurtling forward as I struggle to keep my eyes upon her, the woman in black that is myself.

Only yards away now and just outside the main thoroughfare of Les Puces, and she returns my gaze once more. Now I see her for what she is: her flesh a pallid and mottled blue, lips black and bruised, skin brined with deep ocean water, the dregs of the abyss. She is a drowned woman, this other Anaïs. She is still myself, yes, only after the sea has swallowed me.

My likeness—*ma semblable, ma soeur!*—moves quickly along the meat counter. She rounds the far side, and I hurry around the stall, only to find that she has vanished. The space where she should be standing is now dense with the sticky sweet smell of kief, as well as an incongruous scent of the seaside.

"Maxa?" I whisper. Is this some conjuration of hers, an attempt to communicate with me? What then of her entreaty that we cease all contact? The vision has evaporated, and left me standing in the drowned woman's place.

"Darling?" Hugo, out of breath, places a gentle hand on my shoulder as I scan my surroundings in vain. "What is it? Is everything all right?"

"It is nothing." I shake my head furiously, as if trying to shake away the incident itself, wipe it clean from my mind's uneven slate. I tell myself it was an aftereffect of the opium, but I know it was something else, something inexplicable. It has left me with a lingering and disturbing anxiety. Perhaps I have had a premonition of my own death.

I calm myself as the butcher's wares swing above me, gruesome hunks of pork ribs and pettitoes lashed to wires like sacrificial offerings to a bloodthirsty god. Everywhere I look is carnage. All I am able to do is hold myself, and I stare up at the overcast sky. "I thought I saw someone I knew."

"You gave me quite a fright." He hoists the market bag beneath his arm. "Shall we be on our way, then? Emilia is preparing pheasant, and I offered to deliver the oranges to her."

"That sounds lovely." The words are distant and foreign, spoken in a stranger's voice, as if through another's lips. "Let's go."

I take Hugo's arm, and we reenter the market through the crowded stalls. When I look back, there is no one watching, and we continue on our way.

We arrive at the masquerade in darkness. Fairy lights are strung across the property, lending the evening an otherworldly feel, as, of course, do all the many disguises worn by the guests. Hugo is costumed as the sea king Neptune, bare-chested and adorned with glittering scales affixed to his sides that run up his neck and across his eyes in their own kind of mask. I am Venus arisen from the ocean deep, my breasts covered by two large clamshells, smaller shells woven into the hair pieces that obscure my bare shoulders in golden waves. We are, as they say, of a pair.

Trident in hand, Hugo ushers me through the lush garden, the air warm from a flickering bonfire and reverberating with animated conversation. Blood-rhythmed music echoes across paving stones and through the gnarled crepe myrtles as a band performs atop a raised platform, masked couples swaying on the temporary dance floor laid out across the packed grass. Our hosts, dressed as a monk and a nun, come down from the patio to greet us. A passing waiter offers champagne from a lacquered tray, and though I take a flute I am already made drunk due to the raucous surroundings, the dizzying whirl of light and sound and carefree revelry. As Hugo and our hosts make small talk, I scan the garden, take in the many costumes: the satyrs and nymphs, ballerinas and chained prisoners, an impressive Louis XIV and Marie Antoinette in their own gilded masks. The mood is giddy, the guests shielded and hence emboldened by their chosen disguises.

Across the dance floor, a solitary figure watches me. A man, tall and broad-shouldered and dressed in old-fashioned naval fare, his tricorne hat pointed cowl-like like a bird of prey's savage bill. Dark paint upon his face glistens beneath the lights in an iridescent wave, narrow eyes barely perceptible but for a silvery yellow flicker upon them, cast from the fairy lights overhead. A frisson of excitement spreads across my arms and bared stomach, my thighs beneath my diaphanous skirt, commingled with an unnerving charge of fear. He nods, and tips his hat in my direction.

I take a tentative step back, and look away, over to where Hugo and our hosts should be. Except they seem to have vanished farther into the garden, somewhere past the wide nettle of trees that ring the impressive grounds. I return my attention to the naval captain, who departs across the dance floor through the swirling sea of dancers, silent and unseen as a wraith as he makes his way toward the main house.

I follow in pursuit. Slowly at first, but then I hurry to keep up, my sandals slapping loud against the stone steps as I reach the patio. A cluster of guests chat near the open doorway to the house, a waiter returning from the kitchen with a tray of food, and as I enter the foyer I glimpse a pair of black-booted feet ascending the staircase. I trail after him, and take the steps two at a time, only to find the hallway empty. I pass from room to room, the whole of the house filled with the aroma of boiling coffee and steamed milk. Another scent as well, the burnt spice fragrance of Maxa's flat. Another set of stairs, and by the time I reach the top I am in near darkness. The party below is a quieted lull, and I think of the seaside and the susurrus of waves, rolling in, out, in.

I feel my way along the hall for a light switch, and though the way forward is cast in shadow it is free from impediment. At the end of the corridor is a dim and narrow room, lit only by moonlight from a small round window, the roof bowed like the ribbed hull of a ship. I am reminded of being a little girl, and of leaving France to sail across the ocean to America. Indeed, the scent of the sea is unmistakable, the air thick with a wild and salty tang.

Across the room, a figure emerges from the shadow, and what little light from the window is obscured. My breath catches, and I try to reach for the doorknob, only to find myself unable to move. The stranger approaches, his tricorne hat indistinguishable from his face, his head, his body, so that he is at once a man and a being of irregular angles, his true dimensions difficult to discern. He towers over me, a wall of darkness born out of a larger darkness more impenetrable, vast and unknowable. In a flash, he is at my side, the rough fabric of his suit jacket abrading my bare arm as he reaches to close the door with a soft click.

"What is your name?" It is him, the man from Maxa's flat, the beast disguised in human flesh. His voice fathomless and yet mellifluous, an alluring combination of softness and steeliness, of pleasure and pain commingled. I shudder, and for a moment I cannot answer.

"My name?" I say, and swallow hard. "My name is... Maxa."

"You are not Maxa, no." A heavy sigh, rattling and luxuriant, and above all laced with hunger. "I know Maxa. You are someone else altogether. Your own creature."

"What... what do you want with her?" I begin to say, but "Shh-hh," he whispers. I am silenced. A gloved hand caresses my cheek, and I pull away. I imagine myself leaving, backing through the door and down the stairs, out of the house and across the garden and through the city streets until I am safe at home in Louveciennes. I do no such thing, however, for I am already entranced. The time for leave-taking has passed.

"Tonight is a masquerade," he says. "And so you can be whomever it is you choose." He uses a single finger to guide my face toward his. The leather is supple against my skin, and the tip of the finger parts my lips and slides across my teeth before he removes it. "Tell me, then. Is it Maxa that you truly wish to be?"

"I would never wish to be her," I manage to say, my mouth dry. "Not when she is enslaved, captive to forces beyond her control. Not when you are her soul's tormentor." I want to run but cannot, legs trembling and unsteady like those of a newly birthed fawn.

"Tormentor? Hardly." He chuckles, low and hoarse. "You insult me, and yet it is you who invited me this evening." He touches one of the shells affixed my chest, his finger tracing its scalloped edge. "Even now, you adorn yourself with the very tokens of my realm."

"That is not true," I whisper. But of course it was my suggestion that Hugo and I wear these costumes inspired by the sea, incited by my waking dream in Allendy's box, the sifted-through contents of my own conflicted mind. I had sought to negotiate with my enduring pain, and in doing so I unknowingly invited danger to my door.

"I only grant that which is desired," the stranger says, his tone the low thrum of a wind instrument, the prayer of a parched desert landscape for the salvation of rain. "Do you know what it is that you desire?"

His finger presses against my cracked lips. I swallow hard, and snake the tip of my parched tongue over the leather, which tastes of rare and exotic spice.

"I do know," I say, my open hand against his midsection, hard muscle beneath starched wool. "I do."

"Yes." He places his hand over mine, fingers interlacing with my own. "I know what you want as well."

In an instant I turn and am against the closed door, my body firm against the wood. The whole of him leans against me and I gasp, the door rattling in its frame as his other hand slides between my legs and yanks my underwear down with a quick thrust. My skirt rises, and I steady myself against the door, bracing for his penetration. He lowers himself behind me, however, his tongue at the opening of me, and I widen my legs as far as my tangled garments will allow.

He sucks my clitoris into his mouth, and I bite down on my hand, still pressed against the door. The smell of brine, and the boat that is this room lists so that I am face down on the deck as a wicked squall swirls all around. The sky black, the sea black, everything swallowed whole in a heavy blanket of endless darkness. My thighs slick with a honeyed wetness so powerful I convulse.

He is devouring me.

I want to be devoured.

"Anaïs?" Hugo's voice, muffled and calling from somewhere beyond the door. "Anaïs, are you up there?"

I try to arch my back but I am fixed in place, speared against the door as my body is wracked with a ferocious sensuousness. I bite down on my hand harder, lest I go mad.

"Anaïs," the stranger whispers from my hindquarters, his graveled voice its own aphrodisiac. "What a beautiful name."

"Please," I whisper, the sound of footfall on the creaking stairs through the wood as my husband approaches. "Please, I have to go."

I wrest my hand from his, reach down and yank up my underwear. As I do so my fingers graze his hat, and the tricorne falls free. In the faint moonlight, his hunched form is massive, bestial. His head remains lowered, face shrouded in a nest of wet black hair, from atop which emerge the two gnarled horns I glimpsed in Maxa's bedroom. Now the stranger slowly raises his head, and emits a deep and snarling laugh, his wicked pair of coltish yellow eyes flashing through the dark. What I see of his face is a savage amalgam of leonine features, the proportions of which lend the impression of a second face straining against the first.

The room judders and cants, and I fumble for the doorknob. I finally manage to free myself, and stumble into the corridor before shutting the door fast behind me, my skin burning with stirred desire.

At once I slam into Hugo, who drops his trident as he places a hand on my waist to keep me from falling. "My darling, what is it?" he says, his expression unreadable. "What's wrong?"

"I feel feverish," I manage to get out. "Something must be coming over me. Would you mind if we went home?"

He raises an eyebrow, his glitter-bedizened face contorting with suspicion. "Were you in there with someone?"

"Of course not. Shall we go downstairs? I would like to leave now."

"Is there someone in there? Let me through." Hugo retrieves his trident and forces his way past me. He throws wide the door, and when he turns on a lamp the room is illumined in an electric white.

It is only a simple sewing room. Hugo marches inside, and I hold my breath as he searches the small space from end to end, nothing about it resembling a boat whatsoever. There is no one here, neither person nor creature, and I cannot account for what occurred in this unassuming place, its own kind of sealed room. I do not know whether to feel relieved or tormented, whether my encounter was the result of a demonic visitation or simply a fantastical creation of my own fractured mind.

"See?" I cross my arms over my chest. "Now do you believe me?"

"Of course, my darling. I apologize for overreacting." His expression slackens, and relief colors his cheeks. "Are you sure you wouldn't like to rest for a few minutes? Can I get you something to drink, perhaps? I am sorry you are not feeling well."

"Do not trouble yourself," I say, and shut the door behind us. "Everything will be fine. I am feeling better already."

I feign a smile, and curse myself for deceiving him. I may be a practiced liar, but soon I will become a prodigious one, and eventually Hugo will be unable to see through my deceptions to my authentic self.

"Shall we?" I take his arm and lead him down the hall, my thighs damp with saliva and my own fevered excretions. We descend the stairs and rejoin the party, our fellow revelers blind in their merriment to all that walks among them.

I wake in the night and reach for Hugo, only to find the space beside me empty. And so I step out of bed and throw on a negligee, the dogs fast asleep before the cindering hearth as I slip out of the room and down the stairs in darkness. In the strange, crepuscular shine through the windows, I make my way to the front door, which I discover has been left open. I cross the threshold, the air heady with the scent of night flowers as I enter the garden, the grass beneath my bare feet slicked with cool dew.

I realize now that I am dreaming, and stare back at the house and its wide face, its eleven shutters closed to the evening like slumbering eyelids. All save the center shutter, which is thrown wide, the glass of its window visible in the moon's mellow glow. The sealed room has been opened.

The soft crunch of wet leaves, and I turn. There is a slight figure adjacent to the elm tree, past the drive and the far side of the fountain. A crouched and half-hidden shape, barely perceptible in the blue moonlight but there nevertheless, not ten yards away. I am too scared to move any closer, and yet I know I must puzzle out what is happening, that the answer will comprise the most important truth I have ever known.

"Maxa?" I whisper. Perhaps she has decided to pay me a visit after all, here in this twilit realm. "Maxa? Is that you?" The figure shifts behind the tree so that it is hidden, and I force myself forward. One foot before the next, and it takes all my courage to make the slow and inexorable walk to the tree and the fleeting shape beyond.

When I finally reach the elm, I travel counterclockwise around its formidable trunk, its branches swollen and dripping with moisture. There is no one here any longer, and only now do I realize I am holding my breath. I exhale a cloud of perfumed smoke and lean against the rough bark, my relief laced with a disturbing sense of unease, the source of which I cannot place. I close my eyes, and listen to the trill of a nightingale chirruping in the heavy leafage above.

"Have you forgotten me so soon?"

The stranger's molasses voice shocks me to attention. A melodic baritone spoken everywhere at once, as if sung by a midnight choir of the damned. I attempt to run, but my spine is adhered to the bark, fixed to the elm's rough trunk like a fly drowning in amber. My hands stick to the tree as well, and I thrash and struggle as I try to free myself. Soon, however, I am immobilized altogether.

"Come." The invisible fiend whispers into the shell of my ear, the disembodied word seductive, ravenous. "There is so much more I want to show you."

The heavy branches quiver and bend, and the elm's dense and unseasonal greenery ripples and descends, draping me in a foliate shroud. I am forced against the meat of the tree, pressed into its bark as if into wax. The pressure increases, and I flail in terror, my gaze rearing up toward the house and the darkening sky beyond. At the open shutter, I see the slight figure once more. This time, she stands in the window of the sealed room, her small face staring down at me as I struggle against the tree.

It is myself. Or rather my younger self, maybe nine years old, my tiny hands pressed to the glass and following the proceedings below with an inscrutable interest. Behind my younger self is my father Joaquin, who looks down upon me as well, his gaze conveying a similar stony fascination. He stands very close to her, too close, his large hands on her shoulders, body pressed against her back the way the tree is fixed to mine. He is invading her just the same.

Invading me.

Rather than being crushed against the tree's unwavering mass, I begin to pass into it. My flesh melts against and inside its expanding trunk, until the tree has swallowed me.

Once absorbed, I am released, and drop down onto a ground of coarse sand. My racing heart begins to slow, and I get to my feet, alone inside a humid and dimly lit cavern. The wet surfaces are made of pocked shale or perhaps some kind of coral, the distant echo of crashing waves reverberating against the walls. I shuffle my way toward a slit of light cast upon the far side of the cave, and suck in my breath as I wriggle through the narrow egress.

At once, a vast sheet of churning gray light blinds me. After a few moments my eyes adjust, and I discover I am perched atop a carved pillar of uneven stone. The crude slab rises from the bed of a flooded grotto, the puckered bowl of craggy earth draped in gauzy mist and carved from an eroded cliff face over what must be untold millennia. There are more pillars on the shore around me in a rough approximation of a circle, reminiscent of the pylons of an abandoned dock. A large wave crashes over the enclosure, the impact spraying upward in an angry fan before spilling out and away, back to the rocky shore and sea beyond. Above the smell of the salted sea is another scent, that of incense, and I become light-headed with the holy aroma of sacred space. Another crash, and I throw my arm over my face to shield myself from the angry water. The tide recedes once more, and when I steady myself again, I find I am no longer alone.

Roosted upon the other pillars are a collection of unmoving figures. Two or three dozen of them, women, mostly, though there is a man or two scattered among them. Of varying ages and shapes, every one of them bound with their hands clasped behind their backs, all naked and frozen in the formal poses of classical statuary. They are all blindfolded, eyes obscured with the same tattered material used to bind their hands, the dirty cloth tied in crude knots. One of them is standing, while another is seated, a third crouched, yet another curled onto her side in a fetal position. All are motionless. The roar of the sea, the screeching of famished gulls wheeling overhead, and the battered headland is alive with a charged menace.

The anticipation is broken by a low blast. The blare of a ram's horn, or the keen of an unknown animal, the sound skirls over the encircling cliffs. A shadow appears at the slim parting in the cave walls, long gloved fingers extending and emerging to take hold of the rock before the towering shape emerges. He is attired in the dark loden skins of a sea creature, a dreadful hooded face beneath coiled horns, an uneasy commingling of human and animal. It is the man from the masquerade, Maxa's tormentor, and now my own. He strides toward me in his patchwork armor of ambergris and black leather, and whether to call him man or beast is of little consequence. I decide he is either a thing that was once a man, or perhaps a creature in the process of radical evolution, soon to become something unintended by Mother Nature herself.

I think to leap from the pillar, only to find that my own hands are bound behind my back. I am also naked as well, and aside from the absence of a blindfold I could be any one of them, another bound effigy set out upon a rock as if in sacrifice to Poseidon himself. His narrow yellow eyes focus upon me, and I look away, down at the spot between my feet where I would stare when I was a child and my mother would berate me, furious at whatever fresh shame I had brought to her doorstep.

The creature nears, calcified feet clopping like hooves over the wet stone, the snap and crunch of shells and stones and mermaid's purses as he rears up and leaps with ease to an adjacent perch. He lands with a hard thud of bone upon rock, and takes hold of one of the frozen women by the waist. Only this woman stiffens, resisting his grasp as he pulls her closer. Her feeble effort to squirm free causes him to smile, a flicker of the cruelest face of humanity in his delight.

His hands, which I had thought sheathed in a shiny black material, are in fact formed this way, fingers hooked like deadly talons. He slides one of them down her stomach, through her dark thatch of pubic hair and down between her bare thighs. My eyes return to her face, and I know this woman: it is Maxa herself. She is fixed in a paralyzing rictus, her anguished expression familiar from both the Guignol and her flat alike.

"Release her at once," I command, my voice weak and unassuming. His smile widens at my lackluster demand.

"Why would I do such a thing? She is luxuriant with feeling, is she not? As am I," he says, the taut animal skin at his crotch straining as he grows engorged. "She chose to join me. To become a part of greater things, surrender to a sensuous realm that overflows with a dark voluptuousness. The same way you have given yourself over to me."

"I chose no such thing," I say, with as much volume as I can muster. "And if Maxa made any sort of pact with you, I can assure you that she was unaware of the terms."

I chafe against that which binds me, but my ties fail to loosen. "What are you?" I ask. "Are you man or demon? Or are you both?

What am I to make of you?"

He smiles once more, and my blood runs cold, naked skin turning to ice in the suddenly frigid wind. "I am many things," he says. "Many things, to many people. You may call me Monsieur Guillard."

He leaps across our divide and lands beside me with a hard thud that shakes the stone beneath my feet, the smell of his animal musk commingling with that of the sea, the same intoxicating admixture that captivated me earlier at the masquerade. It is a continuation of the very same exchange of pleasure and pain, a *danse macabre* performed as a *pas de deux*. He can find me anywhere, at any time that he desires, and this dance will continue as long as he wills the music to play.

"What is it that you want?" I whisper. "Tell me, and it shall be yours. Only let Maxa free. I beg of you that."

"You know what it is I want." His hand caresses my breast, skin prickling as he presses himself against me. Slick wet fingers travel down my body to my pelvis, until he finds the moistness between my legs. "I want the light inside of you, sweet Anaïs. As I once craved the light inside them," and he sweeps a gloved hand toward the cliffs and the statues dotting the shoreline, all the many bodies forever suspended in their disturbing tableaux.

"You sought this very same annihilation," he continues, his words a menacing rumble. The sky darkens with clouds, voice accentuated by a heavy growl of thunder as a storm rapidly approaches from the sea. "Like them, you came to me seeking oblivion. And now that you have tasted it, there is no turning back. For oblivion has already tasted you."

He hunches down, his mouth traveling my skin, and my gaze drops to the ground. There upon the sand lies a scattering of shards, and it is only once my eyes focus that I recognize them as the fragments of a sculpture, the shattered remnants of one of the women. The pieces are large enough that I am able to piece them together in my mind, and glimpse the woman that they once embodied, her face long and equine like that of a Modigliani.

I stumble and rear back, and in doing so I face the cave mouth, where the woman with the Modigliani face watches from the darkness. She raises a finger to her lips, her wrist cuffed by torn cloth, though her binds are severed. Another figure hovers in the shadows behind her, an older woman, stooped and emaciated. What I can grasp of the older woman is weathered and formidable, hair a tangle of matted knots, her sticklike limbs corded with muscle and adorned with an array of beaded bracelets of turquoise and amber and gold. She holds a finger to her lips as well, imploring me to remain silent, lest their presence be given away.

I shift my body toward Maxa. Her blindfold is gone now, and she raises her head high, cheeks glimmering in the overcast light. Her once-obscured eyes are sewn shut, wisps of silver thread at her temples. Her jaw drops open and continues to lower, unhinging to an inhuman length so that her mouth becomes its own vast cave. As I watch in horror, she emits a savage cry of terror.

I awaken in my bed, a scream upon my lips. Shuddering and cold, I place my hand upon Hugo's back, his bare shoulders still shimmering with glitter from the masquerade. I want to wake him so that he can hold me and comfort me, tell me that my terrifying encounter was only a dream. Only a dream, a dream. But not a dream alone. A dream also tells the truth, the same way fiction tells the truth, once it is distilled from reality. The same way I use this diary and my emotions and experiences as the fertile foundation for my stories. Indeed, there no longer seems to be a difference between dream and reality, between fiction and real life, as the barriers between realms are shattered one after the next.

Soon, the sun will rise over Louveciennes. Over the city of Paris proper, the whole of the continent and the waking world as well. Come morning, I must have a new resolve, make myself into a new form of creature myself. This being must be capable of resisting the embrace of my would-be tormentor Guillard, of vanquishing this brute birthed out of the vast and wine-dark sea, lest I succumb to the unknowable depths of his nightmare realm. And if I write this new resolve into being, it becomes a kind of truth itself. In order to transform my very life, the diary must turn grimoire. I must become my own sorceress at last.

I cling tighter to Hugo, who can do nothing to help me at all. Only I can save myself, now.

The next day, I return to the Guignol. The main entrance is unlocked, and I let myself in, the heat of the day diminished as I leave the bright sun for the dusty gloom of the former chapel. At once a woman's blood-curdling cries echo across the empty foyer. My stomach knots, and I tighten my cape as I hurry forward, sure that I have found Maxa in her final moments, that the midnight fiend that stalks us both has set himself upon her once more.

When I enter the theatre proper, however, I find two players, a man and a woman, mapping out a scene upon the stage amid their rehearsal. Of course the scream was part of the act: any number of ghastly cries are bound to echo against the walls and ceiling and balcony of the Guignol, on any given day and hour. I linger at the back to watch, beside one of the private boxes that functioned as a confessional when this building was still a chapel.

"Louder, Hélène, louder!" the director barks from the front row, cigarette smoke spewing as he gestures with abandon, his hands glimmering with rings on every finger. "The audience is only going to find the lighthouse keeper menacing if you increase your hysteria. Remember, his face has already been slashed by now."

"Louder. Of course. I understand."

"Then do it again, please," he says, his tone softening. "I've already had enough headaches today."

After a few minutes, a stage manager emerges from the wings. He uses the small set of stairs to step down into the pews, and he approaches me. "This is a closed rehearsal, mademoiselle," he whispers curtly. "I am going to have to ask you to leave."

"My apologies, but I am a friend of Maxa's. Is she here?"

"Unfortunately, no. She has missed the last three performances. We had to call in her understudy," he says, and casts a baleful look at the actress onstage. "If you see her, please make it clear that Monsieur Jouvin is in a rage, and that he plans to let her go if she does not return at once. He is well aware of her vices, and any irresponsibility will no longer be excused."

"I will let her know," I say, the wind going out of me. "Thank you."

Once I leave the Guignol, I hurry to Maxa's place. I hope against hope that I will find her there, that she has not been harmed, or indulged in too much opium for her body to withstand. I ring the bell, and wait at the door to the building. When a distractible family exits the premises, I scuttle inside the vestibule and climb the stairs to her flat.

"Maxa?" I call as I knock on her door. "Maxa, are you inside?" I turn the knob, surprised to find it unlocked, and I slip inside. "Maxa?" I call again. "Maxa? Are you here?"

The apartment emits a chill of loneliness and abandonment, as if no one has been here in quite some time. It is dark as night here as well, the windows and walls draped in their heavy black velvets. I creep down the hall to the bedroom, terrified of what I might discover. That I might find Maxa bound and bloodied, tied to the bedposts in a grotesque display of gore and punctured flesh, a scene of blood-drenched Guignol staged by the unforgiving hand of Monsieur Guillard.

The room is empty, however, rumpled bedsheets the only vague reminder of the carnal scene I had witnessed when last I was here. I search the flat as best I can, comb through her drawers and her cosmetics kits, determined to find any clue as to her whereabouts. Did Maxa manage to flee, as is my profound wish? It is true there is no overt sign of struggle, yet I am no detective, and I wonder anew about contacting the police.

Though what would I say if I did? No doubt they would point to her opium consumption as confirmed by the Guignol, confirmable by anyone who may have crossed her path. Maxa was correct: the authorities would be of no use whatsoever.

Just as I am about to take my leave, one of the pictures pinned to the back of the door flutters to the ground, and I bend to retrieve it. It is the photograph of the young woman in a lace slip, curvy and Amazonian and luxuriating upon a red divan. Something about the woman's ambivalent expression—how it is both welcoming and observant, the eyes vulnerable and unpitying in equal measure—causes me stare at her image for some time. Who is she?

And all of a sudden I know. The young woman standing in the mouth of the cave, her binds untied as she watched from the shadows, an imposing older woman lurking just behind her. The one whose statue was shattered upon the rocky sand, whose face resembled a Modigliani, and I bring the picture closer to my face. The woman on the dark beach, and this woman in the photograph: they appear to be one and the same.

My fingers tremble, and I drop the picture into my bag, nerves frayed like the thief that I am. One final glance about the flat, and I take my leave, the heavy door groaning as I shut it fast behind me.

Henry and I lie in bed, our limbs tangled in the sheets. We hold each other, and watch lazily as dust shivers and dances in the afternoon light that filters through his filthy apartment window. He hums a little song beneath his breath, and I try to keep my mind from Maxa's disappearance, as if this routine of false normalcy will bar Monsieur Guillard from my door. The Dark Angel himself. His disturbing face haunts me, as does the possibility that I conjured him without understanding or intent, perhaps in the very same manner as Maxa. But how exactly?

There is a change in the atmosphere, and it takes me some time to realize that Henry has ceased his humming and fallen silent. I look over at him, and he squints back at me with a bemused concern.

"Little bird, little bird, where did you fly?" he says, and he gives my arm a little squeeze. "You haven't been your playful self lately. Not in bed, and not on the page either."

"I am sorry, Henry. It is just that I have a great deal on my mind."

"Don't think I haven't noticed. It's like fucking a rubber doll, you know? No offense."

"Can a rubber doll do this?" I pepper his face with kisses, his lips, his cheeks and nose, the bald crest of his skull, testing if I can break him of his worry. But when I withdraw, Henry's expression remains unchanged.

"You going to tell me what's going on with you or what?" He leans up on his elbow, as if preparing himself for a lengthy response. I sigh, and sit up myself. Henry knows so much of me, there is no denying this. More than Allendy or my cousin Eduardo, perhaps even more than Hugo. What I have experienced of late, however, is another matter entirely. How can I begin to explain to him the transgression made flesh that walks among us? That a night creature in the guise of a man has come for me in both this world and his own, and now threatens to consume me altogether? These are matters that even a man of Henry's great experience would not be able to comprehend.

"It is one thing to be under the sway of another," I say, an attempt to speak in our common tongue of metaphor and myth, the language of symbol and allusion. "A man, say. Or even a woman," for he knows that I remain entranced by June's lingering spell, just as surely as he does himself. "It is quite another to be haunted by a being that inhabits another world. An angel, or a demon, a creation of light and darkness that cannot be escaped or denied. I have fallen under the influence of such a creature, one I cannot properly begin to fathom. In turn, my life has become a waking dream from which I cannot fully rouse."

"So you're hung up on someone. What else is new?"

"You do not understand my meaning."

"Well *pardonnez-vous*, Madame! Maybe you're just shutting me out with all this mumbo jumbo because you don't *want* me to understand. Ever think about that?"

I get up from the bed. "Maybe it is because I know you are incapable of it."

He reaches for me but I shrug him off, and go into the bathroom to wash myself. I shut the door and run a wet cloth over my face, my breasts, between my legs. All the places where Henry has been, with his hands, his mouth, his penis. My pleasure with him here in Clichy, this once precious place, noticeably dimmed. The same way Louveciennes has grown colorless, Hugo along with it. I know it is because of Monsieur Guillard. The monster that fills me with an evil and unspeakable poison, my usual pleasures steadily drained from the world around me until there is nothing left but the empty husk of a life once lived to its fullest.

I emerge from the bathroom to find Henry seated on the edge of the bed. He stares down at something in his hands, my bag lying open on the pillow beside him.

"So, is this the lucky lady?" He holds up the photograph from the back of Maxa's door, the portrait of the voluptuous young woman upon the divan.

"Who gave you permission to go through my possessions?" I snatch the picture away from him. "If my husband can manage to respect my privacy, I expect nothing less from you."

"Hey, hey, take it easy," he says, and holds up his hands in surrender. "I'm just looking out for you, alright? Let's just say you better make sure June doesn't find out about this girl. Take it from me. She skips town with a broken heart, and you turn around and fall for a whore? Wouldn't exactly make her feel like the belle of the ball, if you catch my drift."

"A whore?" I yank my bag from the bed and tuck the photograph back inside. "What on earth are you talking about?"

"That woman in the picture. She's a professional." He clears his throat. "I don't want to go into any great detail here. Suffice it to say, that's one of Louisa's girls, over at 32 Rue Blondel. Ask me no questions and I'll tell you no lies. It's not a good idea, that's all."

"You do not understand."

"Yeah, you've been saying that a lot lately."

"Listen to me! I do not know this woman, but she might be in grave danger. Regardless, she may well have information about a missing friend of mine. I am going to need your help, Henry."

"Anything you want, kid. You know that."

"All right, then." I straighten up as tall as I can make myself, allow Henry's gaze to travel the contours of my body until his eyes return to my face. I place my hands on my bare hips, and I smile. "I want you to take me to the Rue Blondel."

The taxi lets us out at the mouth of the narrow little street. I take Henry's arm as we make our way to the unassuming building, the number "32" painted in red over the door. He knocks three times, pauses, then knocks three times again, after which he shares a smile both sheepish and mischievous, that of a naughty little boy. The door cracks open, and we slip into the darkness within.

The *patronne* swiftly shuts the door behind us, and we follow her down a crooked hallway to a wall of heavy and torn red curtains, which she parts as she ushers us through with a sly smile of her own. The high commotion of the room envelops me. The acrid smell of smoke and stale spirits, a tinny waltz playing on the phonograph, and above all the laughter of women, who sit naked at various café tables and along the oak bar. A dozen of them or more, dark and pale and every shade in between, drinking and smoking and carousing in stockings and heels, their buttocks and breasts and mounds of wiry pubic hair on proud display. I blush at the banquet on offer, and turn to Henry, who watches me closely beneath the low brim of his hat.

"Like anything you see?" he says. "We're here already. Don't see why we shouldn't kill two birds with one stone, if you know what I mean."

"We are only here to talk," I say, as I scan the room. "You can return to play some other time."

"Suit yourself," he says, and shrugs. "You're the one who's paying."

Two prostitutes approach, and cling to the both of us in a clumsy attempt at seduction. We send them away, however, and circle the room in search of the woman from the photograph. When we fail to find her, I summon over the *patronne* and show her the picture.

"Ah, yes," she says, and nods. "She is one of mine. Her name is Sonia. Unfortunately, she is not working this evening."

"Do you know where we might find her? It is quite urgent." I return the photograph to my bag and produce a handful of bills. "We will compensate you most fairly for delivering us to her."

"But of course." The *patronne* bows in deference, and guides us to the uneven staircase. We follow her up, the sounds and sights and smells of the café setting dissolving below as we reach the landing and continue to the next flight. Here in these dim warrens, any private desire imaginable can be negotiated and consummated. Or so I had once thought, before I encountered Monsieur Guillard.

Harsh grunts and other rutting noises resound beyond the thin walls, the contradictory scents of perfume and sex hanging heavy in the air as we reach a door at the end of the hall. The *patronne* knocks rapidly before she produces an iron key from her apron. "Please," she says, and holds her palm open. I hand over the money, and she bows with an obsequious flourish before unlocking the door, only to turn on her heel and head back down the stairs.

The room is softly lighted, a red glow from a silk scarf hung over a lamp atop a decrepit armoire that gapes open from the corner. Beside it is a rumpled bed and a cluttered night table that bears an almost-drained bottle of *Le Peau Verte*. Two half-emptied glasses and a bowl of sugar cubes as well, alongside a variety of accoutrements.

Barely a moment passes before the woman in question staggers naked from an adjoining room. She is busy pinning her damp hair, arms held high so that her large breasts heave as she works. It takes her some time to register our presence, and which point she freezes in her pose, her own kind of statue.

"What are you doing in here?" Sonia reaches for the dresser and takes up what appears to be a simple hair comb. With a flick of the wrist, however, the comb snaps open to reveal a deadly steel blade disguised in its ivory encasing, which she now brandishes with what can only be described as a world-weary familiarity.

"Whoa, lady!" Henry, ever the gentlemen, leaps in front of me. "Take it easy there. Who comes to a cathouse looking for a fight?"

"Did Louisa let you in? I told that bitch I'm not working to-night," Sonia says matter-of-factly. "You will have to find another girl to entertain you."

"We are not here to be entertained," I say. "My name is Anaïs, and this is Henry. We are looking for answers about a friend of mine. Her name is Paula Maxa. I found your photograph in her apartment, which led us here to you."

"Maxa?" She raises a thinly painted eyebrow and snaps the blade closed before flinging the camouflaged weapon back onto the dresser. "What do you need me for? You can find her over at the Grand Guignol in Pigalle. She is probably on stage getting tor-tured by a psychopathic dentist as we speak. If you hurry, you can still catch the show."

"Unfortunately, Maxa has gone missing."

"Missing? What do you mean, missing?" she says, her voice un-even. "Maybe she took a lover. Everyone needs a break from the world now and then."

"No one seems to have seen her for few days now." I hand her Maxa's letter. "I think she might be in terrible trouble."

"She's flown the coop," Henry says, as Sonia scans the letter. "Sounds to me like she's dug herself a hole she can't get out of. Either that, or someone's dug a hole for her."

"No," Sonia says, and thrusts the letter back at me. "I cannot hear about this now. Not now!" She sinks against the wall until she is curled in a ball on the floor, her hands raking violently through her straw-colored hair until I am afraid she will tear it from its roots. "I already paid my debt," she mutters beneath her breath. "I won't be made to do it again..."

"Henry." I go to him, my voice dropping into a whisper. "Do you think you can give us some privacy?"

"Are you nuts? I'm not leaving you alone with her. Her pupils are the size of dimes. She looks like she's whacked out of her mind!"

"She may be under the spell of the green fairy," I say, and cast my eyes toward the night table. "That only means she requires a gentle hand. Regardless, your presence is only going to upset her."

"There's not a lot this chick hasn't seen by now. Trust me."

"Be that as it may, this occasion calls for a woman's touch."

"Fine, fine. I'll be downstairs, checking out the merchandise. But don't take too long, okay?"

I close the door behind Henry and settle on the floor beside her. "Sonia," I begin softly. "Do you know what might have happened to Maxa?"

"It is nothing I can properly explain to you." She lifts her head, her pink-rimmed eyes still fixed on the floor, on whatever horrors her mind has conjured before her. "It is nothing you can hope to understand."

"He is called by many names," I say. "The Dark Angel of Music. Crocell, the Lord of the Great Deep. Those, and more."

Her gaze meets mine, her wide eyes glassy and no less haunted. "So Maxa told you about him."

"Some, yes. But not all."

"She should have kept quiet. Nothing good can come of speaking of him. Quite the contrary." Sonia lights a cigarette, her fingers quivering. "You should pray that you never come face to face with him."

"I have already faced him. He came to me, at a masquerade in Passy. And then he came to me again inside a terrible dream, a dream that was as real as life."

"You." Her hands move to her mouth, red lacquered fingernails tap-tapping against her lips in a blur of motion. "You are the one from the pool of stone. The woman on the shore." "And you are the one who watched from the cave. The one whose statue lay shattered upon the sand." She looks to the corner of the room, as if someone else is there. "You are the next of us, then," she whispers. "He already knows your name."

"Yes," I say. "Yes."

"Now I know why Therese wanted to..." Sonia trails off, and quickly stands. She stumbles to the night table, where she empties the rest of the absinthe into a glass. "In a few hours, just before dawn, wait for me at the eastern side of the Barrière d'Enfer," she says, her voice newly firm. "I will meet you there. Make sure you are alone. And tell no one. Otherwise, Therese will know, and then she will not meet you."

"And who is Therese?"

"If you do as I say, then you will find out soon enough." She swallows down the drink with a wince, wipes her lips with the back of her hand, and turns to face the window, the leaded glass grimed with soot. "Now go. And take care not to be seen on the street." I want to speak with her more, but I stand in silence instead, my bag with her picture inside clutched to my chest.

As I cross the room to leave, I glimpse Sonia in the scuffed mirror nailed to the back of the door. She remains frozen in place, her voluptuous form framed in the dirty square of the solitary window as I depart.

I already told Hugo that I would be remaining overnight in the city to work on the latest pages of my novel. Indeed, I booked a room at the Hotel Anjou and made it available for Henry's use. No one knows where I am really going, however, as Sonia insisted in her instructions. Not even Henry.

Now, dawn fast approaches as I stand alone at the Barrière d'Enfer, and I try not to pace as I wait. The Hell Gate, fittingly, though I have never thought of the pair of austere tollhouses quite so literally. For what other kind of dark journey must I take tonight, save one that will bring me ever deeper into the unmapped terrain of the Underworld? A dark thought enters my mind, that this clandestine meeting is in truth an elaborate plot to draw me into a trap. That this woman Sonia is not aligned with me, but rather has offered me up as a sacrifice. If so, my recent actions have done nothing but hasten my demise, an ending that fast approaches.

The harsh groan of metal, and a small door near the eastern pavilion shudders open a crack, a flicker of torchlight visible through the breach as Sonia emerges from the gloom. She appears focused, no longer the absinthe-addled wretch that Henry and I found earlier at the Rue Blondel but rather the survivor who watched from the cave mouth, her former self left shattered upon the rocky shore. Her eyes are dark pools, narrow and appraising beneath the cowl of a hooded cape. She smiles grimly, and gestures with the torch for me to enter.

I follow her down into an indentation in the earth, the passage paved and stepped like a cellar. I am reminded of my house in Louveciennes and how it has no cellar, how that fact enticed me from the moment I first crossed over the threshold. Something about the way I could feel the earth directly beneath my feet made me feel as if I were a tree capable of taking root, and, despite my distaste for being tied to any one place, I had found my true home at last. As we descend into these sepulchral tunnels, however, there is no such feeling of the earth anywhere near at hand. Here, I am rootless once more.

Past a set of heavy wooden doors, and we travel through a passageway lined with ghastly walls of bone. We have entered the catacombs, the underground network of ossuaries that spiders its way along the tunnels of this vast metropolis. The remains of centuries' worth of Parisians, unearthed when the cemeteries were emptied and relocated to this series of subterranean vaults. Skulls stacked against the walls by the thousands, ornate patterned archways of rib and femur and breastbone and pelvis, a gothic mosaic of generations past. All the many souls of our beloved city, those who lived here and died here, who ate and drank and made love, the reviled and adored alike. In death, we are all the same.

Sonia and I walk for what seems an eternity. And surely dawn has broken by now, the bells of Notre Dame ringing their morning Angelus. Down another series of passageways, the echo of falling water ahead as my guide steps through a circular entrance. It is like the doorway of *Le Monocle*, the women's bar where June once brought me, where she passionately kissed me one autumn evening before we walked home together beneath the stars.

The damp smell of must, and I step over the low partition into a rounded chamber as Sonia halts ahead of me, the torch flame dancing wildly in her hand. Dozens of candles flicker along the walls and floor, threads of wax dripping from atop the crowns of grinning skulls, from within their hollow eye sockets as well. It is the nightmarish scene of a black mass, a dark vision out of Dante or Goya. I tighten my cape around my shoulders, and move farther into the chamber.

At the center of the dim space are two heavy pillars. Between them is a large cistern, from Roman times perhaps, the basin of which catches a steady beading of water that leaks from the bone-vaulted ceiling. In the shadows of the crypt's periphery, a formation of what appear to be statues watches from beneath their own obscuring cowls, arranged about the chamber in a broad circle. Unlike the stone women from my dream, these figures are unbound and clad in moldering black robes. I look closer, and I see one of the hands is that of a skeleton, the white bones of its knuckles glinting in the uneven light. A renewed chill overtakes me, and I hold myself to keep from shivering.

Sonia brings her torch closer to the wall, where a spindly arm emerges from the darkness to grasp it, a stunted form coalescing as if poured from the shadows themselves. It is the rawboned old woman from the dream, the one who watched from the cave alongside Sonia. She takes the torch and places it into the outstretched hand of a cloaked skeleton, before she steps into the quivering pool of light.

"Welcome, Anaïs." The woman lifts her hood, heavy bracelets shifting as her hair springs forth in a wild snarl of unkempt silver. Her face is sallow, skin a papery yellow vellum around a pair of eyes that bulge green and glittering through a sea of dark paint. "My name is Therese. Rest assured that, despite the surroundings, we are safe down here. Thanks be to priestesses past, who charmed the catacombs for this very purpose, so that no demon could walk their hidden paths. At least not the one who now calls himself Monsieur Guillard. Despite his great hunger, this is one moonless place he is unable to haunt, and for that we are most fortunate."

"What of Maxa?" I ask. "Do you know what has happened to her?"

"She is down here," Therese says. "With me."

"Thank goodness." I exhale a heavy sigh of relief. "She is safe, then?"

"Not exactly." The woman nods at Sonia, who approaches one of the cloaked skeletons staged along the perimeter. Sonia lifts the hood that obscures the figure's bowed head, and I gasp.

It is Maxa. Her eyes shut tight, the whole of her frozen as if in the throes of some terrible pain, and I can only stare unspeaking in confusion. She is pale, hair parted doll-like and combed away from her face. To all appearances, she is only asleep and lacks any hint of deathlike pallor, though her chest fails to stir with breath. She is rendered a waxwork, as if she has become her own example of the Guignol's ingenious stagecraft. Either that or she truly is dead, and preserved by a most gifted mortician.

"How?" I whisper. I take hold of her hand, which in her strange stillness I am surprised to find warm, the skin of her palm supple and smooth. "Is she alive?"

"In name only." Therese shuffles onto the other side of Maxa's rigid form. "She has surrendered to Guillard. Crossed the Rubicon into the realm of the phantom lover, from which there is no return. With much effort, we are able to sustain her body in its present state, but it will not last much longer. If we awaken her, she will begin to decay at once, and soon she will be no more. It would take as little as a day for her to expire. Maybe less."

"What can we do to help her?" I am trembling now, mortally afraid. "What can we do to prevent this fiend from claiming her once and for all?"

"What can we do?" Sonia says beside me. "Nothing." We stare as one at Maxa's corpselike figure. "Maxa pleaded with him to spare her. He only laughed, and called her a fool for attempting to revoke her vows. We saw all this from the dream place, his nightmare realm of stone and sea."

"What vows?" I ask. "Maxa is neither bride nor nun. She made no covenant with him."

"Oh, but she did," Therese says. "We all did. That is why we are here now. Every one of us promised ourselves to him, each in our own way."

She reaches over and caresses Maxa's waxen cheek. "When she was a child, Maxa went for a walk in the mountains with a young man. He set upon her and brutally raped her, stabbed her repeatedly and left her for dead. As she lay bleeding upon the cliffs, she pleaded to God that she be spared. When she received no response, she began praying to a different being instead. Maxa promised herself to him and, in exchange, he restored her to life without injury. As with the rest of us, there was a price, that many years later he came to collect. You must have made a similar bargain yourself."

"Never." I furiously shake my head in refutation. "I never gave myself to him. I would never make a slave of myself, not to any man. Let alone a creature so cruel."

"Not knowingly, perhaps." Therese's voice is gentle, almost pity-ing. "But the phantom lover is clever. It is when you are at your lowest point that he appears, pen in hand, with the kindly manner of a saint. Always in the darkest hour, when you are most in need of the light."

I think of Allendy's office, of sitting inside the isolation accumu-lator. How fragile and childlike I had felt, trapped within the box's enveloping darkness. So small again, and so fearful, and most of all so deeply alone. I recall that long-ago time when I was a little girl as well. How lost I was, and how I prayed for my father to return to me. I held so many confused and conflicted feelings inside, over his unwholesome attentions and his eventual abandonment, all of which led me to start this diary.

The diary. I swore myself capable of becoming my own sorcer-ess, that the words I wrote between these tarnished covers could prove powerful enough to bend my reality and reclaim my life as my own. Only what if I have always been this powerful? The words from the diary, they have already proved to carry a fierce power of their own, my desires realized into the real world, that of flesh, and of blood. Did I not wish as a young woman in my diary for an all-consuming lover, a suitor conjured from the shadows of time to fill the void left in my father's wake?

"No. This is not our fault. None of it," I insist. To Sonia and Therese, to Maxa's unmoving form, to all the many dead and watchful faces encircling us. "This is not our doing! Who would punish a young child, or even a grown woman, for seeking answers or love or companionship in her time of need? Our souls might have cried out for help, yes. But opening the door to despair does not give evil our permission to walk through. Maxa did not ask to be consumed by such forces. None of us did. This cycle of madness must end, and in order for that to happen, we must fight back. And we must win."

"He is formed from the roiling deep," Therese says. "That which is made of the whirl of crashing waves cannot be captured, and will always find its way back into being. He is a storm demon, fashioned from the very depths of the abyss itself. He cannot be drowned, or even burned. He can only be endured."

"Then we will come up with another solution." I puff out my chest, make myself as large as I can. "There is a way to end everything, even a creature such as Guillard. Anything made can be unmade. That is what Mother Nature teaches us to be true."

Therese chuckles at my boldness, her beaded bracelets clacking against one another. "You do not understand," she says. "He controls the twilight realm, the place where we saw each other upon the windswept shore. He can come for you at any time there, and do whatever is in his power to do. In his world, you are his to command. That is his home."

"Then we will confront him here, in Paris. The city that is *our* home. And we shall do it tonight."

I play with the strings of my cape, the satin banding my fingers. "How is it that you are safe from him?" I say. "You, Sonia, whose image lay shattered upon the shore of his domain. And you, Therese, who never appeared captive in the first place. How did you manage to secure your own safety?"

They exchange a look of longing and anguish before Sonia bursts into tears. She hurls herself into her companion's arms, Therese combing Sonia's hair and rubbing her back for comfort.

"Sacrifices were made," Therese says quietly, her eyes unwilling to meet mine. "We purchased our freedom at the expense of others."

"Three girls," Sonia says through her sobs. "Sisters, who worked with me at the Rue Blondel. We summoned the demon, and we gave them to him. He hasn't appeared to us since."

"I am sorry, but I cannot do that." I shake my head. "Neither for Maxa nor myself. I will not offer up another in my stead."

I wait for them to speak, but when they fail to do so I continue. "The Dark Angel, he came to me recently, at a masquerade. He must have felt welcome there, able to operate under cover of the night, his true face hidden from sight. We shall lure him back by promising him more shadows, a place of darkness where he feels most comfortable."

"Do you think you are the first woman to try to destroy him?" Sonia laughs bitterly, and throws her hands up in frustration. "He is not a man, but a demon."

"Then we shall make him otherwise. The way Hera changed Tiresias from man to woman, we shall transform Guillard from demon to man. We will seduce him, the way we have been seduced. Only we shall use the cunning words and the alluring gestures of the coquette, or the virgin, or the courtesan. Appeal to his vanity, the way you would draw forth any man, as the spider lures a fly into its web. And then, like the spider, we shall strike."

"And where exactly do you propose we attempt such folly?" Sonia's eyes widen, with what I can only assume is incredulity. "Where shall we lure the beast to lull him into such submission that he would give himself over to the very women he is so fond of afflicting?"

The crypt falls quiet, the hollow skulls vigilant and waiting. All the many faces of the departed Parisians, who watch as an audience watches, breathlessly awaiting the next twist of fate as our dark drama of violation and revenge plays out before them. It is in them that I find my answer, and smile at last.

Before the car comes to a full stop, Maxa opens her door and steps onto the street, her feet unsteady on the rough cobblestones. I pay the fare and hurry out of the taxi to lend her my arm, and she leans hard against me as we totter our way to the stage door of the Theatre du Grand-Guignol. Already she is fading.

She raps on the wood three times. After a brief pause she raps once again, and I am reminded of Henry's surreptitious knock at the door of 32 Rue Blondel. All the many secret codes and signals, the mysterious pass keys that gain us entry to private places hidden behind heavy doors. Was it only last night that we had ventured out to the whorehouse in search of Sonia? My life entire is now lived in the realm of the incredible, indeed the impossible.

A stagehand opens the door, and upon seeing my wan companion he rolls his eyes with great force. "Maxa!" he cries. "Where the hell have you been? Jack is out for blood." He exhales smoke, his cigarette juddering at the corner of his mouth. "He said if you show your face around here again, to make certain you know that you've been permanently replaced by Hélène."

Maxa straightens up. "You find Jack," she hisses, and I see what a struggle it is for her to marshal her strength, to project her expected air of superiority. "And you make certain that *he* knows it will take a far greater director to get rid of Maxa! Not to mention a better actress than Hélène to replace her." She reaches with a shaky hand to snatch the cigarette from between the stagehand's lips, and she points it back at him, the tip dangerously close to his face. "Now, my dear. Are you going to get out of my way, or am I going to have to put this out in your eye?"

He flattens against the wall, hands held up in submission, and she strides past him. I follow as she staggers ahead through the theatre's narrow backstage passageways, until we reach a cluttered dressing room. "Wait here," Maxa says, "I'll be back," and I take myself inside.

Racks of costumes fill the space. Nun's habits and clerical vestments, corsets and pre-styled wigs, tattered burial clothing and hospital gowns and schoolgirl uniforms and far, far more. Past the racks there is a small and crowded table, the surface overrun with assorted powders and paints and brushes, bottles of cream and pots of paste. The round mirror against the naked brick wall is cracked down the middle, two small lamps trained upon its tarnished surface and casting an unearthly glow. I bend to examine my reflection, turn my face this way and that, searching out any indication of my own potential decay. How calm I appear, given the dangers at hand! By midnight, both of us may no longer be of this world.

As I study myself, the sensation of being watched creeps over me, and my eyes flit across the glass. Cleaved in two by the violent lightning crack upon the mirror, I glimpse an image of the unimaginable standing behind me, that of the most alluring woman on earth. Still as a statue in portrait-worthy silhouette as if captured in bold aquatint by the deft hand of Matisse, glazed hair pinned to one side beneath a plumed hat, her lingering form rests against the doorframe as she watches me through blazing bright eyes.

I turn and face her. Breath trapped inside my chest, my heart aflutter as I take in her wry smile, her lips painted the color of a ripe plum. With one look, she instantly possesses me once more, and it is as if she had never departed Paris in the first place. Her gaze, as ever, is ravenous.

"June?" I manage, once I have found my voice. "Is it really you?"

"Hello, Anaïs." She steps into the dressing room and glances about with a languid curiosity. She parts her cape to reveal a black silk dress, a new one, the neckline low and matched by a lengthy slit that exposes her gartered and stockinged leg. The extended gazelle limb of a taxi dancer, the graceful dancer she will always be, so long as she still draws air.

June slides aside one of the costume racks and nears with the same air of voluptuous nonchalance she exhibited the very first time I laid eyes upon her, in the garden at Louveciennes. Not much more than a year ago now, but nevertheless an altogether different time, one in which I naïvely thought I understood the boundaries of the world outside my door.

"It's good to see you again," she says, her eyes returning to my face.

"I… I don't understand," I sputter, and it is as if I am encountering a ghost. She kisses one cheek and the other, and I cannot help but blush, the heat of desire pumping fresh blood to the surface of my skin. I had forgotten how much taller she is than me, how delicate and small she makes me feel, a hollow-boned little bird that may be snapped in two with ease. "When did you return to Paris?"

"Early this morning. You don't have to worry, I won't be here long. I'm off to Rome tomorrow. I've been hired to dance in an Italian revue. A legitimate one, I might add."

"I am happy you are here. Only... What are you doing at the Guignol?"

"A little birdie told me you might be here," she says, and I wonder if she has plucked the image from my mind in her own deft form of sorcery. She unties her cape and squares her shoulders, the cramped room made more so by her heavy aura of imperiousness. "So. Where is she?"

"Where is who?"

"This other woman Henry told me about." She cocks her head. "The actress I hear you've fallen for. She must be something else if she caught your eye."

"I have not 'fallen' for anyone," I answer meekly. "Henry was wrong to tell you that."

"Yeah, well, Henry's wrong about a lot of things, isn't he?" She pulls the chair out from the table and sits. "My feet are in so much pain," she huffs, and begins to loosen her boot laces. "I walked across half the city today. American Express, Café Viking, the usual haunts. All in search of you. That might not mean anything to you anymore, but I wanted to make sure I saw you in the flesh."

"June, please. You must listen to me." I place a firm hand upon her shoulder and hold her in place, the way you would to ensure the attention of a child. "You cannot be here tonight. This theatre, it is not safe."

"Don't you know? It isn't safe anywhere." She laughs wryly. "The world is a great big terror from one end to the next. Always has been, and always will be. Especially for women like me." She extends her long stockinged legs, her feet coming to a rest on the table edge. "For women such as yourself, however? The ones with means, who can afford to keep their heads above water? Well, I wouldn't know anything about that now, would I?"

June gestures toward me dismissively. "Sure, you play at a kind of bohemianism, typing up your little stories while you trade bon mots with my husband. But it's just a fantasy of poverty, of *feeling*. You daydream your life away, until it's safe to go home again to your banker husband, your beautiful house in the suburbs. Because you're free. Free to live in your safe little world, to hide yourself away at the first sign of trouble. You're too fucking sheltered to know real danger."

"Once, perhaps. But no longer." I lean over her, and we stare at each other in the mirror, our faces inches apart. "Since I have last seen you, I have experienced things I have never known before. Terrible things. Believe me when I say that I have felt fear I never thought possible."

"That's what this whole place is about, isn't it?" she says, and waves her hand in a wide circle. "The famous Grand Guignol! Step right up, and have a look at the freaks behind the curtain. The poor, the deranged, the perverse. Get yourself a little thrill, a safe thrill, because nothing here is going to hurt you, not really. That's not real life, though, is it? Because real life is never safe. Real life is *merde*."

She places her hand against my face, long fingers stroking my cheek. "Remember when we came here together?" June says. "You were so excited! Like you were a child again. I could care less, of course. All the fake blood, the phoniness and melodrama. I still managed to have the time of my life, though. You know why? It was because I was with you."

"I think of that night more than you can know." I crouch beside her, and take her hand in mine. "It was as if a hidden part of myself had only just made itself known." I think of the sealed room at Louveciennes, and all the many secrets inside. "It was like nothing I had ever experienced before. Or since."

"I told you I'd do anything you asked of me, if only for a night. And I still would." She smiles again, tears forming in her eyes. "That's because you saw me, Anaïs. Really saw me."

"And you saw me," I say. "We will always have that. No matter what."

A single tear falls from her eye, and streaks her cheek with black mascara. "I wanted us to be together. But then you and Henry…"

"I am so sorry that it happened this way." I kiss the back of her hand, nuzzle against it, hold it to fast my chest. "I never meant to hurt you, you must know that. How I wish things had been different."

We kiss, her wet lips glazed with the taste of raw honey. "I still see you," I whisper, the words their own invocation. "And I always will."

Maxa lurches into the dressing room. Beads of water cascade from her hands as she closes the door and leans against it with her eyes shut. "All the arrangements have been made," she says in a panting breath, and I wonder if Therese's revitalizing tonic has worn off altogether, if she has even an hour left in her.

Maxa widens her palm beneath the nearest lamp, her fingers blackened with a gangrenous rot. "This entire plan of yours is utter insanity. Even if Guillard does arrive, you'll only have a short time to pull it off before… I mean, would you look at this? I am beginning to fall apart."

She holds her hand this way and that, until she finally notices June, who stares back at her with undisguised irritation. Maxa hides her hand behind her back and waits, wordless. June does nothing to relieve the silence, only looks Maxa up and down as one appraises an eggplant or a cut of meat.

"Who the hell is this?" Maxa finally says, her entire body stiff as a rod.

"A friend," I reply. "June Miller, this is Paula Maxa."

"June Mansfield." She stands as she corrects me, and retrieves her hat from the table. "The pleasure is mine. Unfortunately, I was just about to leave."

"Wait," I say, and grasp hold of her arm. "Maxa, a moment, please. I need to speak with June."

"Be my guest." She drops into the chair between us and rests her head against the table, her skin sallow in the mirror. "But I don't have all night. As you well know."

"She's really not what I expected," June says to me, staring down with distaste at Maxa's crumpled form. "Nice to see you still like them rough around the edges. Always on the lookout for a fixer-upper, am I right?"

"June, listen to me." I take her hands in my own, and draw her attention back toward me. "What you said that night, about doing anything I asked of you. Do you truly still mean that?"

"Why, are you calling me a liar now?" she says, and scowls. "I thought you knew me better than that."

"Answer me. Please."

"Cross my heart, Anaïs. Whatever you want. You know that's the truth. Honest to God."

"Good. Because I need you watch over me this evening. To act as my guardian angel, no matter what dangers may present themselves." I take June's face in my hands, our gazes locked together. "The Guignol is about to see its most unforgettable evening yet."

The audience begins to file inside for the performance. I take my place, not in the usual rows but in one of the confessionals at the rear of the chapel, the enclosed and private spaces lovers are known to occupy for their trysts; Maxa has commandeered a box for me. I settle on the bench and close the confessional door, the mesh partition raised so that the theatre beyond is transformed into a chiaroscuro of light and shadow. I look around the dark box, and my pulse quickens. Perhaps it is the ecumenical setting in which I find myself, but it is all I can do not to clasp my hands together and pray for a steadying hand.

The house lights dim, and soon the sharp pull of the accordion ushers us into the world of the Guignol. The master of ceremonies takes to the stage, and it is only once he has done so that I see just how far I am from the footlights, from where Maxa will deliver her performance in only a few brief minutes. There will be no helping her, just as she will be unable to assist me in my own grim undertaking. The roles have been cast, the twin stages set. There is no turning back.

The curtain opens and I force my breath to lengthen and slow, eyelids fluttering as if I am falling into a waking dream. The first act begins in a classroom setting, Maxa's understudy Hélène as a schoolmistress correcting papers at her desk. A handsome young student peers through the door, his head a halo of auburn curls. "You wanted to see me, Madame?" he asks, and "Yes, George," she replies. "Come in and shut the door, please." He approaches, awkward and stiff, nervous hands clutching a stack of books over his groin.

"What is it you have beneath your books?" she asks, and the audience titters.

"Nothing, Madame," he says. "I swear."

"Do not lie to me." She glares at him over the top of her spectacles. "You are my very best student, but you have been distracted of late."

"I have been distracted, it is true," he says, and scratches at the back of his head. "But that is only because of you."

The crowd continues to laugh as the farce unfolds, and soon the teacher and her student begin making passionate love. Through the crosshatch of the screen, I catch glimpses of their bared flesh: his freckled shoulders as he arches his back to better position himself beneath her, the pale meat of her thighs as she straddles him atop the desk. All the while, my heart races ever faster, the confessional walls are so near I begin to have trouble breathing.

I close my eyes, and caress my face with the back of my hand. Allow my fingers to travel down to my neck and across my collarbone, spidering beneath my cape and bodice, along the curve of my breast. My desire stirs, and I focus on my own powerful sensuousness. It powers an erotic phosphorescence, made brighter by the light of others, yes, but always mine to command. It is as essential a part of my being as breath itself.

Come to me, as you came to me before, I sing in silence. My hand slides down my belly to the cleft between my legs. The bench is hard against my buttocks, only a thin sheen of silk separating my flesh from the rough grain of the wood. *Come to me in this still-holy place, and let us share this dance of death together.*

The door to the confessional slides open. A tall figure crosses the threshold and closes the door, the darkness returned. The bench groans beneath his weight as he sits, a cold and heavy hand dropping down upon my thigh. I stifle a gasp as his fingers interlace with my own, and I dare not glance over. My eyes are fixed upon the stage and the carnal scene unfolding, even as my suitor's sea-water scent engulfs me, his breath rolling like the tide, in, out, in.

"Hello, Anaïs." His voice velvet, as soft as his shirt sleeve is coarse, the fabric harsh against my bare arm. "I am pleased that you called for me."

"Hello, Monsieur Guillard. I am pleased that you answered."

"Oh, George!" the schoolmarm cries from atop the young man. "You truly are my very best student!" The audience applauds, and she tosses high the work from her desk, a swirl of papers cascading across the stage in a wide arc as the curtain draws closed.

"Ah, how wonderful to be back, in the theatre that Maxa once haunted," Guillard says. I attempt to shift down the bench, but his grip tightens so that I am fixed in place. "She was a gifted performer, was she not? A pity I could no longer sustain her talents."

"How can you say that you sustained her, when all you have done is draw away her vitality? Does a parasite cease leeching from its host, only to claim it an act of charity?"

"Maxa summoned me, and I complied. The same way I complied when you called."

"Tonight, I did summon you, it is true." Though paralyzed with fear, I want to face him in all my righteous fury. "On that we can agree."

"Ladies and gentlemen, may I have your attention," the master of ceremonies declares from the footlights. "We have an unannounced performance this evening. Our very own Paula Maxa, The Maddest Woman in the World, is about to grace the stage in a once-in-a-lifetime appearance that will amaze and astonish you."

"Ah. Maxa." Guillard's face nears the partition, and I look over at him now, silver-yellow eyes narrowing beneath his heavy ridged brow as he gazes into the dim of the theatre. "One final performance, then."

"Oh yes, Monsieur. One final performance indeed. And it is dedicated to you."

"To me?" He grins, a mouthful of silver teeth flaring in the scattered light. "This should prove amusing. I thought Maxa no longer fit to walk this world."

"Her pain, it is intoxicating to you, is it not?" I whisper. "You take pleasure in it. The way an alley cat takes pleasure in toying with its prey, before finally killing and consuming it."

"I do take pleasure in her pain, yes." His fingers feel their way up my body, and he finds my collarbone, where he taps with a single sharp fingernail. "But only to a point. Far be it from me to deny Maxa an end to her suffering."

In a flash, his arm clamps tight about my waist. He pulls me onto his lap, the crown of my skull near the top of the confessional, a narrow band of space between the partition and the ceiling so that the screen no longer obstructs my view of the stage.

"Now, I will possess you fully," Guillard says through clenched teeth, a promise he intends to keep. "I will carve my way inside you, into depths of yourself that you have yet to fathom." His long hand moves up my stockinged leg, my body arching as his fingers slide inside me. "I will possess you to your very core."

"Prepare yourselves for a performance unlike any you have ever seen, not even upon this legendary stage of appalling vice and ruin!" the announcer cries, his hands thrown wide. "Here she is, in a tour-de-force that will defy all reason and explanation. I give you The Most Murdered Woman of All Time, The Crown Princess of

Blood and Horror herself, the Great Maxa of the Grand Guignol!"

He steps into the wings as the curtain opens on Maxa at center stage. Lit by a single chalk-white spotlight, she stands motionless in a black dressing gown, her head lowered and face obscured, arms cradling her midsection as if attempting to hold something inside. The audience stills, the absence of sound deafening as they await that which is to come.

"Possess me then, demon lover." I reach behind me, hands raking fistfuls of his untamed hair until I take hold of the twinned knobs of his horns. "Wash over me, the way the ocean subsumes the shore."

"So it shall be," he says, his words a ravenous taunt as he hardens beneath me. "As the earth relinquishes itself to the tide, so too shall you know what it is to give yourself over. Every part of yourself, each inch, within and without."

"Look!" a patron shouts. A gasp from the front of the house, followed by a series of screams as Maxa lifts her head to face the crowd. Now in profile, a green shadow falls over the curvature of her cheekbone. As I writhe against my would-be conquest, my dress yanked to my waist while he frees himself from his trousers, I am able to view Maxa and her greatest performance of all.

Her face is blighted by a swath of decomposition, a dark green infection that rapidly and impossibly spreads across her skin. Only this decay is no stagecraft illusion, no artful deception to horrify and delight the audience. This time, the disintegration is all too real, as Maxa rots onstage before the awestruck crowd.

Another shout from the pews as Guillard thrusts upwards, and I feel him inside as a frozen and inhuman thing, an icy convulsion wracking me. I grasp hold of the mesh screen, fingers scrambling against the metal interstices. Alternating waves of pleasure and pain crash over me, and my hands curl into fists, the partition rattling beneath my grip. A response to my excited state, yes, but also a cue, a signal to the one who watches and waits from her seat beside the aisle.

A wave of startled screams from the audience, and I emit a scream of my own. My dilated body rocks atop Guillard as a boat rocks upon a storm-churned sea, and I cannot help but moan in response. I am back, back inside the hull of the ship that bore me away as a child. Inside Allendy's box as well, where my most monstrous and hidden desires were transmogrified. I inhale, and the aroma of wet sand and tidal pools and my own ripe sex envelops me in a divine alchemy of scent, powerful and fecund and above all alive. The dream turned nightmare has completed its course, spiraling forth to begin anew.

More shrieks from the pews, and a man stumbles from his seat before fleeing up the aisle. He rushes past the confessionals toward the theatre exit, his mouth covered by both hands. A woman in tears quickly follows, as Maxa continues to rot away onstage. Her face festers, the skin of her hands and fingers webbed with bubbling tissue that molts from her exposed musculature in thick droplets. She lets her dressing gown fall away, and a new outcry resounds from the house at the sight of her tumorous midsection, her belly swollen with distension until it puckers and bursts, the front pew splashed with rancid gore. She smiles at the audience, and a clump of flesh sloughs from her cheek like braised meat.

"Anaïs," Monsieur Guillard murmurs. "Anaïs, you are driving me mad." He gathers me in his lap and turns me toward him, his face between my breasts. "You are the only one for me." How much his words resemble those of Henry! How much they resemble those of Hugo as well, or any number of men threaded through the tapestry of my life. Guillard may well prove a demon, but in essence he is only another man. Only a man, before the fall.

"You claim to answer the darkest prayers of desperate women," I say, and grasp his shoulders as he bucks beneath me. "Only it is to your own needs that you respond. One would almost think you a real man."

"I am greater than any man," he grunts. "Greater than any being you have ever known."

"You are demonic in nature. Indeed, you are quite powerful. Yet it is unfortunate that you can never feel true pleasure, not fully. Because pleasure belongs only to the realm of the living, and you cannot live as man lives."

"Oh, but I can," Guillard insists with a lustful snarl. "I do as I wish. I am able to make my blood run as hot as any man's blood. I was once a man myself, and I can take you as one just as readily."

"Show me then," I say. "Show me, and we shall find out together, finally and at last. Fill me with your white blood, and take of my flesh. The way only the animal called man can take."

I feel him warming inside me, the chill of his muscle and bone abating. I breathe him in, his ocean scent shifting toward that of the earth, of land and the living. He has become a man again, like any another. And it shall be his undoing.

"I am what my father made me," he says, and he drives deeper inside me, with such force that I bite my lip and draw blood. "As you are yourself."

A flash of movement outside the partition, as June approaches the confessional from her place at the rear of the theatre. Despite his sensual reverie, Guillard is quick to take notice of my attention, and he leans forward to peer through the screen.

"Even now as I possess you," he whispers, "you have eyes only for another?" I expect him to be enraged, but a wicked smile forms upon his lips. "Your affection for her, it radiates from you like light from the sun. All heat. She is delectable indeed."

"She is but another woman," I say, and place my lips close to his ear. "With the same longings and desires and passions that drew you to me. The qualities that drew you to Maxa as well, to all of us. Only you will never have her obedience. You will never possess her as lord and master. And you will never have any part of her, either here in the waking world or in your land of dreams."

"You underestimate me." Guillard grasps the back of my head, his fingers digging into my scalp as he bends forward again to search out a glimpse of June, who has retreated once more. He possesses me, while he thinks of her. "I can take of whomever I please, at the time and place of my choosing."

"Once, perhaps." I reach behind me and remove Sonia's ivory comb from where it tangles in my hair. "But not anymore."

I snap open the comb, raise it up, and plunge the blade into Monsieur Guillard's exposed neck. He heaves, blood exploding from his lips to splash my face as his hands move to stanch his wound, where my weapon found its mark.

"My father made me, it is true," I say, and I raise the blade once more. Beyond the confessional walls, the crowd roars in disgust, shocked exclamations of perverse appreciation echoing across the rows. The cries are intended for Maxa, yet they sustain me. "But I have long since remade myself."

I strike again, against the heavy hand shielding his face. An arc of blood whips free, and Guillard thrusts me away as he staggers to the confessional door. I spring up like a jungle cat and pounce on Guillard's back. Another swing of the deadly comb, and this time I embed it deep between his shoulders. He stumbles against me, his hands moving to strangle me before returning to his own savaged neck.

"What... have you done to me?" he gurgles, blood bubbling at the corner of his mouth.

"I have freed you from your earthly obligations, you accursed fiend. Now, you may rest at last."

He wrests free and hurls himself against the door. Once, twice, and the door bursts wide, the wood splintered as he lurches bleeding from the confessional. The screams outside are louder now, and I scramble half-naked from the box, my dress bunched around my waist and my face and breasts spattered with blood. I grasp his coattails to slow his progress as he stumbles up the aisle toward the exit.

"June! June, help me!" I cry above the raucous audience. She materializes from her nearby post and throws herself in his path to prevent escape. Startled, he retreats down the aisle, and June and I seize his arms, dark blood pooling on the carpet beneath our feet.

A man seated on the aisle stares up at us in confusion. He studies the blade embedded in Guillard's back before his gaze returns to the stage, where Maxa's putrescent form is near collapse. His attention returns to us, however, followed by other audience members, and soon we attract more stares, a dozen theatregoers gaping in our direction as June and I try our best to hold fast to Guillard.

In a matter of a few heartbeats, the entirety of the Guignol has taken notice. They are unclear of our roles, especially that of the gore-soaked gentleman in our grasp. June glares at me and I look to the stage, to Maxa, who only moments ago had commanded the room as her own. I wipe blood from my face, take a deep breath, and I hold my head up high.

"Hail, Lady Death!" I raise my bloody hand to Maxa in salutation. "Sacred Goddess of the Underworld, we honor you as you undergo your ghastly metamorphosis!"

The audience, mesmerized, turns their attentions back to Maxa. "Now it is your turn," I whisper to June, as Guillard struggles between us. "Go on."

"Hail, Lady Death!" June calls out, and raises her own hand in imitation. "We… We support you in your really disgusting metamorphosis!"

Silence.

"H-hail." Maxa manages to get the word out, black bile spilling from her desiccated lips. "Hail and welcome. S-sisters."

The spotlight trained on Maxa shudders uncertainly before the powerful beam swings in our direction, and we are caught in its unforgiving light. Monsieur Guillard buries his face in his shoulder, but for a brief moment his monstrous visage is made visible, a hideous amalgam of features rendered as if from hot wax poured over cracked stone.

At once, we are shoved forward. The master of ceremonies presses us forward, and we soon find ourselves up the short set of stairs at the foot of the aisle and forced onstage. June, myself, and the expiring Guillard all stand beside Maxa, footlights bathing us in a blood-red glow. We have become a part of the show.

"Accept this sacrifice on behalf of your humble servants," I incant, as loud as my voice will speak. I remember this vantage point well. "And let it be known to all that no man can escape your irrevocable embrace!"

"Accept the sacrifice," June echoes. "And let it be known!"

The demon shrinks in our arms. A dead and dying thing, and even the weight of him seems lessened now. As with all wicked scourges dragged into the light, as with every shameful secret that seeks and fails to remain hidden, his terrible power is at once diminished.

Guillard crumples between us. I tilt my head in the direction of the rear of the theatre, and June helps me drag Guillard's limp body from the stage and back down the aisle. We reach the confessional and thrust him inside, and I scurry after him, June slamming the door behind me. As the audience howls with renewed revulsion and awe at whatever fresh horrors Maxa's flesh has yielded, I drop down to the floor and lower Guillard's head into my lap in a tender pieta.

"How…" he croaks, his life force draining from him, energy depleting as his body begins its own process of mortal decay. "How… can this be possible?"

"Even demons may die, Monsieur Guillard. Indeed, it is the nature of things. In all your vast wanderings and great experience, did you never manage to learn that?"

He stares up and past me, toward the ceiling of the confessional, where his gaze remains eternally fixed. The iron tang of blood commingles with a renewed scent of the roiling ocean, as if I have returned to that rocky shore from the dream. Only now, the demon lover is no more. Now, the storm clouds have parted to let in the light, star shine pricking the heavy blanket of night until all the heavens are aglow.

I stagger to my feet and collapse upon the bench, and stare

panting out through the screen, the audience returning their collective scrutiny to the stage. In a jerking motion, Maxa begins to straighten up like a marionette, her fortitude increasing as her body pulls itself erect. Her limbs lengthen and pulse, swaths of corroded skin rippling and stretching over muscle and bone, taut and unblemished until she begins to regain her familiar composition. The patrons gasp with amazement, their cries no longer those of terror, but rather of a holy form of rapture at this holy miracle of resurrection. The monster's demise has brought her back to life.

Restored to a healthful splendor, the likes of which I had yet to see her possess, Maxa lifts her chin to the balcony and strikes a grand pose of triumph. The crowd leaps to their feet and rewards her with a standing ovation that lasts many minutes, long after she bows and leaves the stage. Finally the curtain draws closed, and beneath the renewed glare of the house lights, the applause continues unceasing, theatregoers left stunned and electrified and unsure of just what it is they have seen. The Maddest Woman in the World is whole again, and the chapel of pain and pleasure glows anew.

"Anaïs?" It is June, on the far side of the confessional screen. "Anaïs, is everything okay in there?"

"It is," I say, and I am startled to find that the words are true. I stare down at the corpse of Monsieur Guillard, the stench of seaweed and brine wafting from his body, as if he is returning from whence he came. "Our terrible problem? I believe it has been solved. Thanks, in part, to you."

I place my palm against the screen. June matches it with hers, our hands separated by the partition but still touching, still connected after all this time.

"What an act, am I right?" Her voice is tremulous, as if she has already begun the process of self-deception that will allow her to bury that which cannot be understood. "I've never seen anything like it! Did you see it, Anaïs?"

"I saw it." An enduring weight lifts, my eyes flooded with tears as a wave of gratitude washes over me, the house lights shining like miniature suns over the sea. A malignant spell has been broken. "It was the performance of a lifetime."

It is another month before I work up the courage to return to Allendy's office. I apologize to the doctor for cutting short our last session, and for failing to respond to his many subsequent inquiries after my well-being. "It was a difficult time," I say vaguely, and smooth my dress hem against the edge of the couch. "My life became as a forest in a fairy tale, one I blithely traveled with neither map nor compass to guide me. How quickly I became lost, and how fast the darkness descended."

Past midnight, June already departed for her hotel, and Maxa and I endure the harsh bounce of cobblestones as we sit in the back of her actor friend's truck. The space cramped and unlit with the weighty clothes trunk positioned between us, I count the minutes until the truck finally pulls to the curb. We emerge along an esplanade overlooking the Seine, the river swirling in the gloom below. Maxa's friend helps us remove the trunk before he drives away, unwilling to help us any further. Alone beside the Pont Alexandre III, Maxa and I wait unspeaking for the others to arrive.

Soon, we spy Therese and Sonia as they emerge from the other side of the bridge. When they reach us, the four of us nod at one another over the tattered trunk, a grim acknowledgment of our collective survival. With no small amount of difficulty, we carry the heavy trunk down the stone steps to the edge of the riverbank and pause at the bottom so that Therese can paint a crude sigil beside the lock and hasp. "To bind him, even in death," she whispers, as she uses a gnarled finger to ornament the trunk with a viscous white paste that reeks of damp wood and pepper.

The twinkle of lights from distant houseboats, the crisp scent of the river at night, and we heave the trunk over the side. It hits the surface with a loud splash, and we watch it sink beneath the water until it is swallowed altogether. We ascend the stone steps, and it is as if the street lamps upon the esplanade burn with renewed strength. As if all the world is brighter now, at least to those who have endured.

"Fortunately, the clouds seem to have passed." I light a cigarette and fix my gaze on Allendy, challenging him to contradict me. "I feel sure of myself, for the first time in many months, if not years."

"I am happy to hear that. It is obvious, however, that you are still conflicted about treatment. Perhaps your childhood feelings for your father have been projected onto me. It is not difficult to see in our therapeutic relationship a classic representation of transference."

Allendy lights his pipe and chews suggestively at the stem. He suspects unwholesome attractions but not their source, the perverse corruption that exists inside me still. Or perhaps he does know, and is attempting to tease a confession from me. I cannot say for certain.

"Regardless of any conflict," he adds, "it is clear that you are ultimately drawn toward chaos. And toward those who provide it most readily."

"Maybe so. Or perhaps I seek them out in order to end it. To stage a final resolution, one that will grant me a new purpose, a new ability to thrive."

Once Therese and Sonia bid us farewell and depart for the left bank, I plead with Maxa to allow me back to her flat, to help her in breaking her opium habit this very night. She simply shakes her head, and smiles sadly. She delivers to me a gentle kiss, one cheek and the other, and last upon the center of my forehead. Even amid the sorrow of parting, she leaves me feeling anointed.

"Thank you for rescuing me," Maxa says with the innocence of a child, the schoolgirl she was before her own trust was first broken. "I hope you understand that you have managed the impossible. But now we must go our separate ways, and never look back again."

I remain at the entrance of the bridge and watch her leave, in the direction of her flat and the Grand Guignol. Once she is gone, I turn to face the river, and study the surface of the water as it flows past.

I wonder if something finished can ever truly begin again. If that which is dead remains departed, or if new life can spring forth from the old.

"I have weathered the storm," I say to Allendy. "Come out the other side, with a rekindled lust for life. For light and for love, the warmth that only human connection can provide." I draw from my cigarette and exhale forcefully, our smoke commingling in the air. "I have my husband, and my writing as well, and I am dedicated to them both. And yes, I still see Henry. He is there for me, when I am not occupied with Hugo. In that way, they are like my fiction and my diary, two alternate sources of inspiration. My needs are the same as those of many women, and I will follow them as long as I desire."

"And what of June?" Allendy says. "What of your feelings for her?"

Later that night, I visit her shabby hotel room. I sink beneath her dress, June listing as I tug down her underwear and bury myself in her sex. She moans, and I find deeper and deeper destinations, my tongue and lips seeking out every part of her. June grips the edge of the dressing table, her long dancer's legs splayed wide to accommodate me, not much time before a new dawn breaks over the Hotel Cronstadt and the whole of Paris awakens from its heavy slumber. Soon, there will be husbands to meet, and old debts to settle, and fantasies to turn away from forever. Not yet, however, because time has no meaning for us. Not here. Not in this endless moment that, delirious with death and sex, we finish between unwashed sheets, my body pressed to hers with Monsieur Guillard's blood still staining our flesh. She becomes mine, and I become hers, in a way that no man can ever undo.

"June is gone," I say, smoke snaking from my lips. "A tour of Italy, and then back to New York, for good this time. According to her own needs as well."

"That is for the best, then. Abnormal pleasures, they…"

"Kill the taste for normal ones?"

"Something of the sort." He taps his pipe into the ashtray. "I believe it would do you good to give the isolation accumulator another go. Step inside the box again, and face your initial resistance. Make a complete circle of it, if you will."

"Doctor, I…" The whistling wind, the sound of the sea rushing in, out, in. Yellow eyes, peering out from the darkness, through the deep. "I do not think that would be wise."

"Come." He gets to his feet and extends a hand toward me. "Let us at least look inside together, shall we? What harm could there be in that?" Reluctantly, I take his hand, and allow him to help me from the couch.

Allendy tells me more about the accumulator's efficacy, how a young doctor at the Vienna Ambulatorium is expanding on the prototype so that the boxes will soon be in the offices of analysts all across Europe, if everything goes as planned. I am not really listening, however. Instead, as he escorts me from the office, I think of this morning, of sitting under the elm in the garden to write in my diary as the bees buzzed through the humid air. Summer arrived early in Louveciennes. Beneath the great tree, I am lost in the act of creation, pages and pages filled with this story I have been so hesitant to tell, for at times it has felt so much like a dream. Yet it is no dream, not any of it. This is the very story of my life.

"Anaïs?" Hugo stands above me with his back to the bright sun, and I squint up at his silhouette, black against the wide blue sky. "I said, I am off to work. Didn't you hear me calling you?"

"I am sorry, my love. I was in another world. But I have returned now." We embrace, and even in this moment I am eager to return to my diary and darken its every page with ink. "Emilia and I will make sure everything is prepared for dinner. All you have to do is return."

"I will be sure to do that. Until then, my darling." We kiss, and when he turns to go, I settle again beneath the elm. "I almost forgot," he says and turns back, his body rendered a shadow once more. "A telegram came for you earlier. It was from your father."

"My father?" My voice trembles, I can barely draw breath. "What is it? Is everything all right?"

"Quite all right, yes. He is finally returning to France. In fact, he plans to be in Paris in a few short weeks. He wants to see us. Wants to see you, that is." Hugo takes the telegram from his pocket and hands it to me. "Won't it be lovely to have him so close, and after all this time?"

"Of course." I force myself to smile up at him. "What a wonderful surprise."

I place the telegram inside my diary, close it up between these brown marbled covers. The way I attempt to trap so many things inside, even with the knowledge that someday it will all come pouring forth, no matter how hard I wish it otherwise. The truth, as they say, will out.

The loud clang of the garden gate as Hugo departs, and I stare back at the house, count the eleven shutters thrown wide until I reach the closed one in the middle. The sealed room, shut tight as ever. I clutch my diary to my chest, and attempt to calm my racing heart, which pounds with fear and apprehension.

Beneath the steady gallop, however, I sense another rhythm. A wilder beat, one that cuts through the air with steel wings, with a wicked and possessed anticipation. I bring my diary to my mouth and press my lips against it, the violent heat of desire overtaking me until I am certain I will be consumed.

Allendy leads me to the parlor, and I step past him and inside. My eyes fall upon the accumulator once more, the imposing wood-slatted box set against the far wall, the door flung wide onto its cold interior. As I slowly approach, I feel its powerful pagan draw, and stand before its open mouth as a naked child stands before the hungry throat of a cave. No powers or magical gifts granted, only my own essential humanity, a woman alone on her solitary journey.

June was correct: it is no longer safe, not anywhere in the world. Especially for women like us. I must choose my path forward wisely.

The creak of a loose floorboard, and Allendy's hot breath brushes against my bare neck, his hands gripping tight to my shoulders. I think of the sealed room, of myself as a little girl, my father as he embraces me from behind. I remember the fear, commingled as it was with fascination, and yes, with a perverse kind of pleasure as well.

I turn, and I face him. I face them all.

AUTHOR'S NOTE

Not so long ago, I took a look at my stories to see if there were any commonalities among them, any recurring subjects that might have escaped me. I was surprised to discover one theme threaded through them in particular, which was a strong sense of longing. This steady emotional refrain—of yearning for something that is missing—resounded over and again, whether it was a longing for an absent parent or a departed lover, a lost past or a future never to be lived.

Soon after I began gathering some of this material into a collection, my life became its own dark tale of loss and longing. Six months into the pandemic, my husband Dan was diagnosed with a rare and aggressive form of cancer; twenty months later, he was dead.

In the aftermath, I was afraid that rereading these stories—written before his death, with nearly all of them completed even before his diagnosis—would be too unbearable, that my broodings on death and trauma and heartache would prove insufficient in the face of my raw and impossible grief. Instead, I took great comfort in them, perhaps as an antidote to the pat bromides our culture usually offers the bereaved. I wrote them myself, yes, but still they made me feel less alone.

I hope that in whatever way possible, these stories made you feel less alone too.

ACKNOWLEDGMENTS

John Joseph Adams, Nathan Ballingrud, Christopher Barzak, Morgan Beatty, Steve Berman, Holly Black, Rebecca Brown, Andy Cox, Ellen Datlow, Mike Davis, Theresa Delucci, Gemma Files, Charles Coleman Finlay, Jeffrey Ford, Rebecca Friedman, Elizabeth Hand, Cara Hoffman, Michael Kelly, Kathe Koja, Nancy Kress, Carrie Laben, John Langan, Eric LaRocca, Kelly Link, Joe Pulver, Priya Sharma, Morgan Talty, Molly Tanzer, Sheree Renée Thomas, Gordon Van Gelder, Wendy Wagner, and Sean Wallace, thank you for publishing, improving, or otherwise championing these stories. It truly means the world to me.

Ross Lockhart and the entire Word Horde team, thank you for all your hard work, and for midwifing this collection into the world. I'm so happy to be in such good hands.

Paul Tremblay, thank you for your time, your attention, and most of all your friendship. I'm very grateful to have you on my side.

Livia Llewellyn, thank you for your thoughtful feedback on just about every piece in this collection. You are the Louise to my Thelma, and I couldn't do it without you.

And Dan. Always, for Dan.

PUBLICATION HISTORY

"Little Flea, Little Flea" — *People Holding, Winter 2017*

"The Closet Game" — *Nightmare Magazine, July 2022*

"The Oestridae" — *Black Static 52* (reprinted in *The Best Horror of the Year 9*)

"The Cenacle" — *Shadows & Tall Trees 7* (reprinted in *The Year's Best Hardcore Horror 3*)

"Ceremonials" — *The Magazine of Fantasy & Science Fiction, July/August 2022*

"Conversion" — *The Madness of Dr. Caligari*

"The Rental Sister" — *Japanese Dreams*

"My Heart's Own Desire" — *Congress Magazine 1* (reprinted in *Wilde Stories 2017: The Year's Best Gay Speculative Fiction*)

"Giallo" — original to collection

"DST (Fall Back)" — *Autumn Cthulhu* (reprinted in *Great Jones Street*)

"The Vault of the Sky, the Face of the Deep" — *Shadows & Tall Trees 6* (reprinted in *The Dark 32* and *Come Join Us by the Fire*)

"Anaïs Nin at the Grand Guignol" — *Lethe Press Novella Series*

ABOUT THE AUTHOR

Robert Levy is an author of unsettling books, stories, and plays whose work has been seen Off-Broadway. A Harvard graduate subsequently trained as a forensic psychologist, his work has been called "frank and funny" (*Time Magazine*), "idiosyncratic and disarming" (*The New York Times*), "ambitious and clever" (*Variety*), "intimate, disturbing" (*Publishers Weekly*) and "bloody brave" (the UK's *SFX Magazine*).

His novel *The Glittering World* was published by Gallery/Simon & Schuster and was a finalist for the Lambda Literary Award as well as the Shirley Jackson Award, and also won an Earphones Award for exceptional audio from *Audiofile Magazine*. Shorter work has appeared in places like *The Magazine of Fantasy & Science Fiction*, *Nightmare*, *Black Static*, *The Dark*, *Shadows & Tall Trees*, *The Year's Best Gay Speculative Fiction*, and *The Best Horror of the Year*, among many others.

Robert is a single dad who lives with his children in Brooklyn near a toxic canal, where he is awaiting his mutant powers to develop any day now. He teaches at the Stonecoast MFA Program in Creative Writing.

Printed in the USA
CPSIA information can be obtained
at www.ICGtesting.com
LVHW090910231223
767293LV00020BA/78